Praise for Harold Coyle

"Coyle is a master at high-tech suspense. He spins his story with such power that you're swept along to the climactic finish."

—Clive Cussler on *God's Children*

"Fast paced . . . Coyle's many fans will need no persuasion to pick up this novel."

—*Booklist* on *No Warriors, No Glory*

"Coyle is best when he's depicting soldiers facing death. . . . He knows soldiers, and he understands the brotherhood-of-arms mystique that transcends national boundaries."

—*The New York Times*

"Harold Coyle has been dubbed the Tom Clancy of ground warfare, and it's easy to see why. He focuses on the grunts because no matter how fancy the weapons are, eventually the military has to send in men to take and hold new teritory."

—*New York Post*

"Pulse-pounding . . . Coyle's masterfully labyrinthine plotlines, pedal-to-the-metal pacing, and brutally realistic portrayal of army life make this another winner."

—*Publishers Weekly* on *Cat and Mouse*

NO WARRIORS, NO GLORY

HAROLD COYLE

FORGE®

A TOM DOHERTY ASSOCIATES BOOK
NEW YORK

This is a work of fiction. All of the characters, organizations, and events portrayed in this novel are either products of the author's imagination or are used fictitiously.

NO WARRIORS, NO GLORY

Copyright © 2009 by Harold Coyle

A Forge Book
Published by Tom Doherty Associates, LLC
175 Fifth Avenue
New York, NY 10010

www.tor-forge.com

Forge® is a registered trademark of Tom Doherty Associates, LLC.

ISBN 978-0-7653-5865-3

First Edition: May 2009
First Mass Market Edition: June 2010

Printed in the United States of America

0 9 8 7 6 5 4 3 2 1

*To the Officers and soldiers who served in 3rd
Battalion, 68th Armor, especially; LTCs Schwartz,
Greene, and Sheer; officers who always gave me
more than enough rope to hang myself but somehow
managed to keep me from doing so; LTC Larry
Lahowitz, Commander of 2nd Battalion, 13th
Infantry and his merry gang of thugs who took me in
as one of their own; Major Tony L. McLain, perhaps
the finest officer I ever served with; Captains A. A.
Stovall and M. T. Johnson, company commanders
who taught me how to be an officer; Captains Bill
Betson and Ken Cross, fellow company commanders
that banded together in an effort to preserve our
sanity; Lieutenant Bill Gwaltney, the other half of
the Whiffenpoof Choir, a true partner in crime and
a lousy pinochle partner; 1st Sergeant John Akerson,
a man I could have never done without; SFC Billy
Hesser, for being the sort of platoon sergeant every
2nd Lieutenant should get; Sergeant Floyd Terrece,
the top gunner in the 8th ID in 1975 and a prime
example of why tankers should never be fed beans;
and my various drivers, who always kept my Jeeps
and me squared away by remembering to wake me
when the colonel was driving by, as well as letting
me drive when no one was looking despite the
terrible things I did to the gearbox.*

"Many wearing rapiers are afraid of goose quills."

William Shakespeare
Hamlet, **Act II, scene ii**

"You should have a clever secretary to write your dispatches, in case you should not be so well qualified yourself. This gentleman may often serve to get you out of a scrape."

Francis Grose
Advice to the Officers of the British Army, 1782

"Four hostile newspapers are more to be feared than a thousand bayonets."

Napoleon Bonaparte

"In war, truth is the first casualty."

Aeschylus, 525–456 B.C.

NO
WARRIORS,
NO
GLORY

PROLOGUE

IRAQ

The shade offered by the low mud and brick wall did little to mitigate the oppressive heat that seemed to radiate from the very ground itself. This mattered little to the gaggle of exhausted soldiers gathered behind it. The heat, like the dust and filth that covered them from head to toe, was an inescapable fact of life the young Americans had long ago come to accept and hate in much the same way they'd learned to despise the people who'd built the wall.

Like the village on the other side of it, the soldiers sprawled about on the ground or leaned against the wall silent. Such was their exhaustion that no one, not even the most vocal cynic among them, bothered to bemoan their pitiful fate. Whatever strength each man had left was expended in vain to become as comfortable as his circumstances permitted. Even Second Lieutenant Ethan Fetterman, their platoon leader, found it quite impossible to whip up anything resembling enthusiasm for doing anything more ambitious than breathing. Given a choice, he would have been quite content to simply stay right where he was, letting the day, like the sweat dripping from his brow, slowly trickle away.

The idea of doing so was incredibly tempting. Without having to give the matter a second thought, the young officer already knew that going over the wall his platoon was currently using as shade and pressing on into the village bordered on insanity. He didn't need to conduct a long, drawn-out assessment of the situation to appreciate that there wasn't a man in his platoon, including himself, who was in any shape to fight if it came to one. Besides, he found himself wondering, what was the point? Whatever was in the village today would still be there tomorrow, be it a cache of weapons and explosives as the battalion intel officer alleged or nothing more than a gaggle of hajjis hell-bent on meeting Allah. The only thing that would be accomplished by completing the mission as briefed earlier that day would be to preserve his company commander's sterling record of achieving all assigned tasks in accordance with an arbitrary schedule established by an operations officer who never set foot outside the wire.

As he pondered his alternatives, Fetterman grudgingly lifted his head up off his chest, gazing out at the drab, dusty landscape that seemed to go on and on forever. The desolation, he concluded cynically, suited his outlook on life to a T. Like his men, he was mentally and physically exhausted by the pace of operations their battalion had been saddled with. That, coupled with having to deal with a company commander who was incapable of saying no to their hard-charging battalion commander, created a near perfect storm that was pushing the young officer toward a precipice, one that he didn't seem to have any idea of how to avoid or deal with. Like the cutting edge of a knife that someone had scraped across a stone far too often, his ability to soldier on had been dulled to the point to where he was worse than useless. Though this was his first tour of duty, Fetterman was astute enough to realize that he was fast becoming more of a danger to himself and his men than the people they were supposed to be fighting. A more attentive commanding officer, one who took the time to see what was—and not what he wanted— would have realized that Fetterman, along with the rest of his platoon, were no longer combat effective. The odds of that happening, Fetterman snorted in disgust, were about as slim as his chances of finding a way to keep from having to lead his platoon into the village that lay on the other side of the wall he was resting against.

The young officer was still mulling over his grim view of the world when he heard his company commander's distinctive voice call out to him over the company command net. Though Fetterman was the only one who needed to answer the call, every man within earshot perked up as they prepared to listen in on the exchange. Before answering Fetterman wondered if there was anything he could say that would convince his company commander that it wasn't a good idea to press on. He already knew that doing so was pretty much an exercise in futility. Still, it was one that he felt compelled to engage in.

With all the predictability of a well-rehearsed stage play, the two officers quickly pitched into a heated exchange with Fetterman, the officer on the ground, putting forth his assessment of the situation as he saw it. His bleak appraisal was immediately countered by his company commander, located some ten kilometers away, who explained that battalion was expecting them to complete their sweep of the village and its surrounding area by dusk. Though he'd already done so, Fetterman once more informed his commanding officer that, in his opinion, his platoon was in no shape to do so. As was his custom, the company commander saw Fetterman's argument as a sign of weakness, which he chose to counter using derisive comments liberally laced with obscenities. It was usually at this point that Fetterman, like his fellow platoon leaders, went silent and, for a fleeting moment, contemplated refusing to carry out his commanding officer's orders. To do so, however, was one of those things that an American officer in combat only gets to do once in his career. It's the ultimate blue chip, one that has to be held for a very special occasion.

This, Fetterman reluctantly concluded as he half listened to his commanding officer's profane commentary on an officer's responsibilities, was not the time to play it. Perhaps, he found himself reasoning, the battalion S-2 was wrong. Maybe the insurgents weren't using the village as a staging area. And even if they were, he concluded, what were the odds that some whacked-out hajjis would pick this godforsaken place as their gateway to martyrdom? Maybe the sight of his platoon coming over the wall would give them pause and lead them to conclude that this just wasn't a good day to die.

With a sigh, Fetterman resigned himself to the necessity of doing what his superiors expected him to do, the consequences be damned. Without a whit of enthusiasm, he gave his commanding officer a halfhearted "Roger, wilco," before turning to his platoon sergeant, a two-tour veteran who'd made his way along the wall to his platoon leader's side as soon as he had heard the initial radio call. With no need to give the matter much thought, he instructed his senior NCO to take the 2nd Squad around the wall to the left in search of a gate or breach. When they'd found one he was to lead them through it and head straight for the center of the village. The 1st Squad would remain in place, deployed along the wall, ready to provide covering fire if necessary. Fetterman announced that he'd lead the 3rd Squad over the wall itself and make for the center of the village as well. If both squads got that far without running into any trouble, he continued, they'd begin a house-to-house search for the weapons and explosives that the battalion S-2—an officer safely tucked away within the confines of a well-secured forward operating base twenty-five kilometers away—knew were there. The platoon sergeant acknowledged his orders with a mirthless chuckle. "Piece of cake, L.T."

Fetterman managed a smile that didn't match his mood. "Yeah, a piece of cake. Now, let's get this over with." He was about to add, "We mustn't keep company commander waiting," but managed to check himself. It wasn't his style to make disparaging remarks about his superiors in front of his men, no matter how deserving they might be of them. There'd be plenty of time later, when he was with his fellow platoon leaders, to heap scorn upon an officer who'd never met a mission he wasn't afraid to volunteer his company for.

Word that the 2nd Squad was ready came down the line. As he took a moment to prepare himself, Fetterman quickly glanced to his left and right at the men belonging to the 3rd Squad. He could see in their faces that they didn't want to go over the wall any more than he did. He knew, however, that they would, just as his company commander knew Fetterman would do as he was told. That was, after all, the essence of how the Army worked. It was simple, brutally simple.

"Okay," Fetterman shouted as he sprang up from his crouched position. "Let's go."

Without hesitation the squad around him followed. Most made it to the other side before the enemy opened fire.

ONE

The feeling of the sheets being pulled away from her, quickly followed by a sudden intake of breath from the other side of the bed, woke Christina Dixon with a start. Lifting her head from her pillow, she peered across at her husband, checking to see if he was awake yet. In the faint light that filtered in through the partially closed blinds, she watched as Nathan clutched the sheet to his chest in a death grip. His lips quivered as if he were speaking. It wouldn't be long before he was awake, Christina sadly concluded. It never was on a night like this. Taking great care, she laid her head back down on her pillow before rolling over on her side, facing away from Nathan. Through trial and error she'd learned the hard way that the best thing she could do was to pretend that her husband's nocturnal stirrings didn't wake her. For some reason, knowing that his nightmares were depriving his wife of badly needed rest only added to Nathan's worries. He had enough on his mind, Christina reasoned. She didn't need to add to them.

With a suddenness that startled him, Nathan Dixon was catapulted from the dark, haunting place where his subconscious had taken him back into the dimly lit bedroom he shared with his pregnant wife. For the briefest of moments, he lay there staring wide eyed at the ceiling, gasping for breath like a drowning man as he struggled to compose himself. How strange, he found himself thinking after he'd managed to regain some semblance of mental balance, to find the memories of a battle long since past more terrifying than the event itself. Try as he might, he couldn't remember experiencing anything even remotely resembling fear that night in the jungle. There'd simply been too much to do, too much going on around him. Had there been confusion? Yes, of course. There always was in battle, particularly that one. Cutting through it and maintaining his focus on tactical concerns were the only things he recalled running through his mind as his company came to grips with Abu Sayyaf insurgents. The fear, like the haunting memories from which it sprang, only came later, long after he'd been medevaced out of the Philippines. And rather than fading with the passage of time, his recollection of what happened that night only seemed to grow stronger, more intense, causing Nathan to wonder if his mind was hell-bent on sorting out the blurred images that he hadn't had the time to pay attention to that night.

Having regained a modicum of self-control, Nathan looked over to see if his stirrings had woken his wife. Only when he was satisfied that she was still sound asleep did he carefully lift the covers off of himself, slip out of bed and quietly make his way

to the guest bathroom just down the hall. Waiting
until after he'd closed the door, Nathan flipped on
the light, turning to face the mirror as he did so.
The first thought that popped into his head as he
stared at his gaunt reflection was always the same on
nights like this: was he going mad? Of course not,
he quickly told himself—perhaps too quickly. It's
just the way things were, he reasoned. It was a new
normal he hadn't quite yet managed to adjust to.
Like the collection of wounds he'd amassed along
the way, the memories of past events were a natural
and not at all surprising psychological byproduct
stemming from his chosen profession. That his late
father had never seemed troubled by his past didn't
matter to Nathan. Scott Dixon had always come
across as being one of those people who were bigger than life, a man who always gave the impression
of being in complete control no matter how dire the
situation. At least, that's the way Nathan and those
who knew him chose to remember Scott. And despite his knack for coming across as a noncon-
formist in a profession where conformity was prized
above all else, more than a few well-placed individuals who were privy to such things had pegged
Scott Dixon as a shoe-in for the Chief of Staff of
the Army.

Without realizing it, Nathan's concern over the
recurring nightmares that plagued him was replaced
by a deep, almost painful longing for his father. If
there was anyone who would understand what he was
going through, who could help him come to terms
with his inability to put things in proper perspective,
it was his father. Whether it stemmed from Scott

Dixon's experience as a long-serving officer or was simply an inherent talent, he had a way of sweeping away all the peripheral fluff and chaff with ease, striking at the heart of the matter at hand with a deftness that inspired envy and confidence.

Planting his hands firmly upon the countertop, Nathan leaned forward, peering at his own reflection. If his father's incisiveness was an inherent trait, he thought to himself, it seemed to have skipped a generation. Even now, after devoting an inordinate amount of time pondering his future, Nathan had no idea what he would say when the question he knew was coming was put to him later that day. Glancing in the mirror at the clock on the wall behind him, he realized that he didn't have much time left to formulate a suitable answer, one that would address all the issues and concerns he found himself burdened with.

Sadly, the younger Dixon concluded that there was little point in returning to bed where he'd do nothing more than toss and turn until he woke Chris. On mornings like this, it was better to head out into the predawn darkness and run. While doing so wouldn't help him reach any sort of decision, pushing his body to the limit would at least give his troubled mind a much-needed break. Besides, Nathan reasoned as he turned to gather his running shorts and T-shirt hanging on the back door of the bathroom, if he did decide to stay in the Army, he needed to get back in shape. Giving into the pain that lingered from his wounds was no longer an option, not if he was going to be the kind of soldier he'd been raised to be.

* * *

The opening of the front door, followed by the sound of someone removing their shoes before venturing any farther, caused Jan Fields to stop what she'd been doing. For the briefest of moments an irrational thought flashed through her mind, one that was as foolish as her efforts to convince herself that the visit by the former Chief of Staff of the Army with the obligatory chaplain in tow had never happened. These absurd little flights of fancy weren't helped any by the fact that her stepson's habits, even the noises he made as he climbed the stairs leading up to the main floor of her townhouse, were all but indistinguishable from those his father used to make whenever he returned from an early morning run. At times like this, Jan almost found herself having to stop whatever she was doing and mutter out loud, "It's not Scott. It is not Scott."

She barely had time to regain her composure before Nathan came plodding into the kitchen where she'd been in the process of slicing up a wedge of cantaloupe. Stealing a quick, fugitive glance over her shoulder, Jan took note of Nathan's limp before turning her attention back to what she was doing. "You're up early," she stated crisply, doing her best to sound cheery despite the pain she felt over her son's suffering.

Before answering, Nathan reached around her, quickly snatching a chunk of cantaloupe from the cutting board. He wasn't fast enough, however, to escape a quick slap on the back of his hand from

Jan, who used the flat of her knife to punish his impatience. "Wait till I'm done."

"Why?" he countered before popping his pilfered prize in his mouth.

"Because you haven't washed your hands, that's why." She was about to add "young man" to her response as she'd done so many times over the years, but didn't. Somehow it just didn't seem appropriate to refer to a captain in the Army, whose name had just come out on the latest promotion list, in that manner.

For his part Nathan found it all but impossible to suppress a chuckle as he made his way over to the sink. "And what's so funny?" Jan asked incredulously.

Knowing better than telling her what was really on his mind, he opted for a response that was in keeping with his determination to keep things as lighthearted and easygoing as possible while he and Chris were living with Jan. "Geez, Mom," he mockingly whimpered. "You're acting like I was a five-year-old."

"Well, when you act like you're five . . ."

Her words were cut short by the sight of a hand reaching around from behind her in an effort to snatch another chunk of cantaloupe. This time she managed to slap her son's hand with the flat of her knife before he managed to secure a piece of fruit from her cutting board.

"Ouch! That hurts."

"Good," Jan replied in triumph. "Now, be a good boy and sit down and give me a chance to finish."

"Gee," Nathan muttered, shuffling over to the breakfast bar where he took a seat, making a great show of rubbing the back of his hand as he did so. "Where's the respect?"

Rather than respond, Jan smiled to herself as she turned her attention back to finishing with the cantaloupe. It was moments like this that vindicated her decision to insist that Nathan and his wife stay with her while awaiting new orders after he'd been discharged from the hospital. Whatever inconvenience and disruption they caused in her life were more than offset by the opportunity they afforded her to once more be part of a family. And though she knew that Nathan and Chris would soon be moving on, just as she and Scott had done with a regularity that was often annoying but always exciting, Jan was determined to make the most of this fleeting opportunity. There'd be plenty of time later, she reasoned, to resume her silent mourning for the only person she'd ever loved. The thought of an eternity of coming home to an empty house, dinner alone and long lonely nights caused Jan to shiver. It was a response she'd learned to keep to herself, lest she burden Nathan, who had more than enough to worry about, from noticing.

Over a light breakfast of fruit, English muffins, orange juice and coffee, Jan and Nathan chatted over the upcoming day's activities. Nathan listened as Jan discussed in detail her schedule. As the Washington bureau chief for the World News Network, her day was pretty much nonstop, from the moment she stepped into her downtown office till she arrived back home in the early evening. Even then, she seldom slowed down, especially since world events refused to maintain the sort of tight, well-ordered schedule that Jan endeavored to live by.

For his part Nathan silently envied the hectic day that awaited his mother. Whatever joy he'd first derived from spending time with her and his wife had been replaced long ago by a gnawing urge to get on with his own life—one that was, at the moment, on hold.

Not that it really was, at least from a technical standpoint. The need to devote time to recovering from the wounds that he'd received during that sharp engagement with Abu Sayyaf insurgents in the Philippines was as much a part of his chosen profession as the training he'd put his ranger company through in preparation for that fight. Such logic, of course, did nothing to dispel a growing unease that left Nathan wondering if he'd ever be fit, physically or mentally, to lead men into combat once more. That was, of course, provided he chose to continue with a military career, a question he found himself brooding over more and more with each passing day.

Noticing her son's expression, Jan realized that she'd reached the point in their idle chat where she'd lost his attention. Pausing with a half eaten English muffin halfway to her mouth, Jan smiled. "So, what's on your agenda today? Another round of physical therapy?"

Caught off guard by his mother's question, Nathan shook his head as if to clear his thoughts. "Ah, no. Not today. I had to reschedule that till Wednesday."

"Well then," Jan continued without bothering to dissect Nathan's wary response, "anything exciting planned?"

Finding himself backed into a corner and knowing full well that he couldn't possibly keep Jan from finding out one way or another, Nathan decided it was time to come clean with her. "I have an appointment this morning in Arlington."

Taken aback by her son's announcement, Jan stopped what she was doing, folding her arms on the table as she leaned forward. Recalling Scott's habit of casually slipping ominous news into the midst of an otherwise innocent conversation, all sorts of possibilities began to romp through her fertile imagination, none of which were very promising.

Recognizing the expression on his mother's face, Nathan realized that this was no time for prevarication. Like it or not, he was committed. The sooner he told her the truth, the whole truth and nothing but the truth, the better. At least, that was the theory. "I received a call from General Stevens's office last Friday," he said, doing his best to fob her off by acting as if it had been nothing out of the ordinary. "He wants to see me."

Jan, of course, knew better. "And what, pray tell, did the good general want?" she asked, making no effort to mask her growing concern.

"Not sure. I only spoke to his executive officer, a colonel by the name of Kaplan who didn't seem to know what his boss wanted to see me about."

"Stevens wasn't exactly on the best of terms with your father," Jan stated in an even tone. "It seems they were in opposing camps on some very important issues—particularly what the Army would look like in the future."

Not having given the matter any serious thought over the weekend, Nathan took a moment to think before responding to his mother. "Dad never discussed such things with me," he responded glumly. "He didn't think it was appropriate that he should discuss the opinions of other senior officers with me, especially when he didn't agree with them. Of course, when it came to someone like Stevens, he really didn't need to do so. Everyone knows Stevens is very much a technocrat, an officer who's staked his reputation on force modernization based on automation. Dad's focus, on the other hand, is always squarely on the soldier, the human factor in warfare as he likes to call it."

Tactfully Jan ignored her son's use of the word "is" as opposed to "was" when referring to Scott. "Stevens is the new Chief of Staff of the Army, isn't he?" she asked, doing her best to keep the conversation moving forward before Nathan realized his mistake.

"As of the first of this month. Prior to that he was C-in-C Southwest Asia."

After a pause, Jan frowned, shaking her head as she dismissed another unsolicited and very troubling thought that popped up in the back of her mind.

"Well, perhaps he wants to convey his sympathies over the loss of your father."

Bothered by his mother's sudden change in mood as well as feeling guilty for having kept this from her, Nathan quickly seized upon her rationale. "I'm sure that's all it is. I mean," he added without sounding very convincing, "why else would someone like Stevens bother with someone like me?"

Having been around the block with Scott and the senior officers he had associated with before his death more times than she cared to think about, Jan found herself thinking that there were any number of reasons why the Chief of Staff of the Army would want to meet with the son of one of the Army's most beloved legends, none of which particularly thrilled her. She, of course, kept her grim speculation to herself, turning her attention instead to dragging the conversation back onto a happier subject. "So," she chirped, sitting up straight while managing to affect something akin to a cheerful smile, "while you're off to see the Wizard, what's Chris got planned?"

Once he'd made it through the layers of security and managed to get his bearings, Nathan found himself actually enjoying his trek through the long, crowded corridors of the Pentagon. It didn't matter that he was very much a fish out of water in a building where anyone lower than a colonel or a sergeant major was all but invisible. After having been out of the loop for so long, it felt good to be back among healthy, fully functional soldiers, sailors, airmen and the occasional

Marine as they went scurrying about at the double-quick with their heads slightly bowed as if the weighty issues on their minds prevented them from holding their heads upright. Rather than regarding the legions of staff officers all about him with the sort of contempt line officers held for anyone who didn't have mud on their boots, Nathan felt the same sort of envy he had earlier that morning when he'd been chatting with his mother. They at least had a purpose in life, people to see and things to do. At the moment, that was more than he could lay claim to. By the time he'd reached the suite of offices belonging to the Chief of Staff of the Army, whatever thoughts he'd entertained earlier in the day about leaving the Army were gone like the predawn mist. Instead, Nathan found himself wondering how he could turn this opportunity to his advantage, perhaps even wrangling a fresh assignment to a troop unit. For the first time in his career, the idea of taking advantage of his unique status as the son of a former general officer didn't bother Nathan in the least. Getting back into the game was all that mattered.

Looking up from the inane memo that he'd been laboring to digest, Colonel Neil Kaplan took note of the captain limping through the open door of his office. There was no need to ask who he was or wait till the approaching officer's name tag was readable. Having seen more photos of Scott Dixon during his tour of duty at the Armor School than he cared to remember, Kaplan was struck by the resemblance between father and son.

For his part Nathan managed to keep his expression neutral when he recognized the look Kaplan was giving him. Bracing himself for the typical platitudes concerning his father, Nathan was thrown when Kaplan made a great show of raising his right arm in order to check his watch. "You're late," the colonel announced.

Befuddled, Nathan hesitated before responding, checking his own watch, then the one on the wall behind him. Both showed it was 10:50. Stopping short of the colonel's desk, Nathan straightened up and took a second to compose himself before reminding Kaplan that his appointment with General Stevens was at 1100 hours.

"And so it is," Kaplan replied with a straight face as he eased back in his seat. "But in this office we go by Vince Lombardi time."

Despite his current surroundings, Nathan found it all but impossible to stifle a snicker as he recalled how fond his father was of proclaiming with mock severity, "If you're on time, you're late." It was a saying that the famed head coach of the Green Bay Packers, Vince Lombardi, was credited with coining and one that Scott Dixon, not to mention countless other officers in the Army, had learned to live by. Not sure how to respond, Nathan countered with an old standby of his own, a retort cadets at the Virginia Military Institute used whenever they found themselves verbally backed into an untenable position by a superior ranking officer. "No excuse, sir."

Pleased with the young captain's response to his unorthodox greeting, Kaplan stood up, walked out from behind his desk and extended his hand as he introduced himself. In the process of doing so, both officers sized the other up. In addition to measuring strength while shaking hands, each man assessed the other's self-confidence as expressed in his eyes. They also took stock of each other's achievements. For military men wearing their full uniform, this last part was rather simple since the row of ribbons and skills badges adorning their chest silently spoke of their abilities, past triumphs and assignments. The patch worn on the shoulder of their right sleeve also honored the unit they'd been most proud to go to war with. Nathan took perverse pleasure in seeing that Kaplan didn't have a ranger tab capping the shoulder of his left sleeve, though the oversized 1st Cavalry Division patch that dominated his right one and the Purple Heart perched next to a silver star on the top row of Kaplan's ribbons told him that this colonel had not only felt the sting of battle, he'd dominated it. For his part Kaplan could not help but admire the patch belonging to the 3rd Ranger Battalion Nathan had opted to wear on his right sleeve as well as the dark blue ribbon trimmed in white and red that represented the Army's second highest medal for valor. All told, the only real differences between the two men was height, which at six foot two gave Kaplan an advantage, age that was a plus for Nathan and of course, their rank—something that mattered less among warriors such as Nathan and Kaplan than most people seemed to appreciate.

With the preliminary round out of the way, the two officers took a seat on a leather sofa off to one side. By sharing it with Nathan, Kaplan was signaling to the junior officer that he wished to engage in

a less formal, more casual conversation than protocol
and rank would have demanded had he opted to resume his position behind his desk. Opening the conversation, Kaplan asked Nathan seemingly innocuous
questions that were, nonetheless, quite probing—
such as how his physical therapy was going, what his
wife's status was and if he'd given any thought to
finding affordable quarters of his own somewhere
in Northern Virginia.

Without betraying his mounting concern over
this last question, Nathan realized that the purpose
of Stevens's invitation was anything but social. He
was being prepped by Kaplan for something, something, he suspected, he wasn't going to like. Crappy
assignments were always heralded by drawn out
banter of this sort.

With this in mind, Nathan was directed to Stevens's office at the appointed hour, presenting himself, as required by regulation, to the most senior
officer in the Army. For his part, Stevens returned
Nathan's salute with one that wasn't quite as crisp
before motioning to a chair that sat off to one side
of his desk. Unlike his executive officer, Stevens
kept things formal, though both officers still engaged
in the ritual of sizing the other up as they exchanged
a few, introductory pleasantries. In addition to the
ribbons, badges and patches adorning his superior's
uniform, Nathan was able to use the photos, personal
trophies and knickknacks the general had selected
to decorate his office with to assess Stevens's background, achievements and what he valued. Like all
Army aviators, Stevens had a finely detailed model
of a helicopter, most probably representing the first

one that the general had flown, predominantly displayed on his desk. Had this been his father's office, that place of honor would have been occupied by a scale model of an M60A1 tank bearing the bumper number of Scott's first command.

Unlike Kaplan, Stevens wasted little time engaging Nathan in social chitchat. "I imagine you've been giving your future a great deal of thought as of late," Stevens stated in a manner that indicated he didn't expect Nathan to answer. "Like most officers who've reached this point in their careers, you have a choice to make, a hard one."

Determined to make this a true, two-way conversation even if Stevens didn't wish it to be, Nathan nodded. "It would be foolish of me if I didn't take a moment to consider my options, sir. I've more than served out my initial obligation, achieving a fair amount of success while doing so."

Nathan's assessment of his career to date caused Stevens to pull back a bit, raising an eyebrow as he did so. "You've more than proven yourself, Captain. Selection for major below the zone and your achievements in multiple theaters of operations attest to that." Unable to think of a suitable response, Nathan remained silent, permitting Stevens to continue, though he did so in a manner that was decidedly more measured. "The Army has reached one of those pivotal points in its history. On one hand we're tasked with fighting two very brutal and very different insurgencies, neither of which are going to end anytime soon."

The manner in which Stevens described the dual wars in Iraq and Afghanistan caused Nathan to raise an eyebrow. General officers, after all, weren't in the habit of speaking candidly with a junior ranking officer in this manner unless that officer was one of the general's trusted aides—or he was about to be handed a big, juicy shit sandwich. Not being on Stevens's staff, his statement meant that it could only be the latter, a fact that fueled the growing apprehensions Nathan felt over where this conversation was headed.

"At the same time," Stevens lamented, "I'm expected to prepare the Army for the next war, one that bears absolutely no resemblance to what's going on in Southwest Asia. And while most people believe the primary players in that war are going to be the Navy and Air Force, I expect the Army is going to have a major role to play in it, one that we're not ready for."

The prospect of a war with Communist China was the Army's version of the eight-hundred-pound gorilla that no one talked about. Even those who were supposed to be drafting contingency plans to address that possibility seldom discussed the subject above a whisper. Since he didn't have anything in his background that would recommend him for any sort of assignment that was Sino-centric, Nathan figured Stevens had something else in mind for him. Of course, he reminded himself, he'd known next to nothing about the Philippines and even less about the Abu Sayyaf until someone in this very building decided to ship him and his company to that island nation to fight those people. It was a peculiar quirk the Army had, a knack for assigning officers to duties they were least qualified to perform.

Most other officers of equal rank sitting where Nathan was at the moment would have been lapping up General Stevens's every word. Nathan, of course, wasn't exactly an average company-grade officer. Having grown up in the Army and rubbed shoulders with more than a few general officers in the process, he didn't view them quite the same way his peers did. If anything, he often found himself dismissing most of what they said, an attitude that gave legs to the old saying, "Familiarity breeds contempt." Whether it was the bored expression that Nathan was unable to suppress or the need to move on to other things, General Stevens brought his lecture on the issues he would need to deal with during his tenure as Chief of Staff to an abrupt end, causing Nathan to involuntarily blink a few times when he realized that Stevens was staring at him. Rejecting an urge to apologize, Nathan returned the general's stare.

"No doubt," Stevens stated rather haughtily, "you've given a great deal of thought as to where you'd like to go next—provided, of course, you stay in the Army."

Having fully recovered his balance, Nathan shook his head, maintaining eye contact with Stevens as he did so since, he figured, they were finally getting to the real purpose of this meeting. "Naturally, sir, I would like to return to Fort Lewis and my old battalion."

"Of course," Stevens stated in an even tone.

When Stevens didn't continue, returning Nathan's stare instead, Nathan began to suspect that he'd once more been backed into a rather awkward corner.

Without having to be told, he already knew that there wasn't a snowball's chance in hell of going back to Fort Lewis, or any other troop unit for that matter. He'd already accumulated more time in the field with troops than most officers of his year-group by avoiding assignments that had nothing to do with combat units, thanks to sheer dumb luck and a few slick maneuvers on his part. Suspecting that this run of luck was about to come to an end, Nathan shifted about in his seat as he braced himself for whatever was about to come his way.

Satisfied that he'd finally managed to rattle the self-assured young officer across from him, Stevens eased back in his seat, resting his elbows on the arms of his tall, leather chair before clasping his hands before him. "One of the greatest challenges I face as the Chief of Staff is getting a clear and accurate picture of what is actually going on out there in the field. Information bubbling its way up through the chain of command tends to become distorted and garbled as each commander and staff officer that touches it adds his own spin to it. For the most part, those officers do so without any malicious intent. There are times, however . . ."

Stevens didn't finish the thought as his voice trailed off. He knew he didn't need to. Instead, he continued to lean back and study Nathan, waiting to see how he would respond.

Suspecting as much, Nathan began by nodding in agreement. "I guess that's to be expected, sir," he stated slowly after giving his response careful consideration. "After all, it's been rumored that even staff officers are human."

For the first time Stevens betrayed a hint of a smile. "You've not had the pleasure of serving on a staff for any appreciable time, have you, Captain Dixon?"

"No, sir. That's an honor that I've managed to avoid, so far."

"But you do know that the day is fast approaching when you'll have to do time in purgatory, don't you? Provided, of course, you do stay in the Army."

Finally, Nathan knew exactly where Stevens was taking this conversation. "I expect you are correct, sir."

Taking a moment to lay his head back against his chair's headrest, Stevens allowed himself a self-satisfied smile, knowing full well he'd managed to snare Nathan. "How would you like to work for me?" he finally asked.

Before he responded, Nathan found himself recalling a story his father was fond of, about a conversation he had with a retired World War II British cavalry officer who had once been offered the command of a parachute infantry brigade by General Bernard Montgomery. Scott, being very much a no-nonsense and to-the-point American, asked the British cavalryman why he'd accepted the command even though he wasn't qualified. The Brit, according to Scott, regarded him in utter amazement for a moment before replying, "When a field marshal makes you an offer, you bloody well don't say no." While not exactly a field marshal, Nathan came to the conclusion that the same principle applied here. To refuse would be akin to Adam slapping away the hand of God as He was reaching out to pass on the spark of life.

Drawing himself up, Nathan paused but a moment to take in a deep breath. "It would be a privilege, sir," he stated, doing his best to keep a straight face.

Having accepted the King's shilling, Nathan found himself handed off to Colonel Kaplan, who immediately took the somewhat dumbfounded captain by the arm and led him down to the cafeteria. There, over an early lunch, Kaplan engaged Nathan in friendly, if somewhat banal small talk. It didn't take him long to figure out what Kaplan's game was. He was playing the role as the good cop in the Stevens–Kaplan tag team. It was a technique Nathan himself had used throughout his career, most recently while serving as the commanding officer of a ranger company. While he, the commander, played it straight, allowing him to come down hard when the company was slacking off or there was a miscreant that needed to be punished, his executive officer was everyone's good buddy, confidant and trusty friend in need. Done well, it was an effective way of running an organization, allowing the commanding officer to be the lawgiver and enforcer while offering subordinates a handy pressure-relief valve in the guise of his number two.

In the course of their conversation both officers were afforded the opportunity to find out more about the other. Kaplan, it turned out, was an armor officer who'd commanded a tank battalion during Operation Iraqi Freedom in the spring of 2003. He'd also served as the division operations officer of the

1st Cavalry Division during a subsequent tour in Iraq and recently commanded a brigade belonging to that same division, again in Iraq. Unable to help himself, Nathan observed that it was no wonder that he'd been tagged to serve as the Chief of Staff's executive officer.

Seeing an opening, Kaplan used Nathan's remark as a segue. "The same can be said about you," he stated in an almost offhanded manner.

Caught off guard, Nathan regarded the colonel across from him for a moment. "Oh?"

"The Chief," Kaplan began, "has been looking for a company grade officer with some solid combat experience, one who is articulate, well versed in military theory and who had the ability to hold his own when dealing with senior officers."

"And what makes you and 'The Chief' think I'm that man?"

Before answering, Kaplan leaned back in his seat, taking a sip from his drink while eyeing Nathan. When he did respond, it was all he could do to hide a smirk. "Get real. In addition to being the son of Scott Dixon, you're the officer who almost single-handedly snatched victory from the jaws of certain disaster in the Philippines. I've been informed by reliable sources you're a person who's not afraid to speak his mind. That, and the fact that you just happened to be in the D.C. area awaiting reassignment made the decision almost a no-brainer. Were it not for your choice of schools, you'd be a perfect ten."

Thrown by the comment about his alma mater, Nathan shot Kaplan a quizzical look. "Excuse me?"

"Though he'll never admit to it, the Chief prefers West Pointers."

"Ah, I see. The West Point Protective Association is alive and well," Nathan countered. "So I take it you're a graduate of Hudson High?"

Reaching out his right hand, Kaplan rapped his oversized class ring on the tabletop. "All the way and then some. When I wasn't at wonderful downtown Fort Hood tending to my domestic obligations or in Iraq making the world safe for Democrats, I was an instructor there."

Sensing an opportunity to find out just how genuine Kaplan's good-buddy act was, Nathan decided to see how far he could go with this colonel. "So, you don't have a college education."

The twinkle in Kaplan's eye and his unabashed smile told Nathan all he needed to know. "Like General Peter Boylan, one of our former commandants said, you can't become Spartan by living in Athens. It's a philosophy the Chief seems to believe in."

"And you, sir?"

"Hey, I'm just the hired help. I'm not authorized to have a philosophy. Especially not in this building," he added as he took a moment to gesture at the senior officers scattered throughout the cafeteria. Now," he stated crisply as he prepared to stand up, "the break's over. Time to mount up and move out."

While making their way back from the cafeteria, Nathan slowed his pace every so often to read the

title posted next to the door of a seemingly important office or to check his bearings. Understanding
exactly what Nathan was doing, Kaplan took advantage of this occasion to begin filling Nathan in on
his duties and responsibilities. "Don't expect to spend
a whole lot of time around here," he stated drily.
"What the Chief has in mind for you is right up
your alley."

Though he didn't say it, Nathan's "Oh, sure," expression wasn't lost on Kaplan, causing him to
chuckle. "Seriously," the senior officer replied, "I'm
willing to bet you you'll spend more time in the
field while working for the Chief than you did as a
company commander."

"Somehow I find that a wee bit hard to believe,
Colonel."

Stopping in midstride, Kaplan turned to face Nathan. "Do you really believe the Chief would pull
an officer like you off the line at a time like this just
to be my assistant?"

"Remember, sir, I've been around the Army long
enough to know that logic and common sense are
two commodities that are habitually in short supply," Nathan shot back without hesitation.

After casting a warning glare at a Navy lieutenant
commander who'd slowed his pace to listen in on
their exchange, Kaplan turned his full attention
back on Nathan. "While your assignment was, in
part, a simple accident of being in the right place
at the right time, the reason for your being here is
not." He was about to elaborate when he spotted a
Marine colonel he apparently knew out of the corner of his eye coming down the corridor toward

them. "I'll explain back in the office," Kaplan stated crisply before pivoting on his heels and marching off.

With no other choice but to follow, Nathan followed. This, he thought to himself, ought to be good.

TWO

From the air, the small U.S. Army installation situated midway between the city of Al Kut and the Iranian border didn't look like much to Alex Hughes. Once on the ground, it looked even less impressive. The manner in which he and his fellow passengers had been hustled out of the UH-60 by a crew chief who didn't look old enough to have finished high school yet didn't help Hughes's opinion of the place or the people around him. The Black Hawk hadn't even settled on the ground before the young crew chief was tossing duffel bags and mail sacks out the door, yelling to Hughes and his fellow passengers to get their butts in gear and get out. "I ain't got all day, people. I've got a hot date with a cute little desert fox back at the FOB and she's not the type to wait around."

While the soldiers who were scrambling out of the chopper took the crew chief's admonishments in stride, even giving him a playful thumbs-up as a way of saluting his amorous plans, Hughes felt slighted. He was more than an ordinary run-of-the-mill twenty-something journalist out looking to earn some street cred. As one of *The New York Times*'s few rising stars and a man who'd already been nominated for a Pulitzer, he had expected to receive the same preferential treatment he'd become accustomed to as he was passed from one command to the next while making his way down the military food chain. None of the old hands back in New York, the men and women who'd already done their time in Iraq, bothered to tell him that after a certain point, he'd pretty much be on his own. No doubt, Hughes thought as he dragged his personal gear across the floor of the chopper under the watchful eye of the impatient crew chief, the bastards were enjoying a good laugh at his expense back in New York.

Without waiting for his recently departed passengers to find shelter from the pelting sandstorm the blades of his chopper were whipping up, the pilot of the Black Hawk pulled pitch. As the disgruntled journalist watched it disappear in the distance, he finally began to appreciate just how much of a Faustian deal he'd made with Chuck Mulder, his editor and an outspoken critic of the war in Iraq. The day he'd met with Mulder over lunch at the Four Seasons to discuss what he'd expect Hughes to accomplish while he was in Iraq now seemed like a dream—a dream replaced by the gritty reality of actually being in Iraq.

"Hey, are you Hughes?" The gruff voice caused Hughes to look around to his left, then his right in an effort to locate the source of the voice. "Behind you."

Startled, the journalist spun about to find himself facing a grinning young officer. "My name's Bedford, First Lieutenant Andrew Bedford. I'm the adjutant for 3rd of the 68th Armor. Welcome to Camp Pacesetter," he added as he extended his right hand.

"I'm Alex Hughes."

"We were expecting you yesterday, Mr. Hughes."

Upon hearing this, the journalist bristled. He'd been bumped, literally at the last minute, from the flight he had been set to take from Forward Operating Base Al Kut the previous day in order to make room for a soldier who'd been medevaced to the rear for a dental emergency. Though the sergeant responsible for making up the manifests and assigning priorities to people going out of FOB Al Kut apologized profusely, explaining that the man who'd taken Hughes's place was tagged as mission essential, Hughes threw a fit. By the time he'd found a sympathetic officer who agreed with him and had the authority to do something, the chopper was long gone. With little more than a shrug, that officer had also apologized, wishing Hughes better luck the next day before turning his attention to more important things.

"Well," Hughes grunted. "I'm here."

Ignoring the journalist's sullen manner, Bedford grinned. "Great! If you'd grab your gear and follow me, I'll introduce you to the Old Man." With that, the young officer pivoted about and began to march off at a brisk pace, leaving Hughes standing there with his mouth agape.

* * *

Seated in the cramped battalion briefing room with nothing better to do than listen to an overworked air conditioner laboring away, Hughes couldn't help but imagine that he was part of a poor remake of the movie *Apocalypse Now*, so much so that he almost expected a colonel bearing a striking resemblance to Marlon Brando to come walking in. The man who finally did make an appearance was anything but a grizzled, brooding copy of the movie's Colonel Kurtz. If anything, Lieutenant Colonel Neil Carrington looked more like a corporate lawyer than a combat arms officer. With another officer in tow and sporting a very unmilitary smile, the energetic battalion commander came over to where Hughes was seated. "Glad you finally made it, Mr. Hughes," Carrington announced. "We were under the impression that you were going to be here yesterday, but I guess we were misinformed." As he was saying this, Carrington glanced over at the other officer, a major who noticeably winced when his battalion commander's eyes met his.

In no mood to rehash his pitiful tale of woe and anxious to get on with what he'd come there for, Hughes simply took the colonel's hand, gave it a quick shake and took a seat as he prepared to listen to what had to have been his tenth briefing on the unique organization of the 3rd Battalion, 68th Armor and its mission to test the Army's newest high-tech toys.

"As I'm sure you know by now," Carrington announced in a voice that was more appropriate for addressing an auditorium than a small conference room that looked as if it had been thrown together

using whatever material the troops who built it
could beg, borrow or steal, "this battalion task force
was selected to serve as the test bed for the Army's
first generation of unmanned ground combat vehicles, or UGVs. We are currently working with two
variants, the Harmon M-10 Assault UGV, named
after General Ernest N. Harmon and the Lee M-11
Reconnaissance, Surveillance and Target Acquisition, or RSTA UGV, which is named after Light
Horse Harry Lee. Like the Air Force's MQ-9 Reaper
UAV and the Navy's X-45 UCAV, or unmanned combat aerial vehicle, the primary goal of the Army's
UGV program is to provide the force with an unmanned system that is capable of gathering timely
and accurate intelligence on the enemy, as well as
deliver devastating fire power under any conditions
in the execution of missions that have been deemed
too hazardous for manned combat vehicles."

Having heard the same spiel delivered in conditions that were far more hospitable than his current
surroundings, Hughes cleared his throat. "I do appreciate you going over this material, Colonel," he
announced, making little effort to check the sarcasm in his voice, "but if you don't mind, I didn't
come all this way to listen to the same briefing I got
back in the Pentagon."

If Carrington was bothered by the manner of the
no-name journalist seated across from him, he didn't
show it. Instead, he turned to the major to his left.
"Well, in that case I'll turn you over to Major Grummond, the task force S-3 or operations officer. He'll
go over the current organization of the unit with
you, fill you in on our mission here and how we

intend to carry it out while testing the new systems we have here." With that, Carrington came to his feet, reached across the table and shook Hughes's hand once more. "If you need anything, anything at all, don't hesitate to ask."

Though Hughes already had a laundry list of things he wanted, he knew he stood a snowball's chance in hell of getting any of them, so he kept his mouth shut and watched the colonel execute a hasty retreat before turning his attention to Grummond. Raising his hand, Hughes attempted to fob off the major by telling him the same thing. "I've already heard this briefing as well, so save your breath, Major."

Unlike his superior, Grummond was neither intimidated by the journalist's arrogance nor willing to simply roll over and be treated like a rank second lieutenant. Slouching down in his chair, the task force operations officer brought his hands together on his midsection, lacing the fingers together as he regarded the civilian across from him with narrowed eyes. "I'm sure all kinds of smart people with a lot more rank than I have told you all kinds of things back in the States and at division. Unfortunately, the crap they've been feeding you is out of date."

Taken aback by the gruff manner with which he was being addressed, Hughes sat up in his seat. "I assure you, Major, I've been given access to all the latest data and information concerning this organization."

"Mister," Grummond replied in a most impolitic manner, "you don't know squat. If you'd had let the colonel finish, you'd know that the realities on the ground out here in Nowheresville have forced us to reconfigure this task force several times since we've commenced active combat operations."

For the first time, Hughes forgot about the massive chip he'd been carrying on his shoulder for days and allowed his journalistic instincts to kick in. "Are your superiors aware that you're changing things?"

"Of course they are," Grummond replied as if he'd just heard the leading contender for the world's ten dumbest questions.

"Then why are they still using outdated information during their briefings?"

Grummond shrugged. "Haven't a clue. I suggest you ask them. I've enough problems to deal with here without going around poking my nose in other people's business."

Unable to tell if the major's comment was meant as a swipe at him, Hughes ignored it. "Okay, Major, why don't you tell me how your unit is currently configured?"

For the next half hour, Grummond described how the original idea of having a mix of conventional, manned combat vehicles and unmanned combat vehicles within the same company had proven to be impractical, leading to all sorts of difficulties. "I've no doubt the concept briefed well back in the Pentagon," Grummond muttered, making little effort to hide the sarcasm in his voice. "We even managed to muddle through our unit train-up back at Hood and at the National Training Center using that configuration. But when we got here, we found that the line company commanders were too overwhelmed trying to deal with very different sets of vehicles, all with distinct operational capabilities. In addition, employing the M-10 and M-11 effectively require command and control techniques that are rather unique."

"When you say unique, what exactly do you mean?" Hughes asked, trying to get the major to stop using broad, general terms so many of the briefing officers he'd run into favored.

Grummond paused and looked away as he thought through what he was about to say. When he was ready, he glanced over at Hughes, giving him a wary smile. "Don't take what I'm about to say the wrong way, as if I'm trying to be funny or treat you like an idiot, but manned vehicles function differently in combat than unmanned ones. A platoon leader can order one of his crewed tanks to advance. Once it's on the move, that officer can turn his attention to other vehicles in his platoon or his own tank. If the advancing tank runs into trouble, the commander of that tank, knowing what the rules of engagement are, will make a snap decision and act. An unmanned combat vehicle, on the other hand, has to report back to its operator, who has to assess the situation and make a decision as to how best to respond. He then has to relay the necessary commands back to the UGV which, if all goes well, will follow his instructions. Not only is there a time delay, there's the whole man-machine interface thing that has to be taken into account."

Sitting up, Grummond leaned across the table and placed his hands palms down on it. "The brain of a well-trained soldier, detecting a threat using the sensors God gave all of us, our eyes, ears, sense of smell and even touch, responds almost instinctively. An M-10 operator seated before a computer display located several kilometers away can only see what the cameras and sensors on the M-10 are showing him. The operator has to understand what the data relayed from the UGV is telling him and decide what to do with that data before he can issue his instructions using keyboards, joysticks and touch screens."

"But surely you're only talking about a second or two, aren't you?"

Grummond regarded the journalist for a moment before answering. When he finally spoke, he did so with a deadpan expression. "Mister Hughes, in combat the difference between walking away alive and becoming a statistic is measured in seconds." Then, after taking a quick glance at his watch, Grummond came to his feet. "I've got an op order I need to crank out and not much time. So I'm going to hand you off to our D Company commander, Captain Ethan Fetterman. When it comes to leading a unit in the field, there's none better. He cut his teeth as a mech platoon leader here in Iraq back in oh five prior to being assigned to 3rd of the 68th. He was serving as my assistant ops officer at Fort Hood when he was handpicked to take over command of D Company just as we were beginning our transition training as part of the UGV project," Grummond added in much the same way a proud father did when speaking of a son who happened to be a football hero at the local high school. "I'm sure he'll be more than happy to answer all your questions about what it takes to run a company of UGVs."

Thrilled to be finally getting down to where the controversial combat systems and, he hoped, a good story were, Hughes didn't notice the smirk that had been on Grummond's face as he'd talked about D Company and its commanding officer.

Looking up from his notebook, Lieutenant Patrick Vanderhoff all but winced as he surveyed the faces of his NCOs. They all wore that bored, been there / done that / got the T-shirt expression that told the young platoon leader he was wasting their time. Were it not for the presence of his company commander, standing off to one side watching and listening to everything that he did, Vanderhoff would have skipped the five paragraph operations order he was expected to give before every mission and simply tell his people to mount up and move out. They all knew what to do and what was expected of them. Their mission that night wasn't any different than previous forays outside the wire. All his platoon sergeant and section leaders needed to be told was where they were going and how they'd get there. Everything else had become so ingrained, so second nature that it would have taken a conscious effort by one of his subordinates to screw things up. Still, there was no getting around the requirement to follow the school-approved troop leading procedures. It was something Vanderhoff's commanding officer insisted on, to include ending his briefing by asking his people, "Does anyone have any questions?" Since this was Captain Ethan Fetterman's third trip to the sandbox, Vanderhoff figured the Old Man must know what he was doing, so he did exactly as he was told, no questions asked.

By way of warning, Vanderhoff's platoon sergeant, Sergeant First Class Benjamin Bohnslav, glared at the two section leaders who stood to his left and his right. Bohnslav was a tanker, through and through. He'd cut his teeth with the 2nd Armored Cavalry Regiment as a gunner fighting the Iraqi Tawakalna Republican Guard Division at the Battle of 73 Easting during Desert Storm. Were it not for his temper and a nasty habit of speaking his mind, he'd have been a first sergeant. Not that he would have wanted the job or the rank. Unlike many of his peers, he was happy to stay right where he was and Vanderhoff was happy to have him.

Having completed this briefing, the young officer dismissed his NCOs before casting a leery eye in the direction of his company commander. If his captain stayed true to form, he'd wave Vanderhoff over to where he was and go over everything the platoon would be doing that night even though the mission and how it would be carried out, like the operations order Vanderhoff had just issued, hadn't changed a wit in almost two months of nonstop operations. Only the appearance of Major Grummond with a civilian he wasn't familiar with saved Vanderhoff from that annoying little ritual. Determined to make good his escape while his captain was distracted by the task force operations officer, Vanderhoff tucked his notebook in a pocket and headed off to hide in his track until it was time to move out.

Oblivious to this little drama, Grummond trooped up to Vanderhoff's commanding officer. "Captain Fetterman, this is . . ."

Before he had a chance to finish, Ethan Fetterman raised a hand to his former superior and mentor, palm out, while turning his attention toward a pair of civilians in coveralls who'd been watching Vanderhoff and his NCOs. "Is Delta 23 Alpha ready to go?"

The pudgier of the pair, a male in his late forties, looked over at Fetterman and nodded. "Yup."

"You're sure it's not going to crap out on me again like it did two nights ago?"

Irked by the captain's belligerent tone but determined to keep his own temper in check, the civilian tech, a man by the name of Kevin McKenzie, sighed. "Captain, we ran a full diagnostics test on D23A's electrical system."

Turning about until he was facing the pair of civilian techs full on, Fetterman planted his fists firmly on his hips, leaned forward and shoved his face to within inches of McKenzie's. "I didn't ask you what you did. I asked you if that diminutive bucket of bolts was going to make it through the night."

Like all the other technicians and field representatives from United Strategic Technologies, McKenzie was tired of the way Fetterman treated them. Just as he was about to respond to the captain, the other civilian tech, a petite female who was a full head shorter than both men, pushed his companion aside and stepped up in front of Fetterman. "There is nothing wrong with D23A except operator head-space and timing," she snapped. "Your people simply have to crank up the engine at the prescribed intervals and keep the batteries charged."

Fetterman was about to have a go at the female when Major Grummond, who'd been watching the escalating confrontation, cleared his throat. "Captain Fetterman, a word please. Now."

Doing his best to stifle his anger, the commanding officer of D Company, 3rd of the 68th Armor, walked over to Grummond, who threw his arm about the captain's shoulder and led him several paces away, leaving Hughes with the civilians.

"So, you two must be with United Strategic Technologies," Hughes ventured in an effort to break the uncomfortable silence.

The petite redhead who'd thrown herself in front of Fetterman, a twenty something by the name of Jordan Sinclair, was still fuming. She made a great show of tugging at the US Technologies corporate logo sewn on her left breast pocket so Hughes could inspect it before looking back up at him. "What was your first clue, Sherlock?"

Taken aback by her response, as well as the way the other people he'd met at Pacesetter carried on, Hughes began to wonder if everyone out here had the temperament of a pissed-off Rottweiler. Never having been around military types before, Hughes hoped not. Otherwise, he concluded, this assignment was going to be even more distasteful than he'd feared.

Sensing that things were becoming a wee bit contentious between his coworker and the stranger,

McKenzie managed to scrounge up a smile as he extended his right hand to Hughes. "The name is McKenzie, Kevin McKenzie. I'm a senior automotive specialist with UST. And this feisty young lass," he added with a nod of his head, "is Jordan Sinclair, Electronics and Communications specialist with the UGV project."

Without warning, Sinclair jabbed her elbow into McKenzie's midsection, causing the man to yelp. When he saw the smirk on McKenzie's face, Hughes relaxed. "I'm Alex Hughes. I'm with *The New York Times*, here to do a story on the unit and the UGVs."

Realizing that he was talking to someone who was, in all likelihood, a cut above your average, run-of-the-mill reporters, McKenzie straightened up and flashed Hughes his most becoming smile. "Well, if there's anything you want to know about the M-10 or M-11, feel free to ask. I've been with the project from the beginning."

Relieved to finally meet someone who was not only friendly and knowledgeable about the system, but actually had access to one, Hughes grinned. "You know, I've been briefed on the UGV project by everyone and their brother, but I've yet to see a real one up close and personal."

"I'm sure Jordan and I can correct that little oversight, can't we?" the older tech stated as he gave his coworker a wink.

In no mood to play show and tell at the moment, Jordan Sinclair made her excuses before heading back to where the UST personnel were billeted.

With the journalist in tow, McKenzie headed over to a maintenance shelter where a UGV awaiting repair was parked. "This is it," the pudgy civilian beamed, spreading his arms out as if he was about to embrace the twenty-ton vehicle. "As you can see, this one is an M-10, armed with the same M242 25mm automatic cannon as the Bradley as well as a launcher for two FGM-148 Javelin antitank guided missiles. The most obvious difference between the M-10 and a Lee M-11," McKenzie stated while running a hand along the armored flank of the vehicle as if it were his pride and joy, "is in lieu of the 25mm gun, the Lee is armed with twin M-240 machine guns and has a more sophisticated reconnaissance, surveillance and target acquisition module mounted where the missile launchers would have been. The primary reason the M-11 isn't better armed is the need to make room in its turret for a pair of Class I unmanned aerial vehicles built by Honeywell. They're used to go into buildings or get a bird's-eye view of the area. This gives one section of M-11s, which is a single, manned M-1209 command and control track operating two M-11s and four UAVs, the ability to cover a large area quickly."

Having heard all of this before, Hughes tuned out the civilian contractor as he slowly began to circle the vehicle, inspecting it as he went along.

"Both vehicles are powered by the same 350 horsepower turbo diesel manufactured by Caterpillar that is used in the Stryker," McKenzie continued, oblivious to the fact that he was being ignored. "Because the M-10 has a lower center of gravity and doesn't have the same crew safety issues the Stryker does, the Army decided not to govern the engine, giving this puppy a top speed of sixty plus miles an hour."

Stopping as he came around to the front of the vehicle, Hughes pointed to a small screen in a pivoting mount that was set into an armored blister. "Aren't these sensors vulnerable to enemy fire?"

Unaware that Hughes hadn't been keeping up with his canned pitch, McKenzie had to backtrack and regroup before he could provide an answer. "Which ones? The LADAR?

Unable to help himself, Hughes shook his head and chuckled. "You're almost as bad as the Army types, tossing those acronyms about as if everyone spoke in military shorthand and understood what you were talking about."

"Sorry. It's just that when you work with the same project and people for as long as I have, you tend to forget yourself when trying to explain things to someone who's never laid eyes on the M-10," McKenzie explained sheepishly. "LADAR stands for Laser Detection and Ranging sensors. Each of these nodding mechanisms contains a laser that determines the distance between the M-10 and any object within its field of vision. When the vehicle is in autonomous navigation mode, the LADAR provides the planning module, the M-10's brain, with the information it needs to move about and steer around obstacles. If the M-10 is being controlled by the human operator, a 3D color camera located there, just to the right of the gun mount, and another on top of the turret provide the human operator a clear view of the same thing on a monitor at his remote location. To test how well a degraded system would function, we disabled up to three of the LA-DAR navigational sensors. While it did slow things down and make driving the M-10 awkward, it was still doable, much the same as if a human suddenly lost the use of one of his eyes. If anything, the M-10's planning module did a better job of coping with the loss of one or more of its sensors than the human operators did when they lost the use of one of the cameras they use when maneuvering the M-10 in manual mode."

Hughes could not help but detect a sense of pride in McKenzie's voice as he made this last point. It was as if the soldiers who were the operators were a handicap and his baby, the M-10, didn't need them.

"Even if we did lose all four of the navigational sensors and both cameras, we'd still have the FLIR, or forward-looking infrared driving camera the operator could use. As a last resort, there's the GPS unit. While the operator or the UGV's planning unit would be blind, both would know where the M-10 is at all times, giving the M-10 a fighting chance to limp its way back to a linkup point with the mother ship."

"Mother ship?"

McKenzie laughed. "Yeah. That's what everyone has taken to calling the M-1209 command and control vehicle, or C2V. That's where the remote operators and their section leader are located. Each M-1209 has two operators, positioned side by side behind control panels and monitors that provide them information about the M-10 or M-11 they're responsible for. They've got a section leader, seated behind them, who has a master display that not only provides him with information concerning the location and status of his two UGVs, but also where the other UGVs in the platoon are. That is added to tactical data concerning the enemy, which is fed to his vehicle via a downlink from Air Force MQ-9 Reaper, other UGVs, or from task force. The section leader also serves as the commander of the C2V, directing the driver of that track."

As the civilian tech rep was going over this with Hughes, the journalist began to understand what the major had been trying to explain to him about the problems with the man-machine interface. He was about to ask this when Major Grummond and Captain Fetterman interrupted.

"Mister Hughes, I'm going to turn you over to Captain Fetterman. You'll be embedded with his unit for the duration of your stay here."

Eager to get started on his story, Hughes asked if he might go out with the platoon that was in the process of moving out. Before answering, Fetterman glanced over to the operations officer, who understood exactly what the company commander was thinking. "I'm afraid that won't be possible," Grummond explained, wearing a very contrived smile. "Captain Fetterman's 2nd Platoon is set and ready to roll. Were we to try squeezing you in, it would delay their departure and badly screw things up. But I assure you," Grummond quickly added, regarding Fetterman with a long hard stare as he did so, "once you're settled in with Delta Company, you'll have free and complete access to our operations and personnel. Now," Grummond stated crisply in a manner that left no one in doubt that this discussion was at an end, "if you gentlemen will excuse me, I've got tomorrow's operations to plan for." With that, he pivoted about and beat a hasty retreat to his ops center, leaving a very ambitious journalist in the care of an extremely disgruntled young captain.

THREE

After adjusting the brightness of his monitor, Specialist Evan Cutty eased back in his seat and rubbed his eyes. He was bored, seriously and undeniably bored. At the moment his M-10, bumper number D23A, was set in autonomous mode, merrily trundling along in column with the rest of the platoon's M-10s one kilometer ahead of 2nd Platoon's command and control vehicles. It didn't matter that the dust being thrown up by the M-10s belonging to the 2nd Platoon's Alpha section, just ahead of D23A and moving along the same dirt road, rendered all its onboard cameras useless. Data being relayed from D23A's GPS tracker kept Cutty posted on where it was, which was exactly where it was supposed to be. To his right was Alexander Viloski, the operator of the section's other M-10, D23B. At the moment he was slouched down in his seat, sound asleep. He had the right idea, Cutty thought. At least he was doing something productive.

Seated behind the two operators was their section leader and commander of D23, Staff Sergeant Justin Plum, better known as Jay. Plum wasn't paying any attention to the pair of monitors at his station that displayed the activities of D23A and D23B, or to the other M-10s and C2Vs in the platoon. Instead, he was riding high with his head and upper torso sticking up through D23's track commander's hatch, scanning his assigned sector of responsibility. Like Bohnslav, he'd served in tank units his entire career, that is, until they'd been assigned to 3rd of 68th Armor. And like Bohnslav, Plum wasn't quite ready yet to put his full faith and confidence in the technological wonders they were responsible for. While the M-10 had pretty much done what it had been built to do, so far, and was superior to any human when it came to a certain function, in particular target acquisition, Plum wasn't about to bet his life on a sophisticated weapons system built by the lowest bidder, especially one that was still experiencing some quirky teething problems. He'd seen what happened to people who didn't pay attention to what was happening around them while outside the wire during previous tours in Iraq. So he kept his eyes open and his mind squarely focused on what they were doing whenever they were downrange, using his own God given sensors just in case the UGVs failed them.

Just ahead of Plum's C2V was Lieutenant Vanderhoff's track, bumper number D21. Though he was just as determined to keep up with what was going on around him, the young officer relied upon the bank of monitors he shared with Corporal William

Zhso, seated to his left. Zhso was the platoon's re-connaissance and information integration special-ist, or RI2S. In a platoon where just about everyone, including the drivers of the C2Vs, were dyed in the wool computer geeks and techno wizards, Zhso was something of a Zen master when it came to the nu-merous computers the 2nd Platoon relied upon and were linked to. Zhso's sole duty was monitoring both friendly and enemy throughout the platoon's area of operation. To accomplish this, he relied upon infor-mation fed to him via direct computer links with all of 2nd Platoon's M-10s, the M-11s in the company's reconnaissance platoon and an Air Force MQ-9 Reaper that was always overhead whenever any part of 3rd of the 68th was outside the wire. Other sources included real-time satellite imagery, when it was available. It was Zhso's task to sort through the glut of data he received, much of it quite raw, and pro-vide his platoon leader with all pertinent informa-tion on friendly and enemy forces he needed to make sound tactical decisions. It was something Zhso excelled at. Were it not for his sarcastic atti-tude, particularly when dealing with non-technically oriented officers, he'd have been a sergeant and the company commander's RI2S. Even Vanderhoff, an easygoing type who got along well with his men, found the Asian-American's sharp tongue a bit too much from time to time. Any talk of replacing the techno wizard, however, gave the young officer night-mares. Given the nature of the platoon, Zhso was arguably the most valuable man in it.

In the eerie glow of D21's dark interior, Vander-hoff and Zhso watched the array of monitors before them. Under normal circumstances neither man had direct control over any of the six M-10s assigned to the 2nd Platoon. That responsibility belonged to Staff Sergeant Aaron Holly, who was the section leader of the platoon's Alpha section; Plum, who had the Bravo section; and Bohnslav, who ran the Charlie section in addition to serving as Vanderhoff's platoon sergeant. Since it had been determined during the project's development and initial trials that burdening the platoon leader of a UGV platoon with M-10s of his own made it all but impossible to run his platoon effectively, Vanderhoff's sole job was command and control.

To accomplish this, his C2V, like all C2Vs belonging to platoon leaders, was configured differently than the other command and control vehicles in the platoon. From his seat, Vanderhoff monitored all the platoon's vehicles, both the M-10 UGVs and the modified M-1209 C2Vs, issuing orders to his section leaders based on information he received from Corporal Zhso, what Vanderhoff himself saw on his monitors by tapping into the data links of his platoon's M-10s and, of course, orders issued to him from his commanding officer, Captain Fetterman. Though he did have the ability to take over the control of any of the platoon's M-10s, standing orders within 3rd of the 68th forbade a platoon leader or company commander of a UGV unit from doing so unless it was an emergency. Just what constituted an emergency was something no one ever bothered to define.

At the moment, Zhso's primary monitor was displaying a map showing 2nd Platoon's location as well as all the operational graphics within the 3rd of the 68th's sector. With the exception of several Iraqi Army outposts set back a safe distance from the Iranian border, there wasn't another friendly unit within thirty kilometers.

Vanderhoff also had a map on the large monitor in front of him, but in a much tighter scale, one that was limited to the immediate area his platoon was moving through. A monitor that sat between them could be shared or used by either man depending on their needs. It was currently displaying the detailed operational and mechanical status of all of 2nd Platoon's vehicles. A wing display to Vanderhoff's right was linked to the gun camera belonging to the lead M-10 in his platoon column while Zhso's wing monitor, situated to his left, kept a running tab on all the intelligence assets and data links that were currently available to him.

Seated directly behind the young officer was Specialist David Larson, a man who was as much a techie as Zhso. He was the platoon's technical and systems integrations specialist. Since the success or failure of a unit equipped with M-10s depended entirely on all computers and related systems functioning properly, it had been decided to assign a systems tech to each platoon. That soldier was responsible for troubleshooting computer related problems wherever the platoon was and either repair it on the spot or come up with a fix that would allow the system to limp along in a degraded mode until battalion techs or civilian contractors could have a crack at it. Since all systems were functioning properly at the moment, Larson had nothing to do, leaving him free to watch a DVD on his monitor. Though doing so while on an operation was in violation of standing orders and could be punished with company grade Article 15, Vanderhoff tended to turn a blind eye to such minor infractions, provided his people were ready and able to switch back to full kill mode, as he called it, the second they ran into trouble.

The last man in the crew compartment of D21 that night was Omer Mohajeri, an Iraqi soldier who served as D Company's translator and liaison with Iraqi Army units and local tribal leaders. While he was supposed to be on the company commander's C2V, when only one of D Company's platoons was in the field, the Iraqi was pawned off onto the platoon leader. It's not that Fetterman didn't understand the need for someone like Mohajeri, it's just that he didn't want anything to do with him, or any other Iraqi for that matter, if he could avoid it. And since Fetterman was the company commander and what he said was law in D Company, Mohajeri went where he told him to go.

When Mohajeri had been told that he'd be working with 3rd of the 68th Armor on its unique mission, he had been excited. A University graduate, he'd always prided himself on being technically sophisticated and well above average when it came to his knowledge of the world outside Iraq. So it came as something of a shock to the twenty-four-year-old Iraqi when he actually met the Americans he'd be working with. To him, it was as if he'd been abducted by space aliens and whisked away to a world that bore no resemblance to the one that lay just beyond

the armor plate of the C2V he often found himself
imprisoned in. And try as he might to play catch-up
to men who'd been born with game controllers in
their hands and a sense of entitlement that was bewildering to him, Sami al-Mohajeri was slowly coming to appreciate that he was fighting a losing battle.
The Americans he worked with, ate with and lived
with were a breed apart. Whether they were to be
admired or scorned was something Mohajeri hadn't
quite made his mind up about.

There was one more person who was always with
Vanderhoff no matter where he went, someone who
exerted an influence that was so powerful he didn't
even need to be in the same vehicle as the young
platoon leader. That, of course, was Captain Ethan
Fetterman, the commanding officer of D Company,
one of two M-10/M-11 companies within the 3rd of
the 68th. It couldn't be said that Vanderhoff, or any
of the other officers in D Company, liked Fetterman. They respected him. They all agreed that of the
company commanders assigned to 3rd of the 68th,
Fetterman was by far the most tactically and technically proficient, not to mention one of the most experienced. As a platoon leader during his first tour of
duty in 2005 he'd earned the Bronze Star with V de-
vice as well as a Purple Heart. He definitely knew
how to get the job done. But to like him as one human likes another? No. No one who knew Fetterman
could really own up to that with a straight face. He
didn't try to be unfriendly or cold. He didn't have to.
It seemed to everyone who knew him that those traits
came to him as naturally as breathing.

At the moment Fetterman was in his C2V, D66,

located a short distance behind Vanderhoff's column traveling along with a C2V from the company's 3rd Platoon, the one responsible for all six of the company's M-11 reconnaissance UGVs. When it came time to establish a table of organization for a UGV company, a number of competing theories had been discussed within the Army's Training and Doctrine Command. One envisioned pure combat companies, consisting of three assault platoons equipped with M-10 UGVs while keeping all M-11 reconnaissance UGVs within the task force consolidated in a single reconnaissance troop. Another configuration saw M-10s and M-11s mixed together within the same platoon, with two sections, the Alpha and Bravo sections, having M-10s and the Charlie section M-11s. The third option given serious consideration advocated equipping two platoons in the UGV company with M-10s while all M-11s were assigned to its third. Since no one knew which would be more effective, Training and Doctrine Command decided to test both the mixed UGV platoons and the pure UGV platoons side by side. B Company, 3rd of the 68th Armor had three mixed platoons. D Company had two M-10 platoons and one M-11 platoon. The remaining companies, A and C, retained their M-1 tanks and M-2 Bradleys, providing 3rd of the 68th with both long-range firepower and the ability to conduct dismounted operations in areas that were unsuitable for the UGVs.

Under the configuration D Company was operating, Fetterman had a choice. He could either attach one M-11 section to each of his assault platoons while retaining one M-11 under his direct control,

or he could keep his 3rd Platoon, the Reconnaissance platoon, together. Without fail Fetterman always opted for the latter, a decision that none of his
platoon leaders were happy about, for it gave Fetterman an excuse to accompany his assault platoons
every time they rolled out the front gate, even when
executing the most routine missions such as the
one 2nd Platoon was in the process of executing.
That meant that the pair of M-11s belonging to the
3rd Platoon's Bravo section, which was currently conducting a route reconnaissance ahead of Vanderhoff's platoon, were not under Vanderhoff's control.
Instead, they were being controlled from D-33, the
other C2V traveling with Fetterman. If Vanderhoff
needed the M-11s to check out something up ahead
of his platoon, he couldn't task the M-11s himself,
he had to go through Fetterman, verbally describing
the situation and the need to task the M-11s. Once
that was done, Vanderhoff had to wait for his company commander to decide if the request was a valid
one. If the answer to that was yes, it was Fetterman,
and not Vanderhoff, who relayed the necessary orders to the commander of D-33, who, in turn, was
responsible for dispatching one or both of his M-11s
to carry out those orders. To Vanderhoff and the
other platoon leaders in D Company, this was a step
that was both totally unnecessary and dangerous.
Even a soldier who was on his first tour of duty in
an active theater of operations knew that the more
moving pieces you have, the more likely it is that
things are going to go wrong. Still, as cumbersome as
this technique was, the practice of employing mixed
platoons was not without its problems, something

that the battalion commander often discussed with his staff. In the end, everyone knew that the final decision as to the best way to go would be made by men who had never been there on the ground when a UGV unit was engaged in active combat or, in all likelihood, had never even laid eyes on either an M-10 or an M-11. It was, after all, the way the Army did things.

An audio cue in Vanderhoff's headset, followed by a computer generated voice alerted him that his platoon was five minutes away from Checkpoint Two, a fork in the road. One hundred meters beyond it was a small farming community. Since the M-10s were at a severe disadvantage when operating in urbanized terrain, Fetterman and his fellow UGV company commander tended to avoid built-up areas whenever possible. Checking out those locations were usually assigned to C Company, the task force's mech infantry unit. In order to avoid the built-up area ahead, the route Fetterman had laid out for Vanderhoff required the 2nd Platoon to leave the road just before the fork and strike off cross-country, deploying into a wedge formation as they did so. They'd remain in that formation until they reached their assigned patrol area along the Iraqi-Iranian border where the platoon's M-10s would establish combat outposts. Once set, they'd spend the balance of the night watching for infiltrators coming into Iraq from Iran.

Despite having thoroughly briefed his section leaders before moving out, Vanderhoff felt it was necessary to alert them of their impending change in formation. "Delta Two, Delta Two, this is Delta 21. Checkpoint Two in zero-five. Acknowledge, over."

In sequence, each section leader responded with a simple, "Roger out." Unlike his fellow armor officers, Vanderhoff didn't feel the need to pop his head up through the hatch and watch his platoon as it deployed from a column into a wedge formation. It wasn't so much that he had supreme confidence in his people, although he did. It's just that he could see everything his platoon was doing on the monitor in front of him far better than he could if he stuck his head up and tried to watch the pending maneuver using nothing more than his own eyes. Besides, doing so would have required him to open his hatch, something he hated to do. Despite an overpressure system that was supposed to keep dust and contaminated air from rushing in through any openings in Vanderhoff's C2V, the fine dust of the Iraqi desert always seemed to find a way of overwhelming American technology with minute particles of dust the tracks of vehicles farther ahead in the column threw up. Besides, Corporal Zhso, who was very protective of the computers and monitors that he relied on, made no effort to hide his displeasure whenever his lieutenant opened the hatch while they were moving.

Aboard D23, the concerns were quite different. When he heard his platoon leader's alert, Specialist Cutty sat up in his seat, squirming a bit as he prepared to switch his M-10, D23A, from autonomous mode to remote control, referred to by M-10 operators as auto and manual, respectively. Normally this

was no big deal. D23A, however, had developed a
slew of quirky glitches shortly after 3rd of the 68th
had commenced operations in Iraq. Most had been
sorted out by the combined efforts of the unit's maintenance teams and the contractors. A few, however
defied their best efforts to diagnose, much less resolve.

The most annoying and persistent fault was with
the electrical system. Every now and then, when
D23A's turret and fire control system was brought
online after the vehicle had been operating for an
extended period of time, the entire UGV shut down.
Diagnostics run back at Camp Pacesetter always
came up negative. Even when Captain Fetterman
had insisted on dragging Jordan Sinclair, the UST
systems integration specialist and James Morgan,
UST's weapons specialist, downrange to run their
tests on D23A immediately after it failed, the civilian contractors were unable to isolate, let alone eliminate the problem. Fetterman's requests that D23A
be left behind until the contractor tech team came
up with a solution that worked were always overrid-
den by Colonel Carrington. "If it can move out the
front gate under its own power," Carrington informed Fetterman in no uncertain terms, "it goes."

It was a decision that no one in Delta Company,
especially Cutty, was thrilled with since every time
D23 crapped out while on a mission a recover team,
supported by a security detachment from 3rd of the
68th's ready reaction force, or RRF, had to come
out and retrieve it. That made for long hours the following day for Cutty, since he, as D23A's operator,
had to be with it while the maintenance and con-

tractor teams worked on it. Even worse, the infan-
trymen of the RRF, who were always drawn from C
Company, never tired of ribbing and ridiculing the
UGV operators whenever they were dispatched to
recover a malfunctioning UGV.

Ducking down from his perch, Staff Sergeant
Plum glanced over Cutty's shoulder as the platoon
was closing on Checkpoint Two. "Five dollars says
she goes tango uniform when you fire up the fire
control."

Cutty didn't answer. He knew it was a sucker bet
and wasn't in the mood to joke about something
that was making him look bad in the eyes of his fellow soldiers. Sweating now, despite the cold air the
C2V's air conditioner was blowing directly onto him,
he grasped D23A's remote controller with his right
hand as he reached up with his left to the box on his
monitor's touch screen labeled *Manual Mode.* "Here
we go," he muttered, more to himself than in response
to Plum.

With a quick tap, Cutty took D23A out of auto
mode and took control of it. "So far so good," Plum
whispered to no one in particular as he watched
D23A's primary monitor over Cutty's shoulder.

"Don't get too excited," Cutty shot back. "I haven't
engaged the turret or fire control."

"Well, now's the time to do it, before we get too
far from the road. If this little beastie of yours is
going to pack it in, I'd prefer it does it where recovery operations will be easy."

Finding no fault with his section leader's assessment, Cutty prepared to switch on D23A's turret
power. "Here goes nothing."

And that is exactly what they saw on Cutty's monitor the second he tapped the box on the screen labeled *FC* for Fire Control. All images disappeared, leaving only the row of pressure-sensitive boxes on the left side of the screen illuminated. Another row of flashing red warning lights arrayed across the top indicated D23A had suffered a total systems failure, again.

In the C2V in front of Plum's, a series of high pitched beeps alerted Lieutenant Vanderhoff that one of his M-10s had malfunctioned. He didn't even bother to glance over at the monitor between him and Zhso to see which one was non-op. Unable to help himself, the young officer muttered, "Son of a bitch."

From behind him, Larson turned away from his screen and peeked over his platoon leader's shoulder. "Which bitch are you talkin' 'bout, LT? D23A or the female contractor who keeps insisting that there's nothing wrong with it other than operator head space and timing?"

Before he could answer, Vanderhoff heard his company commander calling him over the radio, asking him for a status report on D23A. Specialist Zhso looked over at Vanderhoff. "I wouldn't want to be sitting next to the Old Man."

The young officer said nothing as he prepared to tell his company commander what he already knew. Even as he was doing so over the company FM radio net, Vanderhoff could hear his platoon sergeant over the platoon net issuing the order to laager up around the disabled M-10. Though everyone in 2nd Platoon knew it was a waste of time to have Larson

dismount and troubleshoot D23A, doing so was part
of the protocol the M-10/M-11 project officer at the
Army's Maneuver Test Directorate back at Fort
Hood had dreamed up. It was a nauseatingly detailed, step-by-step guide that had to be followed to
a T or there would be hell to pay. The upside was
that by doing so, it took the onus off 2nd Platoon's
back. Once Larson had completed his troubleshooting checklist without success, everyone in the platoon, from Vanderhoff on down, could step back
and watch as the shit defied gravity and began its
uphill journey.

Alex Hughes didn't need to be a military genius to
know that the operation he'd been watching on the
monitors at the command post of the 3rd of the 68th
had hit a serious snag. With a glare that could have
cut through steel, the task force commander turned
and looked over to the corner of his CP to where a
trio of UST contractors were seated. Though Jordan
Sinclair wasn't the most senior of the three civilians
who'd been monitoring D Company's progress in
the task force's tactical operations center, or TOC,
she'd been the one who, a few short hours ago, had
assured Captain Fetterman that there was absolutely nothing wrong with D23A, an assessment
he'd passed onto his commanding officer. The journalist watched as the petite female engineer's cheeks
slowly took on a hue that threatened to match her
flaming red hair.

Hughes wasn't the only person watching this exchange between warrior and arms merchant. Peter

White, the senior United Strategic Technologies field rep, took note of the way Lieutenant Colonel Carrington was eyeing his engineer. Before coming to his feet, he turned and whispered something in Sinclair's ear. Coming to her feet, she hesitated a moment, tightly clutching her fists at her side before spinning about on her heels and beating a hasty retreat, thus avoiding a fireworks display that would have done nothing to resolve D Company's problem.

With his fiery young coworker out of the way, White, a retired Army colonel, made his way over to where Carrington was in the process of coming to his feet. If he was expecting those two men to have at each other, Hughes was sadly disappointed. Instead, after raising his hand to keep White from talking first, Carrington turned to the staff officer on duty and ordered him to roll the RRF and a recovery team. "Give them the coordinates and notify Captain Fetterman when they've cleared the front gate. Then order Fetterman to continue with his mission."

Major Grummond, who'd been seated next to Carrington, looked up at his commanding officer with an expression that clearly showed his displeasure with his decision. Anticipating his operations officer's objection, Carrington looked down at Grummond and smiled. "I don't see any need to have Captain Fetterman stay there with D23 and babysit them. Do you?" While on the surface Carrington appeared to be soliciting an honest answer, even from where he was seated Hughes could tell the task force commander was warning his operations officer to keep his opinions to himself.

Having taken care of that little chore, Carrington turned his attention to the civilian contractor. With nothing more than a nod of his head, he indicated to White that he wanted to talk to him in private outside. Though he would have liked to follow and listen in on that exchange, Hughes was smart enough to know that he wouldn't be welcome. Besides, anxious to quickly learn as much about the UGV program as he could so he could get out of this shit hole of a country, Hughes hung back and watched the show that was unfolding some twenty kilometers away. This, the journalist found himself thinking as he scanned the bank of monitors and computer screens that adorned the TOC, was better than a reality show on TV. Here the players didn't get voted off the island, at least not using paper ballots.

With the rest of the platoon and their company commander gone, there was little for the crew of D23 to do but wait. Perched on top of his disabled M-10 with his M-4 rifle cradled in his arms, Cutty scanned the horizon. Ahead he could see lights in the windows of the huts that lay just beyond the road junction. Between where he was seated and those huts he could barely make out D23B. At the moment it was standing sentry, keeping an eye on what Staff Sergeant Plum determined to be the most likely source of trouble.

Parked a few meters to one side of Cutty's disabled M-10 and just off the road was the section's C2V. Plum was sitting on his vehicle's roof with his legs dangling through the open hatch, watching the

surrounding desert not being watched by Cutty or
D23B. He wore his combat vehicle crewman's helmet, or CVC, cocked to one side of his head so that
he could hear the radio with one ear and listen for
any unusual sounds with the other. Inside D23 Specialist Viloski, now wide-awake, was monitoring
D23B as it automatically scanned the sector of responsibility he'd assigned it to cover. Viloski had
flipped D23B's sights into thermal mode, allowing
him to penetrate the darkness that shrouded the
forlorn little band of American soldiers and their
high-tech machines. The only other sign of life vis-
ible in the pristine night air were a few dim lights
glowing in the windows of the huts, little more than
a hundred meters away and a barking dog.

Unable to ignore the dog's yapping which seemed
to be getting more strident, Cutty turned away from
his assigned sector and gazed off in the direction of
the squat Iraqi dwellings. "Hey, Jay?"

Without bothering to look behind to where Cutty
was, Plum replied in a low voice, "What is it?"

"I thought the hajjis consider dogs unclean."

"They do."

"Why do you suppose that is?"

"How long have you been in Iraq?" Plum asked
as he continued to peer into the darkness.

"Same as you, three months."

"This time around," Plum replied as a way of reminding Cutty this wasn't his first time downrange
in Iraq. "That aside, you mean to tell me you've
been here for three months and you still don't know
anything about these people?"

Cutty shrugged. "According to the Old Man, the

only thing I need to know about them is which ones are the really bad guys and which ones are just plain bad but aren't worth wasting a bullet on."

Plum chuckled. "Spoken like a true American."

"So why do the hajjis hate dogs?"

"That's easy. Muhammad didn't like dogs. That, and their belief that angels won't enter a house that contains a dog makes them unpopular."

"So why do they keep them?"

"Another easy one. Those dogs are there to give hajj a heads-up whenever a redneck dickhead like you comes snooping around."

Cutty thought about that for a moment. "If that's so, then why is that mutt barking its damned fool head off? I mean, I don't remember hearing it when we first got here."

For the first time Plum turned away from the area he'd been watching and glanced over his shoulder at the huts. "That's a good question," he muttered before yelling down through the open hatch to Viloski. "Hey, Ski. You awake?"

From down below, Viloski snarled, "Of course I am. I'm not a total slouch."

"You seein' anything up ahead?"

Before answering, Viloski took a moment to study his monitor as D23B made a full sweep, aware that Plum wouldn't have asked him if he wasn't worried about something. Only when he was satisfied that there was nothing out there that shouldn't have been did Viloski reply, "Nothing. Not a damned thing."

Knowing full well that he had a better view of what was going on up the road because of his higher vantage point, Plum was about to ask Viloski to pass up his night vision goggles when he heard his call sign over the radio. "D23, this is D8 and friends. We're five minutes out, over."

Keying his radio, Plum acknowledged the call from Sergeant Brian Giese, the recovery specialist assigned to D Company. With that, Plum removed his CVC, hanging it from the M151 Remote Weapons Station located in front of the commander's hatch. Standing up on top of his C2V, the section leader stretched before dismounting to give Cutty a hand. "Cutty, Giese is just about here. Get your little beastie ready to go."

"She's ready to go now. All I need is a . . ."

A flash up the road in the direction from which the recovery vehicle and escorting Bradley were coming, followed several seconds later by the sounds of an explosion, sent Plum diving into the open hatch at his feet and Cutty scrambling down off the top of D23A. While he didn't know what exactly was going on, Cutty knew he didn't want to be sitting up on top of a nonoperational M-10, silhouetted against the horizon.

Inside D23, Plum was in the process of ordering PFC Marsden, D23's driver to crank up the track when Viloski sang out with a contact report. "Two possible hostiles, eleven o'clock from 23B. It looks like they've got an RPG."

Plum didn't even bother to check his own monitor. Having been in far too many ambushes like this one during his previous tour in Iraq, he didn't hesitate. "Permission to engage. Light those bastards up!"

Since D23B was in auto mode and its 25mm cannon was already aimed in that general direction,

Viloski simply reached up and hit the target desig-
nate button on his touch screen before tapping the
screen where the thermal images of two Iraqis were
displayed. Without hesitation D23B's turret slew
about till it was trained on the spot Viloski had indicated. As soon as a red box appeared around the
suspected RPG team and he heard a tone in his headset indicating that D23B had target locked, Viloski
hit the fire button on his controller.

From his position in the lee of his own M-10,
Cutty watched as D23B lit up the night with a quick
volley of 25mm HE rounds. While most of the
rounds found their mark, tearing apart the mud and
brick wall behind, which the pair of insurgents had
been hiding as well as the insurgents themselves,
a few of D23B's rounds passed over it, sailing on
through the night until they slammed into the farm
huts beyond.

"Well," Cutty muttered to himself as he watched
D23B's rounds ripping into the huts, "looks like
we've managed to fuck up somebody's night."

It all happened so fast and with so little commotion
within 3rd of the 68th's TOC that Hughes didn't
even know what exactly was going on before it was
all over. One minute he was sitting there, struggling
to stay awake; the next, the radios began to blare, the
duty officer took to issuing orders and the images on
the monitors suddenly went from displaying a dark
tranquil landscape to scenes of utter chaos filled
with tracers ripping through the night and distant
explosions marking their impact. The journalist so

wanted to ask someone what was happening, but didn't know whom to ask.

Everyone around him seemed to be busy, going about their duties with a well-measured ease that belied the seriousness of the situation. A junior NCO was rushing out the door that the task force commander and Peter White had gone, no doubt to fetch him back to the TOC. The duty officer was banging away on his keyboard, trying to tap into the sensors and gun sights on the vehicles that were currently engaged with the insurgents in an effort to provide the operations officer with the best possible view of the situation out there. Major Grummond was on the radio with Captain Fetterman, listening to that officer's assessment of the situation and his intentions. Another officer was on the phone, talking to the air liaison officer at brigade, requesting that the MQ-9 Reaper on station be diverted from its current orbital track near the Iranian border westward, back to where D23 and D8 were being engaged. Hughes seemed to be the only person there who didn't have anything to do, a useless fragment knocking about the workings of a well-oiled machine.

Ever so slowly, it dawned upon the young journalist that he was, in fact, doing exactly what he was supposed to be doing. He was watching, listening and mentally recording everything that he saw going on around him. While it was true that he didn't understand a fraction of what he was seeing or hearing, that didn't matter. When it was all over, when the fog of battle had lifted, he'd write it all down. If time permitted and he felt the need to do so, he'd ask

NO WARRIORS, NO GLORY

someone for clarification. Not that he would. Having dealt with city officials and government spokespersons before, he knew it was best to go with his own impressions of events and ignore the official explanations that were usually little more than well-massaged versions of what had actually happened. Not only did his editor expect it of him, the young journalist knew that if he framed his stories just right, he could very well get the break he so desperately wanted and needed.

Of all the things that occurred to Hughes that night, the thing that left the deepest impression was the casualness with which the officers and soldiers around him went about their tasks and their cold, rather callous attitudes to what was happening. By the time Carrington had made his way back into the TOC, the firefight involving D23's crew at Checkpoint Two, as well as the ambush of D8 and its escorting Bradley, the entire action was over.

Wearing an expression that displayed an amazing lack of concern, Carrington looked over at his operations officer. "What have ya got?"

Grummond, having settled back in his seat, looked up at his commanding officer. "An RPG team tried to light up D8 and the RRF two clicks west of Checkpoint Two while a second one thought it might be a good idea to take on D23."

"And the score?" Carrington asked as if he had missed part of a football game they'd been watching.

"Pacesetters four, hajji nothing. D8 has married up with the crew of D23. They're in the process of recovering D23A. I've already sent word to the UST folks that we're going to have a serious meeting of the minds bright and early tomorrow, immediately after your morning update to decide what to do with their problem child. Other than that, everything is five by five. The rest of Fetterman's people are in place and the MQ-9 is back on station."

Carrington nodded as he reached up to stretch. "In that case," he concluded with a loud yawn, "I think we should call it a night."

Coming to his feet, Grummond grinned. "Sounds like a plan." Then, after giving the duty officer a few last minute instructions, he followed his commanding officer out.

Just why the little vignette he'd just watched play out should have made such an impression on Hughes, and why he found it so appalling, was something of a mystery that he never bothered to delve into. Had the young journalist taken a moment to do so, and had he been totally honest with himself, he would have eventually come to the realization that the behavior of Carrington and Grummond was, in reality, no different than that which he'd observed many times before in *The Times*'s newsroom. Even at his age, Hughes had managed to adopt what many in his chosen line of work considered to be a professional outlook on what they did, one that allowed them to look past the pain and suffering of people involved in events that he'd been sent out to cover and turn them into amusing little anecdotes that he was able to share with his fellow journalists over drinks at parties. But since Hughes was incapable of understanding how any rational human being could ever bring himself to join the military, his ability to relate to the people and events he had been sent to report on and put it all in its proper context was all but impossible. That, after all, wasn't in his job description. Getting a story that was worth printing was.

FOUR

Unable to concentrate on the report he'd been given to review and comment on, Nathan listened in on the sharp exchange that was taking place between Kaplan and another full colonel who was standing in front of Kaplan's desk, leaning forward with his fists planted firmly on his hips. The colonel, who worked for the Deputy Chief of Staff for Logistics was carrying on about a report his superior had forwarded to their office. Ever so slowly, it dawned upon Nathan that the report the colonel was checking on was the one he was reading. Expecting the worst, he straightened himself up, ready to deal with the irate colonel as soon as Kaplan informed him where it actually was.

To Nathan's relief, and somewhat to his surprise, rather than getting all excited, Kaplan eased back in his seat, regarding the colonel before him with a rather bored expression. "The Chief hasn't finished reviewing that document yet," he responded in a rather offhanded manner as he took to rearranging some papers on his desk with the tips of the fingers on his right hand. "I assure you, as soon as the Chief has finished looking it over and making his comments, I'll let you know."

With little choice but to accept Kaplan's offer, the colonel straightened up and grunted. "You need to tell General Stevens that we need to have his answer back on that issue ASAP. Otherwise, there'll be hell to pay when they hold those Congressional hearings on the budget next week." With that, the colonel spun about and left the office Nathan shared with Kaplan.

Having rid himself of the bothersome colonel, Kaplan glanced down at his watch, then over at Nathan. "It's just about quitting time, wouldn't you say?"

After checking the clock over the door, Nathan looked over at Kaplan. "It's only 1725, sir. Besides, I still haven't finished reviewing the report that the colonel was hyperventilating over and drafting up my comments."

"So?"

"Excuse me?"

Kaplan repeated his question as he stood up. "So?"

"I realize that the colonel is probably overstating his case in an effort to expedite things on our end, but he obviously needs it back."

For some reason Kaplan found Nathan's comment funny. "Jesus Christ, Dixon! You mean to tell me you've been here a whole week and you haven't figured out yet that everybody in this building is working on something that is so critical that the universe as we know it will cease to exist if they

don't get an answer, an approval, a signature, a sprin-
kling of holy water or some damned thing on it
yesterday? Just about every swinging Richard who
roams the halls out there thinks what they're doing
is the most important, most urgent, most crucial
project in the world."

With furrowed brow, Nathan took a moment to
consider what Kaplan was telling him. "Forgive
me for sounding certifiably naive, sir, but this is the
Pentagon. I mean, what we do here is important,
isn't it?"

Now it was Kaplan's turn to give Nathan a funny
look. "Dixon, you've been in the Army long enough
to know that the careers of most officers aren't
based upon their ability to lead a cavalry charge or
storm a hill. They're carefully crafted out of paper,
both the papers they write and the paper that enu-
merates their accomplishments. I'm sure you've
seen that at work." The sour expression on Nathan's
face more than confirmed this last point, allowing
Kaplan to continue. "So tell me, what makes you
think that people behave any differently here than
they do anywhere else? Just because someone is a
colonel who happens to be working for a general
here in this building doesn't automatically make
what he's doing the most important thing since the
invention of sliced bread. You could take that report
you're reading, toss it into the shredder and no one
other than the colonel who wrote it would ever know
it was gone. More than half the paperwork that
flows into this office is pure bullshit. That's why the
Chief has us. We're his filters. It's our job to sort
through the avalanche of crap that flows in that

door," Kaplan stated, pointing to the one leading to the outer office, "and decide what needs to go through that one." Kaplan spun lazily about in his chair till his finger was pointing toward the door leading to General Stevens's office. "Besides," he added with a hint of a grin, "do you think I'd give the new kid on the block something that was really important or time sensitive? Not to put you down or anything, but you know how the Army works. As a ranger company commander you'd no more make a new man in your unit a SAW gunner than I would put a rookie straight out of AIT in the gunner's seat of a tank."

Sensing that he needed to tone down his-take-no-prisoners attitude a bit, Nathan, chuckled. "Gee, sir. Thanks for the vote of confidence."

"Don't mention it," Kaplan replied, giving Nathan a wink. "Now," he continued in a tone that made it clear that he would brook no further argument, "secure your classified material, make one more check of whatever is in your in box and then beat feet for the door. You have a hail and farewell that you will be at in exactly two hours."

The mention of that event caused Nathan's heart to sink. At battalion level, where everyone knew everyone and there was a close camaraderie among the officers, the monthly events were usually quite fun. Somehow, Nathan couldn't imagine any gathering involving officers assigned to the Pentagon, either during the day but especially after duty hours, being fun. About the only upside in fulfilling this obligatory social obligation was that it would give Chris a chance to get out of the house and among people. Since resigning her commission, a decision she'd made with great reluctance, she'd been rather down. It wasn't easy for a woman of her caliber, one who'd managed to make it through one tour in Iraq and another in Afghanistan, to suddenly find herself with nothing more important to do all day but decide what she was going to fix for dinner. How she managed to keep her sanity and greet him with a smile every evening was beyond Nathan's ability to comprehend. Maybe what they said about females was true, Nathan found himself thinking as he made his way along the crowded corridor toward the exit. Maybe they were the stronger of the species.

For a woman who'd marched off to war twice, the prospect of attending a simple hail and farewell was proving to be far more daunting than common sense and logic would ordinarily dictate. Yet Christina Dixon found herself dreading that evening with every fiber of her body. It wasn't like she'd never been to one before. If anything, since marrying Nathan she'd found herself having to attend twice the usual number a serving officer was expected to participate in—those held by her unit as well as the ones Nathan was required to attend.

The problem was, things were different now. Then she'd been an officer. Even when she went along with her husband to his social functions, she'd always managed to find a way of avoiding the little clutches the wives tended to gravitate to, hanging out with the officers of Nathan's unit instead. It didn't matter to her if she said nothing for hours on end, she found simply being in their presence and being accepted as one of them as far superior to standing around listening to the mindless chatter that so many of the Army wives reveled in. By no means was Chris Dixon a snob. Just about everyone who knew her enjoyed her easygoing manner, her quirky sense of humor and a streak of common sense that was anything but common. It's just that she was used to having a purpose, of being part of something that was important, an organization that made a difference in the world and associating with people like herself. Now that she was no longer a serving officer, now that she was little more than Captain Nathan Dixon's pregnant wife, she didn't quite know where she would fit in, how she would be able to deal with the people she'd once felt so comfortable being around, and whether she'd be able to relate to those she'd always avoided like the plague. In short, Chris was having a severe identity crisis that only made the trials and tribulations of being eight months pregnant that much worse.

Determined to stick by her decision to leave the Army once she'd learned that she was pregnant, Chris resolved to do her best to meet the challenges her new role as an Army wife presented her as she prepared herself for another, more demanding one: that of being a mother. At least motherhood promised to put some purpose back in her life. Caring for a child, her child, would give her life purpose and meaning, two things that she was sadly lacking at the moment. She'd have measurable goals and objectives. Her day-to-day routine would assume an importance that it currently lacked. Besides, finally giving birth would rid Chris of the rucksack-sized bundle she was saddled with 24/7 and allow her to chuck clothing that bore a striking resemblance to the tent she'd lived in during her tour of duty in Afghanistan.

Being the sort of woman she was, one who had an understanding of the Army that only a person who'd stood their watch on the wall was privy to, Chris kept her personal views on being an Army wife securely bottled up inside. Nathan had enough on his mind already. In addition to dealing with psychological scars that his last assignment had left in its wake, the trauma of going from commanding a ranger company deployed in an active theater of operations to being a third-echelon flunky on the Army staff in the Pentagon left him struggling to find some sort of emotional balance. The last thing she wanted to do was give him something else to worry about. The one duty that all Army wives were expected to perform that Chris was determined to execute flawlessly was to serve as their husband's primary health and welfare officer. If this meant keeping her own counsel, or pretending that she was happy and didn't have a care in the world, so be it. In time, when Nathan managed to settle into his new position and some of the raw edges of his nightmares were smoothed over by the passage of time, she was confident she would be able to reestablish the free and open dialogue they'd once shared and she so cherished.

To his credit, Nathan was not totally oblivious to the fact that his wife was currently experiencing a rough patch of her own. He was far more attuned to

Chris's moods than she gave him credit for. The only problem was, until recently he'd blamed her pregnancy for her morose behavior. That she was suffering from a severe case of identity crisis was something that he'd only recently become aware of, and that was only because his mother clued him in to that possibility. Which was why he felt an outing like the one they'd be attending that evening was just the thing she needed. In addition to getting her out of the house and back among people, he was running on the assumption that being around military types again would have the same effect on her that it had had on him. He had no idea that the opposite would prove to be true. Like all good husbands who set out to help their wives overcome personal issues, his decision process was being driven by pure logic, bereft of the emotional element that often influenced a woman like Chris.

The evening started out well enough. As with all such events, they were met by someone Nathan would be working with. In this case it was Neil Kaplan. Accompanied by his wife Emma, Kaplan introduced Nathan and Chris to people Nathan hadn't had a chance to meet or hadn't been afforded an opportunity to chat with in a relaxed, casual setting. Throughout this ritualistic ordeal, Chris managed to maintain a smile and, when appropriate, answer a few polite questions directed her way. Even during the meal she was able to play along wonderfully, conducting herself in a manner that reflected well upon her husband, though she found that she needed to fight the urge to wolf down her food in a forlorn effort to placate her insatiable hunger.

The death spiral began after the last of the dinner plates had been cleared away and the hailing of newly arrived officers and speeches delivered by those departing began. When it came Nathan's turn to be introduced, the host of ceremonies took his time, mentioning the highlights of his career to date, past assignments and, as was always the case with Nathan, his lineage. So it came as something of a shock when the host introduced Chris by simply stating, "And Captain Dixon is accompanied by his lovely wife, Christina." Period. Full dead stop. At least in the past, when she'd accompanied her husband to his hail and farewells in other units, the host would always make it a point to mention that she was a captain assigned to such and such a unit, that she'd served in Iraq as well as some of her military achievements and, in general, make it a point to let every officer present know that Christina Dixon was more than simply a pretty face, that she was, in fact, one of them.

That this was no longer true, that in the eyes of the gathered officers there, male and female, she was nothing more than another Army wife, was reinforced after the formal part of the evening was over and the party broke up into little groups scattered about the room. Even before they had a chance to leave the table, Neil Kaplan grabbed Nathan and hauled him away to chat with some people he'd need to know better while Emma Kaplan took Chris by the hand to where some of the other wives were gathering.

To their credit, the majority of the women Chris was introduced to refrained from greeting her with the sort of cooing and simpering comments that she and other female officers had often attributed to typical Army wives. A fair number of the women Emma Kaplan introduced her to were professional women—women who were just as accomplished as their military spouses and, in some cases, earned far more than they did. Yet, for some unfathomable reason, once the introductions were over and the serious chitchat began, none of that was discussed. Instead, for the most part the discussion revolved around subjects that tended to bore Chris to tears.

Doing her best, Chris listened attentively, answering questions directed at her as politely as she could when someone made an effort to draw her into the conversation. She was, however, at a loss most of the time as how best to respond. While the women around her had moved seamlessly from high school through college and out into a society where they continued to associate with their female peers in much the same manner as they'd always done, upon receiving her commission, Chris had been submerged into a male dominated culture, where her superiors cut her no slack simply because she was a female. She had learned to deal with men as equals, many of whom took pride in being warriors and not simply goal-oriented careerists. Along the way she'd managed to master the skills needed to survive and thrive in a military culture with surprising ease, thanks in no small part to the fact that she grew up with two older brothers who she competed with and, to their chagrin, often bested. To say that Chris was out of her element that evening when surrounded by women who were armed with an entirely different set of social skills and attitudes would have been putting it mildly. And it showed. Eventually, as the people Emma had introduced Chris to got the measure of the new girl and made their assessment of her, Chris found herself being politely left behind as the discussion drifted from one subject onto the next. In less than an hour, she was so far out of the loop that no one noticed when she eased away from the gaggle she'd been drawn into and retreated to a quiet corner of the room where she made a solemn vow never, ever to come to one of these events again.

By the time Nathan found her, Chris's despair had muted into a simmering rage. She had no idea what exactly she was angry about or who was to blame for her feeling that way. Nathan didn't know either. He did, however, know Chris well enough to understand that there was something going on in his beloved wife's head that was eating away at her. Realizing that the time to pull pitch and leave had come, he told Chris to wait where she was while he made his excuses to the people he was expected to. "We'll go home," he cooed. "I'll fix you a nice cup of tea and we'll talk."

His efforts to placate Chris were greeted with a look that would have reduced a lesser man to ashes. Recognizing all the warning signs that told him that Chris was on the verge of going critical, Nathan wisely backed away. As he went about making his excuses prior to departing, he found himself wondering how best to defuse the pregnant redheaded time bomb he was married to. It was the sort of situation that neither Fort Benning nor his years as a commissioned officer equipped him to deal with.

There was only one person in the world who could help him at a time like this, the one person every boy turns to whenever they need to peek into the mystical realm of the female psyche. His mother.

Nathan found Jan in her little home office, busily pounding away on the keyboard of her laptop. Watching her from the doorway, he couldn't remember a time when it hadn't been like this. His stepmother, a renowned journalist, always seemed to be working on a story. Yet no matter how earthshaking the event she was covering, somehow she always managed to find time for Nathan and his brother.

As he stood there, he wondered if his real mother would have been so understanding, so willing to set everything aside to listen to his latest tale of woe or hear what he'd done that day in school. He liked to think she would have. But having no clear memory of the woman who had given him life, Nathan had no choice but to speculate and imagine that she would have been just as understanding, just as attentive to his needs no matter how trivial they were or how busy she was.

Ever so slowly, Jan realized she had company. Stopping midsentence, she looked over at Nathan and, without him having to say a word, she knew he was troubled. Spinning her seat about, she turned her back on her laptop and invited her son to take a seat. A long night was about to become a little longer, but it was something she was used to. If anything, she relished the challenge of having to juggle career, family and husband; something she missed.

Somehow living alone hadn't brought her peace, just emptiness.

"Things didn't go well tonight, did they?" she asked, though she already knew the answer.

Nathan, both pleased that Jan was able to get to the heart of things with such ease, yet annoyed that she seemed to have known something he should have long before he did, nodded. "You could say that. Instead of cheering her up, I'm afraid Chris feels more forlorn. More lost than ever." Sighing, Nathan shook his head. "God, I just wish this baby would come. This pregnancy is tearing her up."

"Nate," Jan stated firmly, "in case you haven't realized it yet, being pregnant is the least of Chris's problems."

Leaning forward, Nathan rested his elbows on his knees and clasped his hands together. "I know, I know. Leaving the Army was hard on her. But it's what she wanted," he quickly added. "I told her I'd support her decision if she decided to stay, but . . ."

"As far as I'm concerned," Jan stated in a soft, reassuring tone, "Chris made the right choice. While I'm all for women having the right to serve their country, unlike other, less demanding professions, I'm afraid an Army career and motherhood don't mix very well. Most women who try to do so somehow manage to muddle along. Unfortunately, when things don't go right, the price both mother and child pay is heartbreaking."

Surprised by Jan's statement, Nathan looked up at her. Though he was tempted to say something, he didn't for fear that it would divert their attention away from the topic at hand. Instead, he simply shook his

head, signaling his agreement with her stance before asking his mother what he could do. "I'm at a
total loss here," he admitted. "I know how to run a
company of rangers. I know what to do when am-
bushed by a superior force. I know how to plan and
conduct an air assault. And yet I'm totally clueless
when it comes to helping the one person that really
matters to me, the woman I would do anything for."

Jan took a moment to think before answering.
When she did, she didn't hand Nathan a neat, cut-
and-dried solution to his problem in the way his
father had favored. Instead, she gave him a rather
enigmatic smile and wink. "Why don't you let me
think on this awhile," she told her son.

In the twinkling of an eye, Nathan cheered up.
Though she wasn't admitting to anything, he
knew that whatever it was that Jan had on her mind,
everything would somehow be all right. It was what
she did. It was what she was good at. No matter how
bad things were, no matter how grim the future
looked, Jan always managed to find a way to make
things right. That was why Nathan loved her as only
a son could.

Jan Fields never arrived at the offices of the World
News Network D.C. bureau; she assaulted them.
Those who knew better cleared the path that led
from the elevator to her office, everyone, that is, but
her personal assistant, Angela Cardosa. Somehow
Angela instinctively knew when Jan was in the
building and on the way. She was always standing
just inside the suite of offices they shared, waiting

with a cup of coffee in one hand and the morning
update book in the other. That book contained sum-
maries of everything that had gone on in the world
and been broadcast on WNN for the past twenty-
four hours, highlights of stories being run by other
news networks—stories WNN headquarters in New
York wanted to work—and the tentative schedule of
topics the network would cover for the next twenty-
four hours, provided breaking news or an unexpected development didn't force them to reshuffle
the deck. Jan always spent the first half hour of every day skimming through that book while sipping
her coffee before meeting with the heads of her de-
partments to get an update on what they were working on. When they'd finished filling her in, she'd
issue instructions on what needed to be done, repri-
oritize their efforts if necessary and listen to any
new ideas they had concerning stories they felt
needed to be addressed, or technical problems that
would require assistance either from the team of
technicians at WNN headquarters or a local contractor.

This morning, Jan stormed into her office, gra-
ciously accepting the coffee Angela shoved into one
of her hands while deftly catching the briefing book
without breaking stride. She set the book down in
the center of her desk and turned to where Angela
was waiting to see if there was anything her boss
needed before she submerged herself in the book.
"Angie, would you get Frank on the line for me?"

Frank Worley, head of WNN, was Jan's immediate superior, that is if you went strictly by WNN's
organizational chart. Those who had the chutzpah

to do so liked to joke that it was really the other way around. It was even rumored that when Worley stepped aside, Jan would take his place, provided she didn't get impatient and stage a palace coup beforehand.

"What should I tell him this is about?" Angela asked.

"Budget and personnel," Jan responded as she undid the buttons on her jacket and took a seat.

Unable to help herself, Angela rolled her eyes and snickered. "Oh boy. Should I advise his assistant to put the local cardiac care unit on alert?"

Jan gave her assistant the sweetest little smile she could manage, and winked. "Tell Kay I'll be gentle with her boss. I promise."

"Isn't that what the Vandals told the Romans when they opened the gates to the city to them?"

Jan cherished the close, easygoing relationship she enjoyed with Angela. She was the only person in the office she was able to let her guard down with, often dealing with Angela as if she were a friend rather than an employee. Not only did it motivate Angela to do more for Jan than she probably would have if they'd had a more conventional employee/employer relationship, it permitted Jan to tap into the office grapevine, allowing her to keep tabs on what was going on throughout the office, in particular what the latest and hottest gossip was, both work related as well as that which was strictly personal in nature. By monitoring what was going on among her people, Jan was able to head off problems long before they impacted the operation of her bureau. It also provided her with some serious comic relief, as

Angela had a habit of putting a humorous spin on some of the more entertaining stories.

Making a face, Jan shooed her assistant out the door. "Oh ye of little faith. I can do nice when I've a mind to. Now, be away with you, saucy wench, and get Frank for me." With that taken care of Jan settled in to deal with the problems of the day, both work related and strictly domestic, but no less pressing.

The invitation from her mother-in-law to meet her for lunch in D.C. caught Chris by surprise. It wasn't like Jan to interrupt her busy day to indulge in something as pedestrian as lunch with friends or a family member. As fanatical as she was when it came to keeping her work from interfering with family matters, Jan was just as adamant when it came to ensuring that she was seen by all to be a dedicated professional when she was in the office, devoted to giving her job one hundred and ten percent every day, all day. For her to make the time in her busy schedule to engage in casual chitchat with her daughter-in-law struck Chris as ominous. No doubt, she concluded as she waited at the restaurant for Jan to arrive, Nathan had talked to her about the hail and farewell after she'd gone to bed. And while Chris had no idea how their conversation would go, she knew it probably wouldn't be to her liking. Jan, after all, was even more committed to looking after her son's welfare than she was to her profession, as impossible as that seemed.

The conversation started out innocent enough with Jan apologizing, as she always did, for missing her that morning before leaving for work. Chris responded, as she always did, by confessing to be a total slouch, taking advantage of her pregnancy to sleep late. Ever so slowly, with the skill of a predator circling in on its quarry, Jan snuck up on the reason she'd asked Chris to join her.

"I've never been in the position you're in," Jan stated almost wistfully as she poked at her salad with a fork, "so I'm somewhat handicapped when it comes to being able to offer the sort of advice you'd normally expect from a mother, or even a step-mother-in-law."

Before answering, Chris took a sip of her iced tea, carefully eyeing Jan as she did so, wondering where, exactly, this conversation was going. "I think it's a little late for advice," Chris finally admitted glumly, unable to filter out the melancholy she felt over her decision to leave the Army. "What's done is done. I was the one who told Nathan that if we were going to start a family, now was the time. And I was the one who decided that being a mother and being an officer in today's Army just wasn't a good combination. All I can do now," Chris concluded sadly, "is ride this out and hope things brighten up a bit after I give birth to this pachyderm I'm lugging around."

Chris's stab at a spot of humor caused Jan to smile. "Why wait until then?" she suddenly asked.

Having already been to a number of job fairs that catered to former or soon-to-be former servicemen and women in search of employment that would be both fulfilling for her as well as accommodating to a new mother, Chris had come to the conclusion that she'd have more luck finding the Holy Grail. So she'd resigned herself to the grim reality that for the foreseeable future, she was condemned to a life that would revolve around a newborn and the Home Shopping Network. With nothing more than a shrug, Chris sighed. "I imagine in time, when the baby is old enough, I'll start looking for something."

"You know, there's really no need to wait," Jan announced casually. "I happen to know that there's currently a position open that's perfect for you."

Like a thunderclap, Chris finally understood what this lunch date and Jan's roundabout lead-in were all about. Sitting upright, the young woman stared over at the older woman. "All right, you've got my attention."

Jan set her fork down, pushed her plate off to one side, brought her hands together on the table before her and returned Chris's gaze. "How would you like to be a military analyst for World News Network?"

Blinking, Chris cocked her head as she regarded Jan with furrowed brow. "Excuse me?"

"I've been authorized to hire a military analyst for our D.C. bureau. And rather than going with another retired general or colonel, I thought I'd go with a former company grade officer, one who's been to Iraq and Afghanistan and who has recent company command time. In short, what I want is someone who not only knows their way around the service, I want a person who has a firm grasp of what the young men and women in the armed forces actually do and think. Someone who can relate to them. Someone like you."

Before she knew what she was saying, Chris

uttered the sort of words that would have sent shivers up the spine of a feminist had there been one listening in on their conversation. "But I'm a woman!"

Easing back in her seat, Jan gave her daughter-in-law a broad smile. "Exactly." Ignoring the confused look on Chris's face, she went into her prepared pitch. "To the best of my knowledge, there has never been a full-time female military analyst on any of the news channels, this despite there being a high percentage of females in all the services. Not only would you be the first, you'd be perfect."

"And pregnant," Chris added crisply as she lifted her glass of iced tea in one hand and patted her distended abdomen with the other.

Jan brushed aside her comment with a wave of her hand. "You do know that's not a permanent condition, though I expect at times it probably feels like it to you." Jan's comment caused both women to laugh. "Chris, I'm taking about television. The only thing the camera and the viewing audience will see of you is from chest up." Then, leaning forward, Jan whispered across the table conspiratorially. "If truth be known, that's all the male viewers and network executives are interested in when it comes to a female commentator."

Having always regarded Jan as being above that sort of thing, Chris was shocked, causing her to choke on her iced tea and Jan to laugh at her despite the younger woman's distress. "Get real, girl," Jan replied as she once more eased back in her seat. "When was the last time you saw a flat-chested female journalist or talk show host?"

Chris had to admit to herself that there was a

great deal of truth to what Jan was saying. Still, she demurred. "Somehow I don't see myself as being the sort of person you'd want representing your channel."

Once more Jan found herself unable to keep from snorting in a most unladylike manner. "Oh please. Your red hair, a creamy smooth complexion most women would kill for and a pair of blue eyes that will dazzle the camera, make you a natural for TV."

After having spent years doing her best to downplay a natural beauty that even she couldn't deny in order to keep it from interfering with her duties as an officer, Jan's comments caused her to blush. "I don't know, Jan. Even if you're right, how do you know I could pull it off? I mean, for all you know I could totally freeze up on camera or go to pieces when a host or someone with an opposing view lit into me on live TV."

"Give me a break, Chris. I know more about the military than most people give me credit for. Don't forget, I was married to Nathan's father. I know the sort of characters you worked for day in and day out. I know you've briefed officers who would make Genghis Khan sound like a village priest. If anything, I'd have to look out for the people who crossed your path."

Unable to think of anything better to say, Chris tried to fob Jan off. "Let me think about it, okay?"

Realizing that her daughter-in-law was wavering, and knowing how many in the military felt about journalists, Jan decided she needed to go easy, lest she spook Chris. "I'll tell you what. While you're thinking it over, why don't you come back to the studios with me?"

"I don't know, Jan," Chris countered. "I think that maybe, perhaps, I should talk this over with Nathan first. I mean, not only is this a major change in what he and I had agreed to regarding the baby and my working, but taking this sort of job could cause him problems. After all, he is working in the office of the Chief of Staff of the Army. Every time someone on your network uttered the phrase, 'an unnamed Pentagon official,' all eyes would turn toward Nathan."

Knowing exactly what Chris was alluding to, Jan was more than prepared to counter that argument. Waving her hand as if to dismiss the younger woman's concerns, Jan laughed. "Oh, please. Exactly how did my working for World News Network affect Scott's career?" Not being privy to all the times Scott Dixon's superiors had raised the issue of his association with a person so closely associated with a major news outlet, Chris found herself unable to find an effective response. "So what makes you think it would have any impact on my son's?"

Sensing that Chris was wavering, Jan decided that the time was right to give her daughter-in-law that last little nudge. Making a show of looking at her watch, Jan smirked. "Come on, Chris, you can think about this on the way back to the studios. We need to be there in thirty minutes."

"What happens in thirty minutes?"

Jan winked. "You're due in makeup, followed by a screen test with Bob Brant. He's doing his shows from D.C. this week. I've asked him to run you through a mock interview, the sort he's good at."

Stunned, Chris sat there as she watched Jan come

to her feet. Bob Brant, the host of the highly rated WNN prime time show, *Point of View with Bob Brant,* was noted for his take-no-prisoners style of dealing with guests. He wasn't intentionally confrontational, preferring to engage in a calm, evenhanded exchange. It's just that he had zero tolerance for any guest on his show who tried to waffle when answering a question or attempted to feed him something that was patently bull. Facing him would be a challenge all right, Chris suddenly found herself thinking, but nothing when compared to some of the bastards she'd worked for and briefed in the past— men, and the occasional woman, who had neither the time nor inclination to deal with people who weren't prepared or didn't know their stuff. After being verbally beaten to a pulp by some of those characters, how bad could someone like Brant be, Chris found herself wondering.

The young woman was still mulling over the pros and cons when Jan, standing across from her, placed a hand on her hip and began to tap her toe. "Well, are you coming?"

In the time it took Chris to gather up her things and come to her feet, she realized that the opportunity Jan was providing her with was more than that. It was a lifeline, a first-class ticket out of social purgatory.

FIVE

Ever so slowly, Alex Hughes came to understand something that every soldier learns to appreciate long before he finishes basic training: boredom, not battle, is the greatest enemy. Even when a unit rolled out the front gate and headed out on a mission, most of what it did was so routine, so repetitious that everyone had to make a conscious effort to pay attention to what they were doing lest they fall into a near hypnotic state that dulled their senses they relied upon, blinding them to the looming dangers ahead until it was too late to do something. In the short time he'd been with 3rd of the 68th, Hughes had been witness to a number of accidents that were caused by simple inattentiveness. He'd even been in one of them.

It occurred during a road march back to Camp Pacesetter after a long night of sitting at the Iran border, waiting and watching for something that never happened. The driver of the C2V he was riding in, struggling to stay awake and pay attention as the column of C2Vs and UGVs trundled on at a steady speed, missed a turn. When he realized his error, he reacted before he had fully recovered from his stupor, resulting in a radical maneuver that ran the C2V off the road and into a ditch. And while no one was hurt, the track on one side of the C2V was thrown off its road wheels, causing the platoon leader to detach a second C2V with its M-10s to provide security while the crew of the one Hughes was in, the one in the ditch, set about getting the C2V back up onto the road, breaking track, feeding the track back onto the road wheels and reconnecting the track. Although it sounded simple to Hughes when Staff Sergeant Plum explained it to him, when it came time to actually do it, the journalist found out that nothing is easy when you're trying to put a one-ton track back onto a twenty-ton vehicle with nothing more than hand tools and a little ingenuity.

That was also the night Alex Hughes learned that his days of being nothing more than a spectator were over. Plum, not the most soft-spoken man God put on the face of the earth, explained the reality of the situation in rather simple terms. "You can either sit there, scribbling away in that notebook of yours and walk back to camp, or you can get up off your dead ass and lend a hand. Your call." While Hughes knew the sergeant was bluffing, he was smart enough to know that if he wanted to get the men he was with to open up to him and share their thoughts and opinions, he'd have to show them that he was one of them. If that meant getting his hands dirty and sweating a bit, so be it. It was a small price to pay in order to get a good story.

It was this philosophy that now caused Hughes to abandon the air-conditioned hooch he shared with a pair of UST technicians and venture out into the late morning heat to help the crew of D23 work on one of their M-10s. He had thought it would be a simple job. At least, it had sounded simple when Specialist Viloski had described it to him over breakfast with the crew of D23. "All we need to do is replace the seal on one of D23B's road wheels." Of course, like everything else the Army did, there was nothing at all simple about it.

Having helped Viloski and Cutty get the M-10's road wheel arm up onto the jack and remove the road wheel, Hughes sat back in the dirt and took a break as he watched the tow soldiers go about the messy task of wiping away the old grease from the road-wheel arm spindle. "Isn't this something a mechanic should be doing?" the journalist asked after taking a sip of water.

"Yeah, well, I guess," Viloski replied without bothering to look back at Hughes. "Unfortunately, there's not enough mechanics to do everything that needs to be done."

"Why not?"

Cutty couldn't help but chuckle as he looked over his shoulder at Hughes. "Are you serious, man?"

Offended, Hughes stared at Cutty. "Yeah, I am. I mean, you'd think the Army would assign more people to a unit like this."

"Do you think anyone in Congress knows what a unit like this requires?" Viloski asked sarcastically as he wiped off the last of the old grease with a clean rag. "The only thing Congress says is, 'Army, you can have X number of men and X number of dollars. Have fun.' The generals then sit around and decide how many men they need in each MOS. They assign so many to the infantry, so many to the armor, so many to the artillery and so on and so on. Now, because this is the Army, and we're expected to be able to go out and kill people and break things, the Army tends to fill the combat MOS's first since they're the people who are responsible for killing people and breaking things. With me so far?"

Hughes grunted. "Yeah, I'm with you."

"Well," Viloski continued, talking as he peeled off the old seal with the aid of a pocketknife, "eventually, by the time you get down to the people who are supposed to support the killers, you start running out of slots. So the generals and their trusty staff pukes cut corners where they can. Thus, instead of having all the mechanics you need, you have just enough to make do, leaving us no choice but to fill in when the mechanics are off tending to the more interesting jobs, like replacing the transmission on D24B. Besides," Viloski concluded as he wiped his hands before picking up the new seal, "do you realize how many mechanics you'd need in a unit like this?"

Always ready to wean as much information from these men as he could, Hughes shrugged. "I haven't a clue."

"Well," Cutty chimed in as he opened a fresh can of GAA grease, "let's do the math. Second Platoon had four C2Vs and six M-10s. First Platoon has the same. The only difference in 3rd Platoon is they have M-11s instead of M-10s. That makes a total of twelve C2Vs and eighteen UGVs. Add to that D66, the Old Man's C2V, D-55, the XO's and D8, the recovery vehicle that D23A is so fond of. That makes a total of thirty-three tracked vehicles in this company alone."

"B Company's got the same," Viloski continued. "Compared to us, A and C companies are flyweights, number-wise that is. There's fourteen M-1s in A Company and fourteen Bradleys in C Company, period."

"That makes a total of ninety-four tracks in the line companies," Cutty stated, picking up the tread while Viloski checked the alignment of the new seal one more time. "On top of that, you've got to add the tracks in the task force's scout platoon, the mortar platoon, the medical platoon, the tracks that make up the TOC and the task force commander's and operations officer's tracks. That gives us, what, something like 120 tracks in this task force, Ski?"

Easing back, Viloski took a moment to wipe his hands and study his work before moving onto the next step. "Yeah, something like that." Then turning to Hughes, he smiled. "Okay, time for you to grease her up."

The journalist hesitated as he looked at Viloski, the can of automotive grease sitting between his legs and the hub. "How do I do this?"

Viloski grinned. "All ya gotta do is scoop up a handful of GAA, slap it onto the spindle and grease her up like you were lubricating your dick before fucking a dry pussy."

Having worked for as long as he had in a profession where strict adherence to political correctness was expected, the locker room language bantered about by the soldiers within 3rd of the 68th caused Hughes to blush, something that both soldiers found exceedingly hilarious. Embarrassed, but too proud to back down, Hughes did exactly what he was told as Cutty egged him on.

"Yeah, that's it, rub it on there. Just close your eyes and make believe that's your dick. Can ya feel it?"

When he thought he'd put enough grease on the spindle, Hughes backed away. "Enough?"

Like a pair of surgeons, Viloski and Cutty inspected the journalist's handiwork. "What say you, Specialist Cutty?"

"I think Mister Hughes has done a splendid job, Specialist Viloski."

"Yes, our Mister Hughes is a natural when it comes to greasing long, hard objects. I think the time is ripe to carry on and restore the road wheel to its rightful place. Don't you, Specialist Cutty?" Viloski asked.

"Yes, 'tis time," Cutty responded before the two men ended their pretentious banter and set about the task of hefting the road wheel back into place and reassembling the hub.

"So, what you're saying," Hughes surmised as he wiped his hands on a rag, "is that there's not enough mechanics in this unit to take care of everything that needs to be taken care of."

"I didn't say that," Viloski grunted as he struggled alongside Cutty to guide the road wheel back onto the fixed bolts protruding from the road wheel arm. "All I'm trying to point out is that until someone invents another robot that can do this, everybody has to pitch in and do their part."

"The problem is," Cutty explained, "is that every time you add a robot, you reduce the number of people you've got to repair the little suckers. A tank with a crew of four has just one track to take care of. Our crew, D23, has four people to look after three tracks, one C2V and two M-10s."

"If that keeps up," Viloski stated as he began to screw the bolts back onto the bolts that secured the road wheel, "the Cylons will outnumber us in no time."

Hughes looked over Viloski. "The Cylons?"

"Yeah. Haven't you ever seen *Battlestar Galactica*? It's sort of like the movie *Terminator*, only it takes place in outer space. Mankind makes the machines they use to do their dirty work so smart that the machines begin to see men as being redundant, so the machines get together to eliminate them."

Almost finished, Cutty eased back and took a seat next to Hughes. "I for one am looking forward to the day we do become redundant. That way we can send the robots off to shit holes like this to hunt hajji and leave Ski and me back home where we belong."

Coming to his feet, Viloski was about to back D23B off the jack holding the road wheel up when he spotted Captain Fetterman headed over to where a couple of UST tech reps were busily working on D23A. "Oh boy, looks like the shit's about to hit the fan, again."

Both Hughes and Cutty turned to see what Viloski was talking about. "The Old Man really hates those UST people," Cutty muttered.

"Can you blame him? They're idiots. We've been here, what, three months and they still haven't been able to figure out what's wrong with that piece of shit of yours."

"Yeah, you got a point, Ski. And the more they work on it, the worse it gets. I swear, if they don't sort it out soon, the Captain is going to blow up 23A himself, then blow up the whole damned compound where the contractors hang out when they're not screwing up one of the UGVs, drinking beer and collecting all sorts of bonuses for being over here."

Eager to listen in on the pending exchange between the D Company commander and the civilian contractors, Hughes made his excuses and headed over to where he could hear what Fetterman was saying without being too conspicuous. By the time he'd found a good spot, Fetterman was already laying into Jordan Sinclair and Clyde Chase, the UST fire control specialist.

Standing in front of D23A, with his feet planted shoulder width apart and his fists resting on his hips, Fetterman was delivering what amounted to a warning to the civilians who were sitting on top of 23A. "I am way beyond pissed off," the young captain spat. "I swear to God, if this thing craps out one more time while we're downrange, I'll blow the piece of shit up myself."

Having been harangued by Fetterman on numerous occasions, both Sinclair and Chase sat there, pretending to listen to Fetterman while wearing bored expressions. Eventually tiring of their failure to take him seriously, Fetterman made to climb up onto 23A and get in their faces, but was cut short by a booming voice ordering him to stand fast. Looking over to its source, Hughes caught sight of LTC Carrington and Peter White approaching.

Climbing down from D23A, Fetterman turned to face his task force commander. "I know what you're going to say, sir," the young captain growled, "but even you've got to admit that this bullshit has gone on far too long."

Stopping when he was within arm's length of Fetterman, Carrington folded his arms across his chest. "What do I have to do to make you understand, Captain, that part of our mission is to test these vehicles in combat? In addition to finding out how to employ them, we also have to find out what components are susceptible to failure under combat conditions and how to repair them. Believe it or not, D23A is providing the contractor team with a wealth of information."

"It's also proving to be a pain in the ass as well as an impediment to my company's operations," Fetterman shot back. "Every time this thing goes tango uniform out there, I don't lose one M-10, I lose two since D23B is incapable of operating more than five kilometers from D23. And even if it could, it would have to stay within a few hundred meters of 23 in order to provide security since D23 doesn't have the firepower needed to defend itself."

Carrington was unmoved by Fetterman's argument. "That may be so, but that doesn't change my orders which means it doesn't change yours. Our mission is to push these things to the limit in an effort to find out where that limit is. Until such time as the contractor team declares D23A a write-off, it rolls every time your 2nd Platoon moves out. Is that clear?"

Drawing himself up, Fetterman saluted his commanding officer, responding to Carrington's question in a manner that came as close to being insubordinate as he dare go. "Loud and clear, sir." With that, the young officer spun about on his heels and stormed off.

Turning toward White, Carrington jabbed a finger into the contractor's chest. "Look, I've played along with you on this matter for about as long as I can. The time is fast approaching when I've got to say enough is enough. Either your people find some way of making D23A work or I'm going to pull it from service."

Instead of becoming riled by Carrington's threat, White smiled as he reached up and gave the task force commander a friendly pat on the arm. "Sure, Neil, I understand. We'll get to the bottom of this. All we need is a little more time."

"I've given you more than enough time," Carrington shot back. "Fact is, I should have deadlined D23A and submitted a preliminary report on the problems it's been having weeks ago. I'm through covering your ass on this one. One more time," Carrington stated as he pulled his index finger away from White and stuck it up into the air to emphasize his point. "If D23A shuts down just one more time, it's done, fini, kaput." With that, Carrington made his exit, leaving White and his two specialists to weigh their options.

From where he stood on the ground, White looked up at Sinclair and Chase. "Well?"

Sinclair looked over at Chase, who looked back at her before she turned back to White. "Well what?" she asked.

Exasperated, White thrust an arm at D23A and snapped, "Can you or can't you repair this?"

Before answering, Sinclair once more glanced over to where Chase was sitting, regarding her. "Go ahead," the female tech rep muttered. "Tell him what you told me."

Making no effort to hide his reluctance, Chase sighed. "Well, there is one thing I can try, but I wouldn't recommend it."

"Will it work?" White demanded.

"It should, but . . ."

"Then do it!" White snapped.

"But Pete, that would mean I'd need to disconnect . . ."

Tired of listening to Chase's waffling, White threw his hands up in the air. "Goddamn it, I'm in no mood to listen to your technobabble. Just do it." Then without another word, White departed, leaving two civilian contractors staring at each other, and one journalist wondering just what it was that they were so worried about.

SIX

With the sun rapidly receding in the west, D Company prepared to move out. Having received his orders for that night's mission from Lieutenant Vanderhoff, Plum gathered the crew of D23 and passed them on. "We're going to be backing up an Iraqi Army unit that's been given the mission of intercepting a major effort by the Badr insurgents to slip arms and personnel across the border. Before moving out, I want the UGV operators to make sure all fail-safe systems on your UGVs are functioning and engaged. Once we hit the LD, you're to switch to manual mode and stay there. If we do need to go in and bail the IA's ass out, do not, I repeat, do not engage unless you have positive target ID and we have been cleared to do so. Any questions?"

By now Hughes had no qualms about raising his hand whenever Staff Sergeant Plum asked this question at the end of his orders briefing. "What kind of a fail-safe?"

Likewise, Plum didn't have any misgivings when

it came to expressing his feelings to the journalist. Both his expression and his tone of voice conveyed his irritation at having to put up with Hughes, especially at times like this. "All right people, you know what to do," Plum muttered before turning his attention to the journalist.

Folding his arms across his chest, he stared at Hughes as he took a moment to think about his answer, since there were aspects of the M-10's fail-safe system that were still on a need-to-know basis. "The people who designed the M-10," Plum began, "built in some safety features. Because combat is unpredictable, and usually anything that can go wrong does, there are features on the M-10 that are meant to keep it from going medieval on friendly forces or wandering away on its own should there be a breakdown in communications between it and its operator."

"How does that work?" Hughes asked.

"Very well."

Hughes realized Plum was intentionally screwing with him, but ignored it. "What I meant is, what does the UGV do when that happens."

"Should an M-10 wander out of range of the operator's data link or, in a worst-case scenario, the operator's C2V is destroyed, the M-10 stops in place and begins to send out what amounts to a distress call, trying to find another operator in its chain of command who can take control of it. Normally the platoon leader assumes control of the wayward M-10, but if push comes to shove, the company commander or even someone back at the task force

TOC, using a downlink from the Reaper flying overhead, can take charge of it."

"What happens if it's attacked before someone else is able to reestablish control?"

Once more Plum hesitated before answering. "It goes into what is called sentinel mode. In sentinel mode the M-10 scans its surroundings, 360 degrees. If someone approaches it that doesn't have an IFF that's squawking the right identification code, the M-10 sends out a verbal, prerecorded warning, both in English and in Arabic. If the intruder doesn't heed that warning, the M-10 fires warning shots."

"And if they're ignored?"

Plum grinned. "Word of advice, Hughes. If you should ever find yourself alone in the desert with an M-10, don't ignore the warning shots." With that, Plum turned his back on the journalist and set about making his own precombat checks without bothering to mention some of the other, more lethal failsafe features the folks at UST had built into the M-10. The way Plum saw it, Hughes didn't have a need to know. And even if he did, he sure as hell wasn't going to be the one to tell him.

The road march out to the area of operations was uneventful and painfully boring. From his jump seat behind and off to the left of Plum's position, Hughes could clearly see Plum's monitor, which was set higher than those of Cutty and Viloski. He could even see some of Viloski's, who was, as he so

often was during the approach march, sound asleep.
Cutty's monitor, because of Hughes's position, was
totally obscured by the back of Cutty's seat and
head. Not that this was important at the moment.
Like all the previous missions Hughes had been on,
no one expected anything to happen until they were
close to the Ten-K Zone, a ten-kilometer-wide buffer that extended from the Iranian border westward,
back into Iraq. Under the current rules of engagement, no U.S. forces were permitted to enter or operate within the Ten-K Zone without permission
from division or higher. As it was explained to
Hughes, the last thing anyone wanted, given the
current state of affairs between the U.S. and Iran,
was an American unit wandering across the border
by mistake, handing the Iranians, at best, a propaganda windfall and at worse, a fresh batch of American hostages.

For now Hughes was content to sit back and
watch Plum's monitor while Plum stood with his
head and shoulders protruding out of the track commander's hatch, watching and waiting for something that never seemed to happen.

Further along the column Lieutenant Vanderhoff
was watching the monitor in front of him with
greater interest than normal. For the first time in
almost a month all three of D Company's platoons
were operating together. In the lead was the 3rd
Platoon, ready to swing wide to cover the flanks of
the company once they'd reached the designated

line of departure. One section of M-11s would deploy to the left, or north, and two sections to the right, or south.

The 1st Platoon was next in D Company's line of march. It would leave the road they were currently on just prior to the line of departure and deploy into a line formation with all six of its M-10s one hundred meters apart and five hundred meters in front of the platoon's C2Vs, which would also be arrayed in a line.

Captain Fetterman, mounted in D66, was currently between 1st and 2nd Platoons. When it came time to deploy, he intended to place his C2V in line and between 1st Platoon's and 2nd Platoon's C2Vs.

Of the three platoons, 2nd Platoon had it easy. Just shy of the line of departure Vanderhoff would send his Charlie section to the left and his Alpha section to the right, while leaving his Bravo section straddling the road they were on. Rather than basing his decision on how he would deploy his platoon purely on tactical considerations, Vanderhoff heeded his platoon sergeant's advice and placed D23 on the road. "It'll be a hell of a lot easier to recover D23A if it craps out near the road," Sergeant First Class Bohnslav explained back at Camp Pacesetter when Vanderhoff had been issuing his operations order for that evening's mission.

"You mean *when* it craps out," Plum added. It was a comment that neither Vanderhoff nor Bohnslav found any reason to contradict.

*   *   *

Once deployed, D Company was tasked with catching anything that slipped past the IA company deployed five klicks forward of it. Whether or not the intelligence concerning the Iranian based insurgents that set this whole operation in motion was accurate was unimportant to LTC Carrington and Peter White. At the moment both men were located back at the task force's TOC at Camp Pacesetter, seated in front of the oversized monitor displaying D Company's tactical data. Unlike Fetterman's more immediate concerns, Carrington and White were more interested in seeing how a UGV company operated when in support of a non-U.S. unit. It was something they'd never tried before. To ensure that there was close coordination between the two and a smooth handoff of the battle from the forward deployed Iraqi infantry company over to D Company should any insurgents evade the IA positions, a liaison team from the IA battalion had been dispatched to the 3rd of the 68th's TOC for this operation. The Iraqi Army officer in charge of that team was in contact with both the Iraqi officer in command of the unit in front of D Company, his own battalion and Sergeant Omer Mohajeri, Captain Fetterman's Iraqi Army LNO and translator, who was currently riding in D66 with Fetterman.

Even with the entire graphics of the unfolding operation clearly displayed on Plum's monitor, Alex Hughes was oblivious to what was going on around him. Ten days with a unit like 3rd of the 68th Armor was barely enough time for a person with zero military background like Hughes to learn the jargon soldiers so loved to use. Appreciating the complex nature of the sort of operation D Company was currently involved in was simply beyond him. Not that it mattered to Hughes. He wasn't there to learn how to be a soldier or become a student of modern warfare. He was simply there to get a story that the editors back home would find worthy enough to print, and to get his journalistic street cred. Unfortunately for him, in order to do so he had to be patient and he had to go wherever the soldiers he was following went, enduring the same hardships they lived with day in, day out.

"Delta Two, this is Delta Two-One. Switch to manual mode and commence deployment. Acknowledge, over." The sound of Vanderhoff's voice blaring in the headphones of his CVC startled Hughes, catapulting him out of the stupor he'd drifted into and back into full consciousness. Even before he was able to shake his mental cobwebs away, Sergeant Plum was on the radio, acknowledging his platoon leader's order and issuing his own to his crew.

"Okay, everybody," he shouted over the intercom, "it's showtime. Cutty, make sure Viloski is awake."

Letting out a loud yawn, Viloski called out to Plum. "Yeah, yeah. I hear you. Switching to manual now. D23B is manual mode and is green across the board."

Cutty followed suit. "Switching D23A to manual mode. D23A is in manual. I'm green across the board."

Plum didn't respond to the pair of UGV operators. Instead, he keyed D23's FM radio. "Delta 21, this is

Delta 23. All systems in manual mode and green, over."

"Hey, Jay," Cutty shouted back to Plum after he'd finished making his report. "Should I activate 23A's fire control and see what she does tonight?"

Even though Cutty couldn't see him doing so, Plum shook his head. "Negative. If the IAs do their job, you guys won't even need to activate your fire control systems. So why press our luck? Just keep 23A on the road and park it there when we reach our positions. Viloski will cover your sector and his with 23B."

"I hear that," Cutty replied. "It'd be nice to see D23A return from downrange under its own power instead of being dragged behind D8."

Once everyone settled back down and the platoon radio net went silent once more, Hughes keyed his intercom. "What now?"

Looking down from his perch high up in the track commander's hatch, Plum looked down at the journalist. "Now we do what we always do. We wait. If we're lucky, nothing will happen. If we're really lucky, we'll get to kill something."

Never sure if Plum was serious when he said things like that, Hughes returned the staff sergeant's grin with a weak smile. As strange as their language and habits were, Alex Hughes found the philosophy of the men he was living with to be as foreign and as harsh as the desert around them. How he would be able to explain that aspect of modern warfare to the readers of his newspaper was a question that bothered him. Hopefully, he told himself, when the time came he'd manage to find just the right words to describe both the men and what they did in a manner that the American public would understand. He was, after all, a journalist, and that was what journalists did.

Oddly, it was Sergeant Omer Mohajeri, in D66, who was the first man in D Company to learn that the IA company deployed east of them was in contact with a sizable body of insurgents. Captain Fetterman, who hadn't said a word after reporting back to the task force TOC that his unit was in place and set, looked over his left shoulder to where Mohajeri was sitting, jabbering away in Arabic over the radio with the Iraqi liaison officer collocated with LTC Carrington. "Talk to me, Omer," Fetterman demanded without bothering to key his intercom or wait for the Iraqi to finish.

"Several vehicles have crossed the border," Mohajeri shouted back. "They are being shot at."

"Where?"

"I do not know."

"Well, find out!" Then, turning to Sergeant Jeff Kennedy, the Company Reconnaissance Specialist seated to his immediate left, Fetterman asked him if the Reaper was in a position to put eyes on what was going five kilometers east of their position. Glancing over at his wing monitor, Kennedy tapped the touch screen box labeled MQ-9 and waited till a map came up showing its location and the area its sensors were currently scanning before answering

Fetterman. "That's a negative, sir. It's currently on its southbound leg. It's got another ten minutes before it comes about and heads back north."

In the same cool, almost detached manner that he always slipped into when his unit was about to enter combat, Fetterman directed Kennedy to contact task force and request that the Reaper be turned around. While Kennedy was doing that on the task force net, Fetterman contacted First Lieutenant Jared Mosby, leader of the 3rd Platoon, ordering him to have the recon section that was positioned on the extreme left of the company launch a UAV. Once airborne, it was to follow a course going from north to south five kilometers east of the line the company's UGVs formed until it had eyes on the insurgents the IA were engaging. That call was followed by a call on the company net in which Fetterman informed his platoon leaders of what was going on to their front. He had no need to tell them anything else. They already knew what to do.

When word finally trickled down to D23, Cutty turned to Plum. "What do ya think, Jay? Should I see if the fire control system is going to work this time?"

Plum thought about calling his platoon leader and asking him the same question, but decided against it. Instead, he looked down at Cutty, who was wearing an expression that was somewhere between expectant and worried. "No. There's no need to, yet. Let's see what our hajjis can do to their hajjis." In no mood to argue, Cutty turned back around, watching Viloski's monitor rather than his own since the view on his hadn't changed since they'd deployed.

On board D66, Sergeant Kennedy suddenly jumped up in his seat. "We've got MTIs six klicks southeast of 3rd Platoon's southernmost element."

Having been fixated on the area directly east of his company's position, it took Fetterman several seconds to shift the display on his monitor until it matched the one on Kennedy's. As soon as he saw the line of computer generated symbols that marked the unidentified moving targets Kennedy was talking about, Fetterman zoomed in for a closer look at the images that the Reaper's thermal sights had picked up by pure luck during its turn to the north. "Contact task force again," he ordered. "Have them keep the Reaper locked in on those targets. See if they can get a better read on what they are."

Once more, while Kennedy was talking to the Air Force liaison officer at the task force TOC, Fetterman contacted his 3rd Platoon, this time ordering it to launch a pair of UAVs, from the recon section on the far right of D Company's positions. He wanted to have as many eyes on the enemy as he could in an effort to determine what they were facing before he made any decisions as to whether he needed to reposition any of his units. It was more than an overreliance on the technology that so many American officers had become wed to that, that it stayed Fetterman's hand at the moment. It was the memory of leading a platoon of soldiers

over of a mud wall into a hail of enemy fire—one
that always seemed to leap to the fore at moments
like this.

Twenty kilometers away, at 3rd of the 68th's TOC,
Carrington, Grummond and White were seeing exactly the same thing that Fetterman was. Because
there was nothing else going on within the task
force's area of operation at the moment, Carrington
had directed the duty officer to set a spare radio on
D Company's command net in order to monitor
what Fetterman was doing. Since he had no problem with the way Fetterman was handling the situation, Carrington had no need to insert himself into
the situation. So he lounged in a folding chair set up
before the master monitor with White to his right
and Grummond to his left, quietly chatting among
themselves while the battle staff of the task force
carried out their assigned duties with a measured
efficiency that would have puzzled Alex Hughes if
he'd been there and not cooped up in the back of a
crowded C2V.

The Iraqi Army liaison officer, tucked away in
one corner of the TOC, could not find it within himself to remain as calm or detached as the Americans around him. Long before the senior American
officers seated in front of the large TV screen understood what was happening, the Iraqi officer read
the situation and came up with what he thought was
the right answer. In Arabic, the liaison officer informed his battalion commander that the insurgents

the IA company was engaging were nothing more
than a diversion. The real threat was to the south, the
one the Reaper had stumbled upon. It was an assessment his battalion commander concurred with,
one that left him with the horrible realization that
once more he'd been outsmarted by the insurgents.
In an effort to remedy his error and prevent Iranian
supplied arms and explosives from finding their
way into the hands of his government's enemies, he
ordered the commanding officer of the IA company
to personally lead two of his platoons to the southwest in order to intercept the main body of insurgents before they reached a point where they could
disperse and scatter. Once the commander of his
forward deployed company acknowledged his order
on the internal Iraqi battalion command net, one
the liaison officer with 3rd of the 68th wasn't monitoring, the Iraqi battalion commander left his command post to rouse his reserve company and
personally lead them east to establish a blocking
position while leaving orders for his last company
to be prepared to follow if needed.

Captain Fetterman first knew the IA company in
front of him was moving back toward his position
when the first UAV launched by 3rd Platoon's north-
ernmost recon section spotted a column of trucks
moving west. Unfortunately, although the images
the UAV were sending back clearly showed that
they were trucks, it could not tell with any degree
of certainty who was in them. In an effort to find

out what was going on, Fetterman turned to the
Iraqi seated behind him. "Sergeant Mohajeri, find
out if any of your people are moving back along the
road."

Dutifully, the Iraqi NCO with Fetterman contacted the Iraqi liaison officer at 3rd of the 68th's
TOC seeking whatever information he had concerning the activities of the forward deployed Iraqi
company.

The young Iraqi lieutenant who'd been selected to
serve as the link between 3rd of the 68th and
his parent battalion was, at that moment, suffering
from a unique version of cultural shock and awe.
Though he had worked with Americans before in
the field and was well aware of the many wonderful
technological aids they employed to rain down
death and destruction on their common enemies,
the futuristic command, control and communications 3rd of the 68th enjoyed astonished and intimidated the young Iraqi. If truth be known, he was
even a bit embarrassed given that all he had to work
with was a single radio that had been cast off by the
American Army as obsolete more than a decade
ago.

Even more disorienting than the plethora of gad-
getry the Americans relied upon was the way they
went about the serious business of waging war.
Were it not for the rank the senior officers wore on
their uniforms, the Iraqi officer would have found it
difficult to tell, with any degree of certainty, who

was in charge. Junior officers no older than he chatted and joked with their task force commanders as if they were equals. The task force operations officer went about issuing orders as if his superior wasn't there while that officer exchanged whispered remarks with the civilian to his right. It was all so confusing, so bewildering to a man who'd been nurtured in a culture where unflinching deference to your elders and obedience to your superiors was the very fabric that held together the community and society in which he lived.

So it should not have come as a surprise to anyone that he found it all but impossible to seamlessly mesh with the high-tech American military machine he'd been tossed into at the last minute. The idea that he should aggressively seek information from his battalion commander on his current situation and intentions, especially when that officer was in the midst of running a battle, was as foreign to him as were the habits and practices of the Americans who surrounded him. So he did exactly what he'd been ordered to do by his battalion commander. He kept his superior informed of what the Americans were doing by passing information up his chain of command and, when he was told to do so by his battalion commander, he informed the Americans of what his unit was doing.

This seemingly minor glitch in the intricate web of twenty-first-century command, control and communications that 3rd of the 68th relied upon could have been avoided had 3rd of the 68th seen fit to dispatch a liaison party to the IA battalion. That neither Carrington nor Grummond felt the need to do so was little more than a simple oversight, one of those things that causes a person to slap their forehead after the hidden flaw has become a glaring error. But since the 3rd of the 68th had avoided working closely with Iraqi units since arriving in the country, it wasn't in the habit of sending any of its valuable and highly trained officers off to an Iraqi command post that a Vietnam-era American officer would have found to be primitive. It wasn't arrogance. Nor was it ignorance. It was simply an oversight, the sort that gets people killed when men armed with sophisticated weapons clash in the dead of night.

"We've got movement to the front," Specialist Viloski sang out, catching Alex Hughes by surprise. He'd been busily taking notes on the small laptop he was struggling to balance on his knees, not paying attention to any of the monitors Plum, Viloski and Cutty were watching.

Dropping down from his perch topside and into his seat, Plum took a second to study the images on his split screen, the one that showed what the thermal sight on D23B was observing. "I make it to be four trucks, coming on fast," he called out over D23's intercom.

Viloski confirmed his count. "Roger that. We have four, maybe more headed our way, coming on fast and dumb."

Without waiting to see if there were more, Plum keyed his radio. "Delta Two-one, this is Two-three.

Delta Two-three Bravo has four trucks moving east to west on the road toward my position, over."

It took Vanderhoff, who'd been following the events that were unfolding off on the company's right flank several seconds to reorient his attention back onto his own platoon's sector and tap into the data link that connected him to D23B and its operator. Once he had a firm grasp of the situation, he verbally reported Plum's situation to his superior on the company command net.

On board D66, Captain Fetterman reached across with his left hand and tapped the little box labeled *D23B* on the wing monitor to his right. In an instant, the exact same image and data that D23B was sending to Viloski and Plum was displayed on his monitor.

Twenty kilometers away, at the task Force TOC the duty officer eavesdropping on the D Company radio net entered the appropriate code, using a keyboard that allowed him to tap into D23B's data link and display what D23B was showing its operator. The image on an auxiliary monitor to the right of the master tactical monitor that dominated the TOC. Within the span of a minute, maybe two, operator, section leader, platoon leader and task force commander were all seeing the exact same thing. Pleased that everything was working as it should, Peter

White eased back in his chair wearing a Cheshire cat grin.

With the trucks barreling down on their position, Staff Sergeant Plum and his crew automatically slipped into kill mode. While he hit D23's IFF interrogator, PFC Marsden cranked up D23, adjusted his seat so that he could see through his driver's night viewer and prepared to move out the second Plum gave the order. While Viloski continued to track the unidentified trucks, Cutty looked over his shoulder and up at his section leader. "Well?"

Plum didn't need to ask Cutty what he was talking about. The time was fast approaching when Cutty would have no choice but to activate D23A's fire control system, giving Plum either two combat ready UGVs or one functional UGV and one high-tech, multimillion-dollar speed bump. Well, Plum thought as he watched the trucks draw nearer, if 23A was going to be a speed bump, he'd make it the best damned speed bump money could buy. "Cutty, before you do, turn 23A sideways and park it right in the middle of the road. Ski, I want you to back 23B off, making sure that it can cover everything on the road from where 23A is and off toward the east."

Needing no further explanation as to why their section leader was issuing those orders, both operators got down to implementing them.

Their platoon leader, on the other hand, was caught off guard when he saw the symbols representing

D23A and D23B on his tactical display begin to move, even though he'd yet to issue a single order. "Delta Two-three, this is Two-one. What are you doing?"

Before he could explain, Captain Fetterman was after Vanderhoff via the company command net, asking him the same basic question. Upon hearing this on the radio set to D Company's command net, LTC Carrington sat up in his seat, glancing over at Grummond who mirrored his commanding officer's puzzled expression. All the while, the Iraqi liaison officer, fascinated by what was going on, moved closer to the task force's tactical display in order to watch how Americans fought a battle.

At the center of this sudden flurry of radio calls was Lieutenant Vanderhoff, doing his best to fend off his company commander while waiting for his section leader to explain what he was doing. Fetterman naturally won this verbal tug of war, ordering Vanderhoff to have Plum resume his previous positions and prepare to engage the trucks if they proved to be hostile. Unable to clearly hear what Plum was telling him over the platoon net because he had the volume on the company net turned up higher, Vanderhoff acknowledged his commanding officer's orders and passed them on down to Plum. His response of, "But sir!" was cut short with a crisp, clear, "Just do it!" from Vanderhoff.

* * *

Since Cutty had heard everything that passed between his section leader and their platoon leader, he
didn't need Plum to relay the order over the intercom. "Okay boys and girls," he announced as he
took a deep breath and reached up to engage D23A's
fire control system. "Here goes nothing."

Had nothing happened when Specialist Cutty activated D23A's fire control and turret drive, just as it
had on so many other occasions, no one on D23
would have been surprised. Peter White, on the
other hand, would have been embarrassed while
everyone above Plum in the 3rd of the 68th's chain
of command would have been royally peeved. That,
however, would have been preferable to what actually did happen.

At first Cutty couldn't believe his eyes. The system showed green across the board. He even found
himself momentarily befuddled as he stared at his
screen, not knowing what to do. It was only when
D23A's turret spun about and the fire control system
trained the UGV's 25mm cannon on the lead truck
and began to calculate a ballistic solution that Cutty's
confusion morphed into concern.

From his position, Plum watched all of this on
the split screen that showed what D23A was target-
ing. "Cutty, what are you doing?"

Caught off guard by his UGV's unexpected gyra-
tions, Cutty took a moment to scan his UGV's status. The indicators on his control panel showed that
his UGV was in manual mode, which told him that

it should not have been doing a damned thing. But yet, even as he watched, D23A was electronically reporting back that it was transmitting an IFF challenge to the oncoming trucks. "Christ! I think 23A is in sentinel mode."

Plum wasn't sure what to do, or even if he needed to do anything at the moment. Without having to be told, Cutty was already going through the process of troubleshooting 23A, which included remotely rebooting the UGV's entire system if all else failed. It was a risky move at a time like this, one that could result in the sort of total shutdown to which 23A was prone. Not that that would be a bad thing, Plum reasoned. If nothing else, 23A could still serve as a roadblock, causing the trucks to slow down as they approached it. If they were full of insurgents, 23B, sitting to the right side of the road, would be able to place effective fire on them. D22B, one of Staff Sergeant Holly's UGVs deployed south of the road, was also in position to engage. Caught in the crossfire of those two UGVs, the insurgents wouldn't have a chance.

"Two-three Alpha coming back on line," Cutty announced.

Holding his breath, Plum watched as that portion of the screen displaying 23A's primary sight flickered, as they tended to do when coming back online. This was followed by a jiggling of the image, indicating that 23A's onboard computers were in the process of applying a fresh ballistic solution to its 25mm gun, which, at that moment, was trained on the lead truck. "What have you got?"

"I think we've got a rogue, Jay. Everything on my end is telling me we're in manual mode, but 23A's behaving like it's in sentinel mode."

"Well, we're about to find out," Plum muttered. Squirming in his seat, he watched and waited for 23A to execute the next subroutine it was programmed to perform when in sentinel mode.

"Those assholes in the trucks aren't going to hear the challenge," Viloski offered up as he leaned back in his seat in order to look over at D23A's monitor to see what Cutty's M-10 was doing."

"Well, if they don't hear that, I've no doubt they'll see the tracers when 23A cuts loose with some warning shots," Plum concluded before keying his radio to warn his platoon leader that they were having problems.

Because everyone in Plum's chain of command was seeing the same images he was, and was receiving the same erroneous status from D23A that Cutty was struggling to correct but couldn't hear the exchange between Plum and Cutty, they all thought he was in control of 23A. So no one, not even the crew of D23, was prepared when 23A began to take the lead truck under fire, hammering away at it with deadly accuracy.

Stunned, everyone who had access to D23A's data stream watched in disbelief as 25mm high-explosive rounds tore it apart.

* * *

Not yet having established whether or not the trucks coming toward his company were hostile, Fetterman called for an immediate cease-fire over the company command net. Without bothering to acknowledge that order, Vanderhoff did the same over the platoon net, thus blocking Plum's efforts to call and inform him that 23A had gone rogue, a term that the unit had adopted for an M-10 that failed to respond to commands or began to behave in a manner contrary to its programming. Eventually he did manage to get that word up to his platoon leader, but not before 23A's sensors signaled that the most dangerous target in its sector of responsibility had been destroyed, causing the fire control system to automatically lay the 25mm cannon onto the next greatest threat.

Whereas 23A had responded to Cutty's previous command to shut down and reboot, if in fact it had gone into self-defense mode as both Plum and Cutty suspected, all external signals were blocked. This was one of the fail-safe features that was designed to prevent someone other than a UGV's designated operator from hacking into an M-10's computer system while in combat, taking control of the system and either shutting it down or turning it against other M-10s or even its own crew. Frustrated, Cutty took to mashing down on every command escape key and system shutdown button he could over and over again, spitting out a stream of obscenities while Plum did his best to inform Vanderhoff that they were doing their best to carry out his repeated demands that they cease fire.

At least the crew of D23 had only one superior to deal with. Vanderhoff had to listen to his own company commander, who was giving him the same order the young lieutenant was repeatedly screaming out over the platoon net as well as the voice of his task force commander who'd chucked aside all protocol and was using the radio in his TOC set to D Company's command net to relay his orders directly to Vanderhoff. Carrington felt that this breach in the stringent military chain of command was more than justified when the Iraqi liaison officer in his TOC informed him that the trucks were IA, a piece of information that even the IA sergeant with Fetterman was now aware of and had passed on to him. Unfortunately, neither Fetterman nor Carrington were privy to an equally important bit of information, information Plum was desperately trying to relay to Vanderhoff, who was too busy doing his best to get Plum to comply with his orders while mentally blocking out the dueling incoming traffic on the company command net.

Frustrated and at a loss, Plum ripped the CVC off his head. "Viloski, move 23B onto the road and in front of 23A." It was a desperate move, one that the various UGV section leaders and their platoon leaders had often theorized about from time to time during their train-up but had never attempted because of safety concerns. The resulting damage that could occur if they were proven wrong would be monumental. Plum was hoping that by placing another M-10 in 23A's line of fire, the rogue M-10 would recognize 23B as a friendly vehicle via the IFF system both UGVs were equipped with and stop shooting. Failing that, he was already mustering up the nerve to move onto an even more and equally desperate measure.

In the TOC, Carrington stopped yelling into the radio hand mike when he saw the symbol for D23B began to advance toward D23A. "What in the name of Christ is he doing?"

Grummond was the first person in the TOC to grasp what was going on twenty kilometers away. "D23A is a rogue. The section leader is going to place his other M-10 in D23A's line of fire."

For the first time Peter White spoke out. "He can't do that. If D23A really is a rogue, it might engage D23B."

Grummond looked the civilian contractor in the eye. "Maybe, maybe not."

"Have you thought of shutting down D23A from here?"

Peeved at having White interfere at a time like this, Grummond planted his fists on his hips and shoved his face into White's. "What makes you think we're going to have any more success doing that twenty klicks away when D23A's operator or the platoon's technical specialist hasn't been able to do that?"

"For Christ's sake, we don't even know if either of those stupid bastards have tried that yet! For all we know the comms on D23 might be down."

Grummond was about to counter that lame argument by pointing out that D23B seemed to be under positive control when Carrington raised his hand, signaling his operations officer to cease and desist before turning to the duty officer. "Punch in the code for D23A and see if we can do something with it from here."

With the ease and speed of a person who was banging away on a computer keyboard before he learned how to hold a pencil, the duty officer tapped directly into D23A's data link and attempted to shut down the rogue M-10. After using every combination of commands he knew, the duty officer looked up at his task force commander and shook his head.

At a loss as to what to do now, Carrington looked over at White. The gray haired civilian was a team leader and the onsite rep for UST, not a technocrat. None of them had yet to respond to the desperate call an NCO on duty at the TOC had made over to the civilian quarters. Embarrassed by his inability to do something more meaningful, White turned away, leaving Carrington no choice but to watch and hope Plum's maneuver succeeded.

Moving D23B as fast as he dare up onto the road ten meters in front of D23A, Viloski muttered, "Here goes nothing."

At first it seemed as if Plum's plan was working as D23A's 25mm cannon went silent the moment the image on Cutty's monitor of the third IA truck was replaced by that of D23B as it moved into 23A's line of fire. For a few precious seconds, it looked as if the friendly-fire incident was over as the two M-10s, with their turrets oriented on the other, stared each other down like a pair of Old West gunfighters standing in the center of the street, waiting for the other to make his move.

D23A made the first move. Following another subroutine written to address situations like this, but which were not part of the sentinel mode program, D23A began to maneuver around D23B in order to get a clear shot at the target it had been engaging before its field of fire had been blocked by a friendly vehicle.

Realizing that he was fighting a losing battle, Plum keyed his radio and asked permission to fire on D23A using D23B. Even before he'd finished that transmission, Viloski trained D23B's 25mm gun on D23A, switched the gun's sight into tracking mode and selected armor-piercing ammunition.

With the images of what D23A's gun sights were seeing and what D23B's sights were fixed on, as well as watching the status lights of D23B displaying what its operator was doing, Fetterman knew exactly what Plum was contemplating. Knowing full well that this was the only way they could keep D23A from opening up on the IA soldiers again, Fetterman preempted Vanderhoff's radio call and granted permission for Plum to engage and destroy D23A.

When the senior officers and civilian contractor back at 3rd of the 68th's TOC heard this, chaos broke out as White screamed to Carrington, "NO! He can't do that! Order him to stop."

Grummond countered. "We have no choice. Those are friendlies out there."

Throwing the chair he'd been sitting on out of the way, White stepped up to Carrington. "You can't let them do that. How in the hell will we be able to find out what went wrong with D23A if you let that idiot blow it up?"

Carrington wavered even as Grummond stepped between the two men. "You've got to be shitting me," he bellowed as he shoved his face into White's. "That machine is murdering Iraqi soldiers."

Determined to stop what was about to happen, White grabbed the radio hand mike out of Carrington's hand and ordered Fetterman to stop D23 from firing.

In D66, Fetterman was bewildered, not only by the order but also by who was issuing it. In an effort to confirm it, he called back to the TOC, using his task force commander's call sign, asking him to repeat his last transmission, knowing full well that it hadn't been Carrington who'd given the hold to check fire.

Since all of this was being transmitted on the company net, Vanderhoff had monitored White's order to check fire as well as Fetterman's request to Carrington for clarification. Unsure how this would play out, Vanderhoff did what he thought was best and ordered Plum to check fire.

Oblivious to what was going on further up the chain of command, Plum looked down at Viloski in utter amazement. The operator of D23B returned Plum's bewildered stare before looking over at Cutty's monitor where he saw that D23A now had a clear line of sight and was preparing to finish what it had started. Unable to watch the slaughter, Plum pulled his CVC on, stood upright in the open hatch and ordered his driver to move out. Since blocking D23A's line of sight wasn't enough and he didn't have permission to blow up D23A, he figured his last best hope was to wedge D23A between D23B and his C2V, a maneuver that would obstruct 23A's line of sight while preventing it from moving into a new firing position.

At the moment, no one at the task force TOC was monitoring what was going on downrange. All eyes were on Carrington and White who were staring at each other. Grummond, who had taken a step back, watched and waited for someone to say something. The person who broke that silence was Fetterman, who repeated his request to Carrington that he either confirm or deny the order to have D23B check fire.

Like an animal signaling its submission to a rival, Carrington gazed down at the ground as he reached out and took the hand mike from White. "Delta Six-six, this is Pacesetter Six. I say again, do not fire on Delta Two-three Alpha. Acknowledge, over."

* * *

While everyone back at the TOC was somehow
finding it easy to ignore what was actually happening, Fetterman could not. After drawing in a deep
breath, Fetterman keyed his company command
net. "Delta Two-one, this is Delta Six-six. Engage and
destroy Delta Two-three Alpha. I say again, engage
and destroy Delta Two-three Alpha, out."

Now it was Carrington's turn to lose it as he screamed
at the duty officer to switch the radio frequency
they'd been on over to D Company's 2nd Platoon. As
soon as the duty officer gave his task force commander
a nod, Carrington keyed the hand mike. "Delta Two-
three, Delta Two-three, this is Pacesetter Six. You will
not, I say again, you will not fire on Delta Two-three
Alpha. Acknowledge over."

Staff Sergeant Plum heard his task force commander's order and understood it. He also heard the order
that his company commander issued in its wake,
one that demanded that he destroy D23A. Disgusted
with the way his officers were behaving at a moment like this and finding it all but impossible to
direct his driver into position, Plum reached down
and turned off his radio.

Sitting quietly in his little corner of D23, Alex
Hughes watched and listened as he realized that not
only had he just been handed the story of a lifetime
on a silver platter, the incident he'd just witnessed
provided him with the perfect excuse to bid 3rd of
the 68th Armor adieu. That the men around him

would soon be engaged in a very different sort of struggle, a fight in which he would soon be very much a part of didn't matter to Hughes. He was, after all, a journalist with a job to do. As he saw it, the sooner he got back to New York and did that job, the happier he, not to mention his editor, would be.

SEVEN

Sitting at the table in the breakfast nook of his mother's townhouse, Nathan Dixon looked across to where his wife was poring over a script, holding a cup of tea in one hand and a red pencil in the other. He still wasn't quite sure who to be angry with, his mother for offering Chris a job at WNN, a job he had little doubt she'd pulled strings to make available, or his wife for taking it without first talking it over with him. He knew that at some point Chris would find a position to her liking, one that was challenging, but not until she'd given birth or the baby was old enough to be left in the care of a sitter. And while they'd never quite figured out how old "old enough" was, in Nathan's mind it definitely wasn't D Minus 30.

Still, he could not help but realize that this was exactly what Chris needed. Well, he grunted to himself as he took a sip of coffee and peered out the window across the Potomac River, maybe not exactly, but better than the way things had been going.

Nathan knew things had been hard on Chris since his return from the Philippines. First she'd had to deal with his long and difficult convalescence, a painful and somber period in his life made more difficult by the recent loss of his father. Had it not been for Chris being there with him, setting aside all her own feelings and concerns in order to keep his spirits up, he'd never have made it through the grueling and painful physical gauntlet he'd crawled through in order to regain full use of his left leg and arm.

That crisis had barely been surmounted when Chris reached the point in her pregnancy where she felt it was time to resign her commission. And while that decision had been hers and hers alone, it was one that had impacted both of them in ways that neither had anticipated and were still struggling to come to terms with. It had been especially hard on Chris. The logic she had based her decision upon did little to ease the loss of purpose and prestige she experienced when she set aside her career. Until that moment, her military career had defined who and what she was, just as it did for Nathan.

The emotional trauma Chris had experienced over losing something that was so important to her was compounded and exasperated by the onset of a late-term pregnancy. The physical discomfort of carrying around a ravenous and ever-growing fetus was accompanied by hormonal imbalances that were as unpredictable as they were dramatic. One minute Nathan would be talking to a calm, rational woman and the next, he'd find himself having to deal with a blubbering mass of tears.

Since no one at VMI, Infantry Officer Basic or
Camp Darby had found the time to teach him how
to deal with pregnant women, Nathan was pretty
much on his own. It left him longing for simpler
days, when all he needed to worry about was leading a ranger company through the jungle and into
a night attack.

Without looking up from the script she was editing,
Chris grunted. "You'd be appalled by the ignorance
most people have when it comes to the military," she
muttered before taking a sip of tea. "I mean, you'd
think journalists who were covering military affairs would take the time to bone up on what it was
they were looking at before mouthing off on it. But
then again," she concluded as she peeked up at her
husband through her lashes, "if they did that, they
wouldn't need me, would they?"

Looking back at Chris, Nathan found himself unable to resist that quirky little smile of hers or keep
from becoming ensnared by a pair of blues eyes that
reached down into his soul and touched a spot he
never knew he had until he'd met her. How, he found
himself wondering as he returned Chris's smile,
could anyone be angry with this woman?

As he watched her dive back into the script, Nathan decided that if he really needed to find someone to be upset with over Chris's decision to become
a military analyst, it would have to be his mother, a
task he already knew would be akin to raising the
Titanic. At least she'd finally agreed to keep Chris
off the air until after the baby had come. That, Nathan figured, would give him plenty of time to figure out how he was going to break the news to the

general that his wife had sold her soul to the devil
and gone over to the dark side.

Had Chris managed to land a job with Homeland
Security, any of the letter agencies that she'd applied
to, or even a defense contractor, Nathan doubted if
he would have even considered going to General
Stevens to inform him of it. Most of the people he
was now working with had a spouse who was employed by someone who either worked as part of the
Federal government or for it. While Nathan knew
from listening to stories his father had shared with
him and items he'd read in the newspapers that such
relationships could create conflicts of interest, it
was part of the Army's institutional culture that was
so ingrained that no one really questioned it unless
something really, really bad happened.

Having a spouse who was employed by a major
news media outlet, on the other hand, was an entirely different matter. While few of the officers he
knew ever owned up to their hostility toward the
media when he was around because of what his
mother did for a living, the intelligence officer of
the ranger battalion he'd served in always listed
journalists as part of the enemy order of battle. This
hate—really a hate relationship between the military and journalists and Chris's acceptance of her
job as a military analyst would have been tough
enough to deal with under ordinary circumstances.
Unfortunately, his present assignment placed his
desk but a few steps away from the most senior officer in the United States Army, leaving Nathan in a

rather precarious and unenviable position. Every time someone on a WNN broadcast uttered those infamous words, "an unnamed Pentagon source," he knew all eyes would turn toward him. Whether or not this was something Chris had factored in when she'd been deciding if she was going to accept Jan's offer was something Nathan had never found the courage to ask. And though this might seem strange to some that a combat arms officer like Nathan, a man who'd faced enemy fire on numerous occasions, feared his own spouse, it wasn't. Nathan only had to kill the enemy. He had to live with his wife.

Slowly treading his way over to his desk, he plopped down in his seat, clasped his hands in his lap and stared up at the ceiling. He spun his seat about to the left using his feet, then to the right as he did his damnedest to figure out how best to broach the subject with his superiors. It was more than a simple question of how. There was the issue of timing that he needed to consider. Without having to be told, Nathan knew it would be certifiably dumb to dump something like that on the General when he was in a foul mood or he didn't have the time to address the issue in the manner that it would, no doubt, demand. Perhaps, Nathan reasoned, he could wait until the next hail and farewell to bring the subject to Stevens's attention. After all, both his mother and Chris had told him that she wouldn't be doing anything major at the network over the next few weeks except going over scripts and news stories that were related to the military, checking them to make sure that the facts were correct and the writers who'd drafted

them were using proper military terminology. He
had time, he finally concluded, to formulate both a
strategy as well as find the right time to tell General
Stevens that he was now officially sleeping with the
enemy, or as close to the enemy as you could get in
the D.C. area.

He was still lost in thought, pondering this almost nonduty related issue when Neil Kaplan came
bursting out of the Chief's office. Without stopping,
he made for his desk while addressing Nathan.
"There you are. You're late, you know." Confused,
Nathan glanced up at the clock. Though he saw that
he was twenty-eight minutes early, he didn't bother
mentioning this to Kaplan, who knew very well that
he wasn't.

Having retrieved the file he'd come out to fetch,
Kaplan spun about on his heels and headed straight
back into Stevens's office. "Well, what the hell are
you waiting for?" Kaplan sang out as he sailed past
Nathan's desk without bothering to look over at the
befuddled captain. "A personal invitation?" Grabbing his leather-bound writing pad and scheduling
book, the weapons of choice for a staff officer assigned to the Pentagon, Nathan came to his feet and
followed Kaplan.

From the head of the small conference table General Stevens used for small meetings, he called out
to Nathan to close the door behind him. Having
been clued in by Kaplan on the Chief's habits, Nathan knew that the subject about to be discussed
was important and that anything said during the
course of the meeting was need to know. After taking his seat, Nathan opened his writing pad on the

table and armed himself with a pen in preparation for whatever it was that was about to come his way.

"How much do you know about the M-10 UGV program?" Stevens asked by way of an introduction to the subject.

"Only what I've read about in *Army Times*, sir."

Arching an eyebrow, Stevens looked over at Kaplan, who didn't hesitate to counter his Chief's concerns. "While I am sure there are technical aspects that Captain Dixon will need to address, the primary issues we are dealing with here concern how the chain of command dealt with the situation and whether or not we've got a real problem with the unit conducting the combat evaluation of the M-10 program."

Clueless as to what the colonel was talking about, Dixon watched as the two men regarded each other. While Stevens was mulling something over in his mind, Kaplan held the Chief in a steady, unflinching gaze, signaling that he felt he was right and was prepared to stand his ground. Finally, Stevens nodded and admitted as much.

Having already managed to get the measure of the men he was working for, Dixon looked at Kaplan before turning to Stevens. "Excuse me, sir. But what, exactly is Colonel Kaplan right about?"

With another nod, the Chief of Staff gave Kaplan permission to fill Nathan in. "Third of the 68th Armor is currently running combat trials of the M-10 and M-11 unmanned ground combat vehicles in Iraq. They're operating out of a camp located northeast of Al Kut near the Iranian border, covering a sector that has become quite popular with commercial smugglers and Badr insurgents. Yesterday, while conducting a joint operation with units of the Iraqi Army, 3rd of the 68th Armor was involved in a friendly-fire incident in which a number of IA personnel were killed and wounded."

Slouching down in his seat, Stevens looked over at Nathan, taking up the narrative. "What we have here is a goat screw of biblical proportions." Raising his right hand, he began to tick off each point he was making using a finger. "To start with we have an unproven weapons system that many in the Army believe is the key to our future malfunctioning in the worst conceivable way. Two, you have a friendly-fire incident involving American forces doing all the shooting and an Iraqi unit doing all the dying. Three, we have rumors of a civilian contractor interfering with a combat operation. And last but not least, there seems to have been a breakdown in 3rd of the 68th's chain of command in the middle of it."

"This incident has already resulted in a letter of protest written by the Iraqi President to our President that was delivered to the Iraqi ambassador last night," Kaplan pointed out.

"We've got an avalanche of dung coming our way," Stevens surmised as he peered into Nathan's eyes with an expression that left no doubt in Nathan's mind that, in all likelihood, that avalanche was about to land right in his lap.

Once more Kaplan took over. "You're to go over there, conduct a preliminary investigation and report directly back to the Chief on who, what, why and, more important, what we need to do."

"We?"

"Because of the unique nature of the unit involved and its primary mission, that of testing the M-10, and the fact that this involved a unit of a foreign army, there are all sorts of mitigating factors and concerns that cannot be ignored, all of which will have an impact that go way beyond those normally associated with an ordinary friendly-fire incident." Never having heard any friendly-fire incident described as ordinary, Nathan couldn't help but grimace, something Stevens noticed.

In an effort to make it clear to Nathan what was involved, Stevens described the circumstances that were in play. "Robotics and combat vehicles like the M-10 are here to stay," he stated making no effort to hide his distaste for what he was saying. "Whether or not the M-10 is going to be the tip of the Army spear in the future or simply a stepping-stone on the way to something better has yet to be determined. What is important here is that we figure out what we want in the way of unmanned ground combat vehicles and how, when and where we're going to employ them. That's the primary mission of 3rd of the 68th Armor, a mission that will continue despite this incident."

"So the unit is still in the field and engaged in active combat operations," Nathan stated in an effort to clarify that point.

Stevens nodded. "And it will continue to do so unless you determine that conditions on the ground dictate that we stand the unit down."

Unable to help himself, Nathan looked away as he let out a nervous chuckle. "Nothing like a little pressure, sir."

This caused both Stevens and Kaplan to snigger. "Welcome to the big leagues," Kaplan remarked drily before picking up the thread. "You're well aware that the drawdown of U.S. forces in Iraq has led to an uptick in insurgent activities. To support that effort, the Iranians have been slipping weapons, explosives and volunteers into the country using the same routes smugglers have been using for years. Many friendly tribal leaders along the Iranian border, and kin on the other side of it, depend upon that illegal trade, trade that the Iraqi government has decided to turn a blind eye to. That makes the task of the 11th Airborne Division, the unit responsible for securing that part of the border where this traffic is the greatest, complicated and difficult. Third of the 68th Armor, with its ability to cover large portions of the division's sector is an important part of that effort. If the 3rd of the 68th is stood down, there'll be a gaping hole we won't be able to fill, one the insurgents will pour through."

"Which is why the Iraqi government has agreed to allow 3rd of the 68th to carry on while we conduct a thorough investigation before taking any further steps," Stevens explained. "Provided, of course," he quickly added, "we do so in a timely manner."

"Could you describe 'timely,' sir?"

Once more Stevens eased back in his seat and planted his clasped hands on his stomach as he warily regarded Nathan. "To be determined."

Figuring that he wasn't going to get a straight answer on that one, Nathan moved on to the next item of importance. "When do I leave?"

Unable to help himself, Stevens smirked. "What are you still doing here?"

After giving Nathan some additional guidance, Stevens dismissed both officers. Back in their own office, Stevens provided Nathan with additional details. "You know," he admitted in the midst of doing so, "I envy you."

Nathan looked up from the copy of the travel orders Kaplan had handed him. "Excuse me?"

"You're getting out of here."

"This isn't exactly going to be a boondoggle, you know. I mean, how would you like it if your battalion screwed up like 3rd of the 68th did and have a shit-for-brains captain like me drop out of the sky, sent by The Man himself, to decide if you're going to keep your head on your shoulders?"

"First off," Kaplan replied with a knowing grin, "we're not sending a captain."

"Excuse me?"

Picking up another set of orders, the colonel slipped it over the one Nathan had been reading. "Effective immediately, you're a brevet major." As Nathan was reading those orders, Kaplan opened a drawer and fished out a pair of bronze oak leafs that he tossed across the desk. "You can borrow mine."

After picking one of them up and studying it as if it were a precious stone, Nathan gazed up at Kaplan. "Why?"

"The Chief decided that it would add just the right touch. You'll be equal in rank to everyone at

Camp Pacesetter save the task force commander, but not so far up the food chain that some of the enlisted people you're going to need to talk to will be intimidated by your rank. That," Kaplan concluded, "was what kept me from getting this plum. It seems a colonel has too much rank and would be seen by the people you're going to have to deal with as being too far removed from his muddy-boots days to be effective."

Nathan chuckled. "Well, hell! If you wanted to go so bad, why didn't you ask the Chief to give you a temporary reduction in rank?"

Kaplan wiggled a finger at Nathan. "Be careful there, Major. It's not advisable to be too smart for your own good around here. Now, according to my watch, Mickey says you have just enough time to run home, pack your kit bag, give your wife a quick slap on the bum and make your flight."

Kaplan's comment reminded Nathan of the potential problems Chris's new job created for him. Hesitating a moment, he debated whether or not this would be a good time to tell General Stevens that she was now a card-carrying member of the fourth estate.

Kaplan didn't give him the chance. "If you don't get your butt in gear, Major, you're going to blow your chance to give your wife a long, lingering good-bye kiss."

Shaking his head, Nathan managed to scrounge up a smile. "Yeah, that would be unforgiveable." Doing anything that would jeopardize his chance of getting out of this office, if only for a few days, and back in the field where he belonged was equally unforgivable, Nathan concluded as he gathered up his orders. With the next hail and farewell still weeks away and Chris safely tucked away in a tiny cubical somewhere deep in the bowels of the WNN building till after she'd shed a few pounds and one very feisty baby, there'd be plenty of time to tell Stevens when he got back.

As she made her way back to the small office after what seemed like her fiftieth trip to the bathroom that morning, Chris could not help but notice the stares she got. Everyone knew she was the boss's daughter-in-law, just as they knew, as Chris now did, that the position she was filling hadn't existed until a few days ago. When she mentioned to Jan that hiring her might not be a good idea, lest people accuse her of nepotism, Jan howled. "Girl, this is Washington, D.C. If it wasn't for nepotism, half the people in this town would be unemployed." While Chris knew that Jan was exaggerating, she was astute enough to know that favoritism in the civilian world didn't carry the same stigmatism that it did in the military. The fact was, Chris was finding out rather quickly that any effort to compare the civilian work force she now found herself in with the warrior culture she'd only recently left was pointless. One of the producers she'd become fast friends with put it quite nicely, "Girl, you're not in Kansas anymore."

The most startling differences Chris noticed concerned the attitude many of her coworkers held when it came to their responsibilities and work. While

she'd come across more than a few people in the
Army who were unwilling to do anything that was
not spelled out in their job description, when push
came to shove and something really needed to be
done, everyone set aside their pettiness and pitched
in. That mentality didn't seem to have a counterpart
in an organization that was built upon fragile egos
and staffed by union members, or people who be-
haved like they belonged to a union.

Not that Chris had anything against unions. Her
father was a Teamster. On many occasions that
union had made all the difference between living
comfortably and teetering on the brink of disaster.
Still, in Chris's mind at least, even a good thing can
be carried to extremes, something that many of her
new coworkers didn't quite understand.

Upon entering her office, Chris was startled by
Nathan who called out from the other side of the
door he'd been seated behind. "Hey there, good-
looking."

Spinning about as quickly as her swollen ankles
allowed, she bawled her husband out. "Jesus Christ,
Nate! Do you want me to drop this kid right here
and now?"

Ignoring her admonishment, he came to his feet
and moved to where she was standing, doing his best
to put his arms about his wife's distended waist in
order to give her that long, lingering kiss Kaplan had
suggested. It was his default response whenever he
had done something to rile the passionate redhead
he'd married.

Caught up by this sudden and totally unexpected
but most enjoyable diversion, it took Chris a moment

NO WARRIORS, NO GLORY

to realize that Nathan was wearing the rank of major. Stepping back, she gave him a quizzical look. "When did this happen?" she asked. She gingerly touched the metal oak leafs with the tips of her fingers.

"Don't get too used to them," he cautioned her. "It's only temporary. As soon as I get back it'll be plain old Captain Dixon again."

"Get back?"

"Ah, yeah," Nathan mumbled after clearing his throat. "I'm going to be gone for a few days," he explained as carefully as he could lest he find himself dealing with a hormonally induced emotional outburst.

In an instant, Chris knew that something was up, something that she wasn't going to like. "Oh? And where is this last minute TDY boondoggle taking you to, *Major* Dixon?"

Knowing he was not at liberty to say, not even to the person he trusted above all others, he shrugged. "Away."

Cursed by having been in the Army herself and knowing that the boyish grin on her husband's lips was nothing more than a ruse, Chris said no more. Instead, she pulled herself as close to Nathan as her condition would allow, hugging him fiercely as she lay her head against his chest. She turned her face away so he wouldn't be able to see the tears forming in her eyes.

So it begins, she thought to herself.

After an early lunch together, Nathan took his leave of Chris and headed back to Alexandria to pack his kit. Doleful and in no mood to deal with anyone, she hid in her small office, doing her best to carry on but knowing full well that Nathan was, in all likelihood, headed off to the Sandbox where he'd be with his kind of people, people who had once been Chris's as well.

In the midst of struggling through a script she'd been given to look over and comment on, one in which she had absolutely no interest in at the moment, Chris was startled yet again, when Jan's assistant, Angela Cardosa, knocked on her door and opened it without waiting for an answer. "Chris, Jan would like to see you."

Giving her head a shake as if that would help cast away her prevailing despair, Chris pushed herself up out of her seat and followed Angela. In Jan's office she was greeted with a side of her mother-in-law she still wasn't used to seeing. At home Jan was soft-spoken, easygoing and calm as a millpond. In the office she always on the go, from the moment she left the elevator in the morning till it came time to leave. And while she'd yet to hear Jan raise her voice, those who had been working for her told Chris it was something you didn't care to be around, much less be the reason for it.

Without being told, Chris waddled over to the sofa in Jan's office and took a seat. That was when she took note of a man who was quite familiar but whom she'd yet to meet. "Chris, I take it you know who Ian Hall is," Jan stated as a way of opening this little impromptu meeting.

"Yes, our man at the Pentagon."

"And you," Hall replied giving Chris a warm smile, "are Ms. Dixon, our new military analyst."

"You're almost right, Mr. Hall. It's actually *Mrs.* Dixon," Chris replied, giving Hall a shy smile as she patted her belly. "And it's Chris."

Throwing his hands up, Hall nodded. "Well, one can never be sure, so it's always best to play it safe."

Chris's reflections on another aspect of the radical political correctness that seemed to be the governing principle at WNN was cut short by Jan. "I expect you two will be working together closely in the weeks ahead. As I was telling you, Ian, Chris's knowledge and experience as a company-grade officer will be an asset you'll come to cherish, keeping you from making another boneheaded blooper like you did last month." Though neither Jan nor Hall elaborated on what Hall had done, it must have been a biggie for his cheeks took on a bright red hue at the mere mention of it.

"Now," Jan announced, all businesslike as she brought her hands together on her desk and leaned forward. "I just got off the phone with the folks up in New York. It seems *The Times* is working on a major story, real front-page stuff according to our sources. No one knows for sure when they're going to release it, but it seems that it's going to be huge. Ian, I want you to sound out your usual sources, see what they're willing to fess up to. If you find something of interest, run it past Chris and see if it passes the smell test. I'd love to scoop *The Times*, but only if we're right. Clear?"

Hall nodded, leaving Jan to turn her attention

to Chris. "Once Ian has something, I need you to check and verify everything. Nothing goes on the air here until we're one hundred and ten percent satisfied that we've got this right. I'm sure you know how that works," Jan added, giving her daughter-in-law a quick smile and a wink. "Now, away with you wretched creatures. Have some coffee, get to know each other, but do so someplace else. I've work to do."

After struggling to get up, Chris stood there for a moment, wondering if she should tell Jan her son was gone or wait till that evening. Jan, noticing that Chris was still in her office, looked up from the document she'd begun to study. "Yes? Is there something else?"

Chris shook her head. "It can wait."

EIGHT

FORWARD OPERATING BASE AL KUT, IRAQ– SEPTEMBER 16

"Hey Major, we're here." Blurry-eyed and severely disoriented, Nathan gave his head a quick shake before peering up at the grinning crew chief hovering over him. "Welcome to wonderful downtown Al Kut, home of the 11th Airborne and some of the ugliest women God ever put on the face of the earth," the NCO shouted in an effort to be heard above the whine of the Chinook's engines. Since kissing his wife good-bye, he'd been in almost continuous motion. The only spot of luck he got during the entire trip had been during the transatlantic leg of his trip, when he was able to stretch out on the nylon jump seats of a C-17 that was hauling critical supplies, high-priority spare parts and a half dozen troops returning from leave.

Sitting upright, Nathan stretched and yawned before checking a watch on his right wrist, set to Charlie, or local time. It was 0410 hours, just after four in the morning. Then he checked a watch on his left wrist, set to Romeo or Eastern Daylight

Time. Chris would be back home by now, stretched out on the sofa in his mother's living room enjoying Häagen-Dazs chocolate chocolate chip ice cream from a bowl preciously resting on her stomach as she watched Bob Brant's show, the hottest show in WNN's evening lineup. Had he been there, he would have been on the sofa with her, massaging her feet and swollen ankles as they rested on a pillow set on his lap. It was a thought that did more than put a smile on Nathan's lips.

The habit of wearing two watches was one Nathan had gotten into when he was a young lieutenant, after he'd screwed up during an exercise when making the calculations between the time zone his unit was in and Zulu, or Greenwich Mean Time, the time the operations orders he was following were based upon. The incident had proven to be embarrassing, very embarrassing. Still, it could have been a lot worse. Had it occurred during combat, it could very well have been fatal. Knowing how easy it was to screw up calculations like that when fatigued or under pressure, Nathan had resorted to what he considered an idiot-proof solution. From time to time he caught grief for it, but he never made that mistake again.

The moment he felt the wheels of the CH-47 touch the ground, Nathan went about gathering his gear. He didn't have much, just an aviator's kit bag and a military-style computer bag. It was the lightest load he'd ever carried going into a combat zone, leaving him feeling naked and somewhat self-conscious since his crisp new ACUs, a conspicuous lack of battle rattle, and the patch he wore on his left sleeve would mark him as an outsider. Though that's exactly what he was, he felt the need to do something to blend in as best he could, if he could. When and where he'd be able to scrounge some of the gear he felt he needed was a question that had been bugging him throughout his long trek. Much to his relief, he didn't have long to wait for an answer.

Nathan had barely stepped off the Chinook's ramp and onto solid ground when a captain hailed him. Rendering a crisp salute and a greeting that was way too chipper for that hour of the morning, the young officer introduced himself. "Major Dixon, I'm Captain Halerin, General Hannigan's Aide. Welcome to FOB Al Kut, home of Hell's Angels."

If being saluted by a captain was disorienting, being met by a division commander's aide was downright ominous. Not that Nathan minded, of course. The prospect of bumbling about at oh dark thirty in the morning, trying to find someone who was in charge and could direct him to the headquarters of the 11th Airborne, better known as "Hells Angels," wasn't something Nathan was looking forward to. Acting as if all of this was no big whoop, Nathan returned Halerin's salute. "I take it there's a plan."

Grabbing the kit bag out of Nathan's hand, the aide threw it into the back of a waiting Humvee. "I'm to drop you off at your quarters where you'll have a chance to catch a few hours of zees. At 0915 I'll pick you up and run you over to the mess hall, after which you have a meeting with General Hannigan at 1000 hours."

Without so much as batting an eye, Nathan took all of this in stride as he climbed into the front seat of the division commander's Humvee. Sensing he had an opportunity to exploit his good fortune, along the way he asked Halerin if there was a chance of borrowing some field gear from someone.

"No problem, sir. We'll fix you up with whatever you need. All you have to do is ask and it's yours."

Unable to help himself, Nathan glanced over his shoulder at the young officer in the back of the Humvee, wondering if that man knew how dangerous that sort of statement was. If he didn't, he was about to get a first-class education from an officer who'd learned that there was never any harm in asking for more than you expected to get, and then some.

Freshly showered, shaved and with just enough sleep to recharge his batteries, Nathan followed Captain Halerin into Major General Hannigan's office at the appointed hour. When he entered, the commanding general of the 11th Airborne Division, a full colonel wearing armor insignia on his collar and a 4th Armored Division patch on his left shoulder, as well as a JAG lieutenant colonel came to their feet. Before Nathan had an opportunity to salute, Hannigan offered him his right hand. "Welcome back to Hells Angels, Major."

If his reception came as a surprise to Nathan, the fact that Hannigan knew he'd once served in the 11th Airborne didn't. No doubt his aide or another trusty lackey on his staff had scrambled to find out just what sort of officer the Chief of Staff was sending over to rummage through the dung heap 3rd of the 68th had managed to get itself mired in. Accepting the general's hand, Nathan smiled. "It's always good to be back home, sir. In fact, it's good to be anywhere but where I just came from."

This caused Hannigan to chuckle. "Having done a tour of duty in Sodom on the Potomac, I understand. That seems to be an honor Colonel Madina over there has yet to be blessed with," Hannigan added as he nodded toward the colonel.

Following his commanding officer's lead, Colonel Madina took Nathan's hand once Hannigan let it go. "I expect the day will come when I'll have to serve my time in hell. Until then, I'll be happy to stay right where I am, commanding the 3rd Brigade of the 4th Armored Division, even if it *is* currently attached to the 11th Airborne."

Unable to help himself, Nathan smiled. "Well sir, I'm glad to see you're keeping better company these days."

"Well played, Major," Hannigan snickered before waving a hand at the JAG officer. "Lieutenant Colonel Grotten is my divisional SJA." Unlike the others, Grotten didn't say a word. He couldn't even find it in himself to return Nathan's smile before the four officers settled down into a group of comfortable chairs that had once belonged to a high-ranking Baath Party official. The setting, an informal one, set the tone for the meeting.

"I spoke with the Chief of Staff last night," Hannigan announced as a way of signaling that it was time to get down to the matter at hand. "He wanted to make sure I understood your charter."

"Then you do understand, sir, that this is not a formal investigation," Nathan stated in an even tone.

"Not yet, at least," Grotten added.

A quick exchange of glances between the general and his SJA told Nathan the two had had a long and meaningful conversation before he showed up. Returning to the subject, Hannigan expressed his concerns. "Although a decision has yet to be made as to how this matter will be handled, I don't see how we'll be able to put this incident to bed without nailing some poor bastard to a cross now that the Iraqi government is involved. Which is why I asked General Stevens to temporarily assign you to the 11th Airborne and grant me the authority to appoint you as an Article 32 officer, if it should come to that."

Having been warned by Kaplan that this could happen, Nathan was prepared. "While I agree, sir, that there will be some sort of formal investigation and someone will face charges under the UCMJ, I would prefer to keep my investigation as low key as possible."

Upon hearing that, Hannigan snorted as he eased back in his seat. "Good luck on that score, Major. I hope you realize that you're going to be as welcome as a drug-crazed, machete-wielding, plague-infested leper by any and everyone associated with 3rd of the 68th and this incident."

Despite the seriousness of what was being discussed, Nathan couldn't help but chuckle when he recalled a saying his father was fond of using whenever he was preparing to face a hostile reception.

Unable to help himself, Hannigan asked what was so funny. "This isn't exactly my first rodeo, sir. Besides," Nathan went on to explain, "as a wise old soldier always told me, they can kill you, but they can't eat you. That's against the law."

As Nathan dwelt on the realization that this had been the first time since his father's death that he'd been able to joke about something his father had said with other officers, Hannigan and Madina exchanged knowing glances, satisfied that the Army had, for once, picked the right man for the job.

It would be bad. Everyone in 3rd of the 68th knew that. The only question was just *how* bad. As he stood in the midafternoon heat waiting for the chopper bearing the officer who would have a major say on that, Carrington found himself wondering what, if anything, he could do at this point to limit the amount of damage his career would suffer. The idea that he could escape any consequences for what his unit had done was a fantasy he had no intention of indulging in. Even if he somehow managed to make it through the coming ordeal with his record intact, he knew his name would forever be associated with this incident and what he himself realized had been a breakdown in the chain of command under the worst possible conditions.

Standing behind Carrington and off to one side, Peter White had different concerns, but the same goal in mind. He had become a believer in what he was doing. In his eyes UGVs were the Army's future. The days of sending men over the top to face enemy fire with nothing more than their personal courage and body armor that covered only a few select spots were numbered. In the future, autonomous weapons platforms more sophisticated than the M-10 and M-11 his company was producing would render manned combat systems such as the M-1 Abrams and Bradley obsolete, just as airplanes replaced captive balloons for observation and steam-driven steel ships put an end to the days when navies were beholden to the whims of wind and tides. But to get there, to ensure that progress was not slowed or even stopped by those in the Army who saw the UGVs as a threat to their chosen profession, the M-10 program had to be a success. If that meant a handful of military careers had to be sacrificed, or even worse, so be it. Pioneers always paid a price for pushing the boundaries of science and technology. White just needed to make sure that it was someone else and not him or UST who made that sacrifice.

Upon landing, Nathan hefted the rucksack he'd drawn at FOB Al Kut to replace his kit bag up over his left shoulder. Grabbing his computer carrier in his left hand, he headed for the ramp of the Chinook with far more confidence than he had just a few short hours ago. Not only was he armed with the full support and confidence of the entire chain of command from brigade level all the way back to the banks of the Potomac, he felt like he now fit in. While the combat gear he was wearing, a 9mm pistol secured in a shoulder holster under his arm and an 11th Airborne patch on his left sleeve wouldn't make what he had to do here any easier, at least he

wouldn't be seen by the officers and men of the 3rd
of the 68th as a total rogue. In a profession where
men still judged each other by measuring just how
much of a badass you were, such cues had real
meaning that made the difference between being
accepted as worthy of a soldier's respect or becoming nothing more than an object of scorn and ridi-
cule.

Of course, Nathan fully realized that he wouldn't
be embraced by the personnel of the 3rd of the 68th
simply because he looked like one of them. Whereas
the greeting by General Hannigan's aide had taken
him completely by surprise that morning, the sight
of the commanding officer of 3rd of the 68th and
the tall civilian clad in the distinctive coveralls of
United Strategic Technologies was something he
expected. If anything, had they not been there glaring at him as they were, Nathan would have been
shocked.

Drawing himself up, Nathan purposefully made
his way over to where they awaited him, stopping
when he was but a few feet in front of Carrington.
Easing his tactical computer bag onto the ground
while dropping his ruck next to it with far less fi-
nesse, Nathan rendered a crisp salute, reminding
himself as he did so that it was Major Dixon, not Captain Dixon, a mistake officers tended to make when
introducing themselves immediately following a
promotion.

The expression on Carrington's face, the manner
with which he returned Nathan's salute, and the
care with which he chose his words as he spoke told
Nathan that Carrington understood what was at

stake and was determined not to say or do anything that would prejudice the major against him, one way or the other.

"While you are here, Major," Carrington stated in a tone of voice that was as warm as a New England winter morn, "you will have my complete support as well as that of every man under my command." The exaggerated emphasis he put on the word *Major* also told Nathan that Carrington wanted to ensure that he remembered that he was, in fact, a lieutenant colonel and Nathan was a mere major, leaving him to understand why the Chief had found it necessary to frock him. Had he shown up wearing the twin bars of a captain, Nathan suspected Carrington would have done his damnedest to lord over him. Doing so to a major would be a wee bit more difficult, especially this one, Nathan thought.

When he saw that there was to be no handshaking, Nathan clasped his hands behind his back and assumed a rather relaxed position of parade rest. "I will do my best to carry out my orders as quickly and thoroughly as possible, sir, doing so in a manner that does not interfere with your operations or create undue hardships or difficulties on you or anyone in your command." Just as Carrington had been most deliberate in his choice of words, Nathan had been just as purposeful when he'd inserted the word *undue* in front of hardship and difficulties, making it clear to Carrington that he wasn't here to slap a coat of paint over the problem or put a happy face on it.

Whereas the task force commander was cautious

and measured in his approach, the UST civilian sought to impress upon Nathan that he wasn't in the least bit intimidated by his presence or his mission. "I'm Colonel White," the older gentleman announced as he stepped out of Carrington's shadow. Unlike Carrington, White made no effort to extend anything even resembling a greeting. Instead, he folded his arms across his chest and leaned back a bit as he looked down the bridge of his nose at Nathan.

This was a challenge Nathan had more or less expected. "So," he stated as dismissively as he could without going overboard, "you're the civilian."

"I'm the senior field representative for United Strategic Technologies."

Without so much as batting an eye, Nathan turned his attention back to Carrington. "There'll be another officer arriving here in a couple of days from Army Materiel Command to review all maintenance records and operator and unit maintenance procedures that have been used since your unit arrived in theater. Until then, I request that all records, logs and documentation concerning anything done to D23A, as well as D23 itself, be turned over to me."

The task force commander was about to respond when White grunted. "I'm afraid I'm going to have to disappoint you, Major. Some of those records are the property of UST. I don't know if you realize it or not, but as a private company your authority over UST is limited. Before doing anything, I need to clear it with our corporate headquarters."

Suspecting that White was merely bluffing in an effort to see how much he could get away with, rather than arguing with the retired colonel, Nathan cocked his head, looked down, and sighed. "I see. Well, if that's the case, Mister White . . ."

"It's *Colonel* White, *Major*."

"Whatever," Nathan muttered dismissively with a quick wave of his hand before bending over and reaching into the pocket of his tactical computer bag. When he found his satellite phone, he stood up and began to scroll through its directory, speaking as he did so. "General Stevens was hoping that we wouldn't need to go drag the Department of Justice into this until after I'd had a chance to investigate it. But since you leave us little recourse, I need to advise him that the Army is going to need to execute that court order we were sitting on to deal with this sort of contingency, which," Nathan emphasized looking up from what he'd been doing, "Mister White, they will be delivering to your company's corporate offices within the hour. Ah, there it is," Nathan announced when he found the number he was looking for.

The possibility that the major standing there before him was bluffing was one White wasn't prepared to bet on. His orders from his superiors had been to make this problem go away as quickly and as quietly as possible. They were, White imagined, just as clear and unambiguous as the major's. So rather than stand his ground, the retired colonel caved. "*Fine*," he grumbled. "You'll get what you want."

With that, he stormed off to make sure that his people had completed their review of all the records they had and had purged anything that could prove embarrassing to them or detrimental to the project.

Having decided on a top-down approach, Nathan started by obtaining a copy of the task force operations order that had been issued for the 13 September mission, a copy of the log kept by the TOC duty officer that day, and all digital and audio records of the operation that had been made during the operation within the TOC. Since space on Camp Pacesetter was at a premium, Carrington offered Nathan the use of either his office or the task force conference room. In order to show that he had been sincere when he'd told the task force commander that he wanted to stay out of his way, Nathan took over the conference room. With only two doors, both of which could be locked and one that led to the outside, he asked that he be permitted to bunk in there as well, something that all the officers in the task force bought into since it saved them from having to spend more time with the drug-crazed, machete-wielding, plague-infested leper than they had to.

It also allowed Nathan the freedom to call back to the Pentagon and brief Kaplan on his progress whenever he felt the need to do so as well as chat with Chris at two in the morning without having to get out of bed and go sneaking around in search of someplace where he could hold a very personal conversation with her without the fear of being overheard. He made his first call home after he'd finished going over all the official records and statements written by the various personnel involved in the 13 September incident. It provided him with a much-needed break from the grim issues he'd been sent to deal with but proved to be a little awkward at first as Chris did her best to wean out of him where he was by using every trick in the book.

"So Nathan," Chris asked as sweetly as she could, "how's the weather?"

"It's about what you'd expect this time of year."

"Have you run into anyone we know?"

"No, not really."

"Have you had a chance to get out and about yet, see any of the sights or sample the nightlife there?"

Knowing full well that the determined redhead he'd married wasn't going to stop till she managed to weasel something out of him that would clue her into where he was, Nathan realized that the only way he was going to be able to stop her from poking into his professional affairs was to get her talking about hers. That ploy worked like a charm. The shy, little girl cutesy voice she used on him whenever she was trying to get her way disappeared in a heartbeat as she took off telling him about her experiences at WNN at the double-quick, barely taking time to catch her breath as she did so. While Chris could be as cold and calculating as the most seasoned staff officer he'd ever run across, when she was truly enjoying herself, she bubbled over with an enthusiasm that was irrepressible.

Any reservations Nathan had had over Chris's decision to accept his mother's offer to work at WNN were forgotten as he listened to her. It had been a long time since he'd heard her this excited over anything. Only now was he able to appreciate just how difficult the past few months had been on Chris. The loss of his father, the ordeal he'd gone through in the Philippines while serving under an officer who bordered on being incompetent, and the wounds he received there, had all but blinded him to the personal upheaval she'd been struggling with at the same time, leaving him to wonder how he could not have noticed.

Well, he found himself thinking as he pretended to take an interest in what his wife was saying, that was all behind them now. If she was happy, he concluded, he was happy. And if there were professional consequences that he'd have to pay for having a wife working for an organization such as World News Network, so be it. As dedicated as his father had been to the Army, he never seemed to forget what he was fighting for.

Lost in his own thoughts, Nathan somehow managed to miss the importance of what his wife was telling him. Much of her enthusiasm, it seemed, was due to a story she was working on with Ian Hall, a name Nathan was vaguely familiar with but couldn't place at the moment. Nor did he notice that she was being just as evasive when it came to giving him a clue as to what the story was about as he'd been in telling her where he was. As with much of the communications that passes between husband and wife, all too often it's not what is said that is really important. Just hearing each other's voice, having an opportunity to share a few brief moments was what really mattered. Unfortunately, in this case, that theory fell short of the mark.

*   *   *

Even before he met Captain Ethan Fetterman, Nathan knew he would like him. Not as a friend, the
sort he'd go out of his way to share a beer with.
Rather, Nathan's opinion was purely professional,
one based upon what he read in the TOC duty officer's log and heard on the audio files that recorded
the radio transmissions made during the course of
the "13 September Incident," the tag everyone in
3rd of the 68th used when referring to the friendly-
fire incident. Whether his ability to identify more
closely with a company commander who'd been put
in a tough spot by a superior who did not have a
firm grasp of the situation he was facing was the
real reason that Nathan chose to interview Fetterman first was something that he didn't concern
himself with. In his mind it made sense to start with
the D Company commander. He was, after all, the
officer who had actually planned how the American
unit involved was deployed, issued the orders to it
and was physically there on the ground, not more
than a few hundred meters from where the incident
occurred.

Fetterman's written statement was also a factor.
Knowing full well that there would be an investigation of some sort, Major Cody Hogan, Carrington's
executive officer, recommended that all the princi-
pal players involved, including witnesses such as
the TOC duty officer, write statements while the
events of the 13 September Incident were still fresh
in their minds. Without fail everyone except Peter
White did so, turning them over to Hogan, who was

NO WARRIORS, NO GLORY199

the most senior member of 3rd of the 68th not involved in the incident and thus, the logical choice to handle them. Already suspecting that his career was in the balance, the last thing Carrington wanted was for anyone to come back at a later date and claim that his actions in the wake of the incident had been inappropriate or questionable. He therefore adopted his executive officer's suggestion as his own. Upon his arrival at Camp Pacesetter, Hogan had passed a copy of those reports on to Nathan, along with the other material he had requested, saving him the trouble of asking each of the participants to provide him with a written statement.

Of all the statements provided to him written by the key players, Fetterman's was also the only one that seemed to be of any real value. Carrington's was riddled with all sorts of equivocations and long, tedious explanations that addressed issues that had little direct bearing on the focus of Nathan's investigation. The language in Major Grummond's was very guarded, to say the least. Lieutenant Vanderhoff's rambling prose reflected both that officer's confusion and a desire to play it safe. Staff Sergeant Plum's was terse and limited in scope, addressing only what he and his crew did while avoiding mention of the orders and counterorders he received from his superiors. The TOC duty officer's statement was little more than a regurgitation of what he had recorded in his duty log. Quite naturally, there was nothing from White or anyone from the UST contact team since, according to White, this was purely a military matter.

With a highlighted copy of Fetterman's written

report before him, as well as a notepad on which he
had a list of handwritten questions, Nathan sat at
the conference table across from the commanding
officer of D Company, listening to that officer verbally walk him through the events of 13 September.
As he did so, Nathan checked what he was hearing
against what Fetterman had said in his statement.
With few exceptions, the two accounts matched
word for word, leaving Nathan to believe that Fetterman reviewed a copy of his statement that he had
retained just prior to seeing him. It was the smart
thing to do, the sort of thing Nathan knew he'd have
done were he in Fetterman's boots. When that officer was finished, Nathan turned to the questions
he'd written down beforehand. Most were little
more than points of clarification, items that Fetterman had touched upon but were not clear to someone who was not part of the 3rd of the 68th or was
familiar with that unit's unique command and control network or the UGVs they were equipped with.
The really important questions, the ones that everyone seemed to have glossed over in their statements
and no one had mentioned since he'd arrived at
Camp Pacesetter, would come last.

Before he continued, Nathan took a moment to
look over his next few questions, checking to see if
he needed to amend any or add new ones based on
what he'd heard during the interview. He also
needed to mentally regroup, for he was now venturing into areas that could very well impact on how
this matter was dealt with. Any thought of reminding Fetterman of his rights under Article 31 of the
UCMJ were dismissed out of hand. While the 11th

Airborne Division's SJA had recommended that he do so, Nathan felt it would cause those who had been involved in the incident to withhold information, lest anything they say be held against them should the matter be referred to a general court-martial. His mission, the one General Stevens had given him, was to find out what had happened and how things had gone as badly as they had.

When he was ready, Nathan looked at Fetterman. The expression on that officer's face told Nathan he knew what was coming. "Captain, did you monitor Lieutenant Colonel Carrington's order to Staff Sergeant Plum not to engage D23A with D23B?"

"Yes, I did."

"Did you understand that order?"

"When you say understand, Major, are you asking me if I was able to comprehend what he was saying? Or are you asking me if I understood why he was bypassing the entire chain of command and issuing that order?"

"I am asking you if you understood that it was your commanding officer's desire that Sergeant Plum refrain from destroying D23A."

"Yes, I understood that."

"Then why did you countermand that order?"

There was no doubt that Fetterman was prepared for this question, for he answered it without missing a beat. "At the time, I was under the opinion that the people back at the TOC had lost control of the situation, that they did not have a clear understanding of what was going on and, as a result, were not in a position to issue orders appropriate to the situation my unit was facing."

"What caused you to arrive at that conclusion, Captain?"

"Have you listened to the recordings of the radio traffic, sir?" After Nathan nodded, Fetterman continued. "Then you heard the transmission made by a civilian who is not in my chain of command, a man who has a vested interest in seeing that the M-10 project succeeds. Because he is not in my chain of command, I did not feel I was under any obligation to follow his orders."

"But Colonel Carrington is in your chain of command. He is your immediate superior. And yet you chose to countermand that officer's order."

"In my opinion, sir, Colonel Carrington not only did not have a firm grasp of the situation, I believe he was unduly influenced by Mr. White to buy into a decision that was wrong, both tactically and morally."

Nathan fought off the temptation to ask one more, straightforward question, one that he already knew the answer to and one Captain Fetterman would have answered without hesitation. Deciding that he'd heard enough, Nathan crossed it off his list.

It came as no big surprise to Nathan that when he interviewed Carrington, the commanding officer of 3rd of the 68th presented a verbal narrative that pretty much matched his written statement, just as Fetterman had. Major Grummond followed suit, as did Lieutenant Vanderhoff and Staff Sergeant Plum. Suspecting that neither Specialist Cutty nor Specialist Viloski would be able to add anything of value to their accounts, Nathan decided to try something different with them. Rather than having them report to him in the task force conference room, a setting that was sure to intimidate them, he decided to talk to them where they'd be most comfortable. It would also provide him with an opportunity to learn about UGVs. To this end, upon wrapping up the first full day of his investigation into the 13 September Incident, Nathan requested that he be given a hands-on orientation and demonstration of the M-10 system by the crew of D23 the following day. Major Hogan, having been charged by Carrington to assist him in his investigation, made the arrangements.

An e-mail to Kaplan, summarizing his activities thus far, concluded his official duties for the day. After securing his notes, computer and other sensitive items, Nathan took advantage of the relatively cooler temperatures of early evening to get in a bit of PT, the first he'd done since arriving in-country. He used this time to clear his head as well as consider how best to go forward. He knew he'd need to talk to Peter and any of his people who'd worked on D23A. Unlike his interviews with the members of the 3rd of the 68th, Nathan expected his dealings with them would be contentious and, in all likelihood, of little value.

Unlike the military, the people who made up the United Strategic Technologies tech team were not bound by the same ethical code that the officers and men of the 3rd of the 68th were. While Nathan knew there was a certain amount of fudging going on within the ranks of the task force in an effort to cover their collective and individual asses, hiding it was difficult, if not impossible. There were simply too many people involved, all with their own self-interest or careers to protect. There was also way too much evidence in the form of a paper trail and digital information available that documented the event. Any effort to play fast and loose with the facts in a case that had as much command interest as this one did would not only be foolish, it would be suicidal. Waffling on a written statement or during an interview was one thing, a natural human response that could almost be forgiven. Obstructing the investigation of an officer representing the Chief of Staff of the Army or tampering with evidence could not. The UST folks, playing under an entirely different set of rules and ethical code, provided they knew what the word "ethics" meant, were a different matter, one that would require Nathan to understand what they were responsible for. It would also help if he had a working knowledge of what the UGV was capable of and how it worked. The only way to do that, he decided, was to arm himself with as much technical expertise as he could before dealing with the civilian contractors.

As he had the previous evening, Nathan ended his day by calling Chris. Excited over what she was doing at WNN, she made no effort to weasel any information out of Nathan as to what he was up to. Instead, she regaled him with stories of what life on the outside was like and some of the strange things nonmilitary types did and said. The phrase, "You would be appalled," cropped up several times in her description.

One thing she never mentioned in their conversation was the story she was working on with Ian Hall. Through one of his sources in the Pentagon, Hall had managed to get a handle on the story Jan was convinced *The New York Times* was about to splatter across their front page. Unable to resist the urge to scoop *The Times,* Jan put Chris to work on finding out everything she could about the Army's unmanned combat vehicle program, as well as the activities of a unit that was currently testing them. That her efforts were about to collide with Nathan's was something Chris was oblivious to and Nathan never even considered.

NINE

The ease with which he was able to master the basics needed to control and maneuver D23B both amazed and pleased Nathan. It also raised his stock in the eyes of Specialist Viloski, who sat in Plum's seat, and Cutty, who was in his own. Staff Sergeant Plum, who said little during the orientation his crew had been directed to provide Nathan with, watched with mild amusement from the jump seat that Alex Hughes had used when he'd been with them.

"The real trick to this," Viloski informed Nathan as he was in the middle of steering 23B through an obstacle course set up just outside the camp's perimeter fence, "is to become so familiar with the manual mode controller and location of various commands on the touch screen that you don't have to think about what you're doing."

"Yeah," Cutty chimed in. "Once you've mastered that little trick, you can focus your full attention on what you want the UGV to do and not worry about what you need to do in order to make it execute your commands, if that makes any sense."

Without taking his eyes off the monitor, Nathan nodded. "That makes perfect sense. I guess it's no different than ordinary muscle memory, like the ability to reach out and pick up a glass of water without having to think about what each and every finger on your hand needs to do in order to accomplish that task."

Cutty looked up over his shoulder at Viloski and gave him a wink, something Nathan noticed out of the corner of his eye. He had 'em hooked. Now all he needed to do was carefully reel them in. "Okay, I'm pretty sure I understand how the UGV maneuvers in both manual and autonomous modes. Now, what happens when you come across a potential threat?"

Unable to help himself, Plum snickered, knowing full well what the major was up to. Still, he said nothing as he watched his two operators walk that officer through the acquisition and engagement sequence with the sort of enthusiasm all soldiers show when they're afforded an opportunity to showcase their individual skills and knowledge, especially to someone like the major. Besides providing them with a break from the mind-numbing routine that dominated so much of what a soldier did, it would supply them with countless stories, all of them embellished of course, to share with their friends about the rookie mistakes the major from the Pentagon had made while trying to perform a task that was second nature to them.

"Okay, Major," Viloski ordered as he watched

what Nathan was doing on the section leader's monitor, "I want you to drive Diabeł on over to those two yellow and black barrels you see on your screen off to the right. When you get there, park between them with your main gun oriented downrange and pointed between the two range fan markers you'll see once you get there."

"Diabeł?" Nathan asked as he was carefully maneuvering D23B off the driving course and over to the area Viloski had directed him.

"It's Polish for devil. We were allowed to name our M-10s so long as the name started with a D. Since all the good names were taken before I could come up with one, I called my mom and asked her how to spell devil in Polish."

Nathan glanced over at Cutty. "What do you call 23A?"

Before he could answer, Viloski laughed. "Originally he named it Damien, like the kid in the movie *The Omen* who was supposed to be Satan's son. We figured we'd stay with the devil theme on 23. But after it started breaking down everytime you looked at it the wrong way, we changed it to Dumbo after the elephant that tripped over its own ears."

Irked at being mocked by his friend like that in front of a stranger, Cutty turned red. "Ha-ha, very frackin' funny."

In an effort to keep his two operators from getting into it, Plum cleared his throat. "Children, behave. We don't want the major to think we're a bunch of juveniles."

Unable to let things end there, Viloski looked down and behind to where Plum was. "I thought you said we weren't supposed to lie to the major." This earned Viloski a dirty look that caused him to snicker before turning his attention back to watch what Nathan was doing. "Okay, sir. That's good enough. Now shut her down while I get clearance to fire."

"What's that involve?"

"I call the TOC on the camp's admin net, tell them we need to test fire our weapons and wait for permission to go hot."

"The TOC puts out a net call and sounds a siren to warn all the hajjis in the area," Plum explained. "Then we wait ten minutes. That's usually enough time for any hajjis who have goats or kids down-range to get them out of the beaten zone."

Used to the stringent restrictions of stateside live-fire ranges, Nathan was amazed. "Has anyone ever killed a goat?"

D23's crew exchanged guilty looks before Plum answered. "Officially, no sir."

"And unofficially?"

"Pat Emerson over on Sergeant Bohnslav's track plugged one a few weeks ago by mistake, of course."

"Yeah," Cutty chimed in, sporting a broad grin. "And don't believe what you hear about goats. It didn't taste like chicken, at least not any chickens I've ever eaten."

Nathan grinned. "No, I imagine it wouldn't. I'd rather expect it tasted like goat." His response brought a smile to everyone's faces.

While they waited for the ten minutes to pass, Nathan took advantage of the relaxed mood every-

one on D23 was in to ask some technical questions
that had a bearing on his investigation. "Could someone explain to me about the fail-safe system on
these UGVs?"

He'd been looking at Cutty when he asked his
question. Cutty, however, looked over his shoulder
at Viloski. "You're in the seat," he stated, indicating
Viloski's current location, the one the track commander normally occupied.

"Well Major, you see it's like this," Viloski began
in a deep, officious sounding voice intended to
mock the tone Plum always used when training his
crew. His effort earned him a loud slam on his thigh
from Plum.

"At ease, trooper," Plum admonished Viloski in a
manner that was anything but serious.

Rather than being annoyed by this behavior, Nathan was pleased. It told him that the crew of D23
knew in the way soldiers often did without having
to be told that they had nothing to worry about.
They'd done everything expected of them on September 13 and more. It had been Plum's quick
thinking and unconventional solution, and not the
chaotic orders from his superiors that had stopped
D23A's slaughter of IA troops. If anyone was going
to be hung out to dry for the friendly-fire incident,
Plum and his crew knew it was going to be an officer or the contractors, not them. So they were able
to interact with the officer sent to investigate the
13 September Incident in a manner that would have
appalled everyone in their chain of command.

"As I was saying, sir, before I was so rudely

interrupted," Plum continued, "the fail-safe on the
M-10s are designed to prevent the enemy from tampering with it as well as preventing an M-10 from
going rogue, that is doing something that it's not
programmed or ordered to do. All commands, re-
gardless of whether they are autonomous or manual
mode commands, are routed through the fail-safe
module before going out to the component that is to
carry out that command. If the command does not
meet certain criteria, it is not performed."

"Can the fail-safe system be bypassed, disen-
gaged or disabled?"

Cutty answered this one. "If you know what
you're doing, sir, you can do just anything with the
M-10's computer systems. Dave Larson, the platoon's tech specialist proved that during our train-up
at Hood."

Viloski sniggered. "Yeah, he really ticked off the
UST folks. They'd just gotten done explaining all of
this to some VIPs who were visiting our unit back
at Fort Hood when D12A, the M-10 that they were
using to demonstrate the system, did Larson's version of the *Swan Lake* ballet instead of maneuvering its way through the obstacle course."

"We have that on a DVD if you want to see it
later, sir," Cutty added before Plum told his people
to knock it off.

"As I was saying, sir," Viloski continued where
he left off, "in order to gain access to the fail-safe
and master control panel on a UGV, you need a key
to open the ballistic cover that's located on the rear
of the turret. Once that's open, you have to punch in

the vehicle's access code to open another cover before you can reach the actual control panel where the fail-safe switches as well as other controls are located."

"What if the UGV's batteries are drained and there's no power? Can you still access this control panel?"

Once more Cutty interjected himself into the conversation. "No problem, sir. There's a place under the ballistic cover where you can insert a flashlight battery that provides enough power to open the access covers and enter commands."

"Once you're in," Viloski continued, "you've still got to enter another code, like you do for a home security system. You've got two chances to do it right. If you screw it up a second time, the system sends out an automated signal telling everyone on the net that someone is screwing with the UGV and it locks up the system."

"There's talk about adding a self-destruct sequence to later models," Plum stated in a rather matter-of-fact manner, "but no one knows if that would be a good idea. At present, if one of our Tonka toys is in danger of falling into the wrong hands and there's not another M-10 in position to do the job, the Reaper that's always on station while we're out is capable of taking it out with a Hellfire."

"So what you're telling me," Nathan stated in an effort to make sure he got this right, "only someone who knew the code to the control panel cover and the UGV's access code could have tampered with the fail-safe."

Only then did the crew of D23 understand what Nathan had been driving at by asking his questions. Without waiting for him to say another word, Plum made an important point. "While that is true, sir, it's equally true that someone who was working on an M-10's computers or fire control, someone who knew what they were doing, could have done something that either bypassed the fail-safe or did something to the computers that screwed up D23A's programs or subroutines."

"And who has the ability to do that, Sergeant?"

Plum stared into Nathan's eyes before answering. "At present, only the contractors."

The chill Nathan's questions had generated thawed the second he began to engage an assortment of derelict vehicles and plywood panels that had been set out as targets on 3rd of the 68th's ad hoc gunnery range. The experience reminded Nathan more of a video game than what it actually was, causing him to realize that this was the reason he and the young soldiers assigned to Bravo and Delta companies took to the UGVs so easily. They'd already received their basic training on the M-10 while they'd been growing up, playing video games in their homes on PlayStations and Xboxes. It was a revelation that was revealing and more than a little disturbing. No doubt sociologists were going to have a field day studying that phenomena to death once they figured out how to obtain government grants to underwrite their efforts.

It took Nathan a while to notice that there was

something missing from the experience of engaging targets with a remote weapons platform. Though he had always been assigned to airborne, ranger or light infantry units, he had, on occasion, been on a combat vehicle during a live-fire exercise. During those instances, no matter how good the vehicle's internal filtration system or effective the main gun's bore evacuator was, inevitably the crew compartment would quickly reek of burnt cordite and hot gun oil that cooked off the coaxially mounted machine during firing. It wasn't an unpleasant smell. If anything, it was one that always seemed to cause a soldier's pulse to kick up a notch or two. That smell, and hence the excitement it evoked, was missing on D23, making the experience of engaging targets with a UGV almost sterile, even more like a video game. Perhaps, Nathan thought, those who said the day of sending robots out onto the battlefield to die for their creators was closer than he'd imagined. And while the death of each and every soldier who followed him into battle was something he took to heart, the idea of turning the process of killing for God and country into nothing more than a mechanical process orchestrated by men seated in comfortable chairs in front of color video monitors hundreds, perhaps even thousands of kilometers away from the slaughter was disturbing. It was, he concluded as they prepared to wrap up his orientation, a future he wanted no part of.

Upon returning to the motor pool, Nathan stayed with the crew of D23 as they pored over it, watching

them as they performed after-operations maintenance and prepared the UGV for that night's operation. He'd be going out with D Company, riding in
the company executive officers C2V, which had a
layout that matched Fetterman's. It was seldom used
since First Lieutenant Keith Austin, the company
XO, was kept back at Camp Pacesetter by Fetterman to tend to the administrative and maintenance
needs of the company. Even when all three of Delta's platoons rolled out the front gate, as they had on
13 September, Austin remained behind. It was a
practice Nathan had seen before, one he personally
didn't care for but never commented on. No doubt
there were things he had done when he'd commanded a company that struck other officers as odd
but had somehow worked for him. Commanding a
line company was a unique experience and doing so
successfully, especially in combat, was more of an
art, one that was very much personality driven.

Ignoring the halfhearted protests of D23's crew,
Nathan was in the process of cleaning the M240
coax machine gun when Viloski grunted. "Oh no.
Pissed off captain at ten o'clock coming our way."

To a man everyone looked up from what they'd
been doing in the direction Viloski had indicated.
Coming to his feet, Staff Sergeant Plum prepared to
greet his commanding officer, who had his platoon
leader in tow. "What can I do you out of, sir?" Plum
asked warily as he wiped his dirty hands on an
equally dirty rag.

"Get over to the contractor maintenance area and
pick up D23A," Fetterman ordered with a deadpan

expression meant to hide his true feelings. "It's going out with us tonight."

From his perch on D23B's turret, Cutty couldn't help himself. "You have got to be shitting me!"

Ignoring Cutty's comment, Fetterman looked at his watch. "Sergeant Plum, you've less than two hours to get this vehicle back together, 23A prepped, your crew fed and mounted up, ready to roll. Is that clear?"

Astonished by what he was hearing, Plum simply stood there, mouth agape, staring at his company commander. He wanted to say something, something that he felt he needed to say. The look on Fetterman's face, however, told him that he'd already fought the battle to leave D23A behind with the task force commander and had lost. Since there was no point in repeating it here, Plum sighed and turned away without uttering another word to his commanding officer. Instead, he looked at Viloski and Cutty. "All right, people, you heard the man."

While D23's crew returned to what they'd been doing, Fetterman looked over to Nathan. "Sir, I was told to inform you that there's another major from Washington inbound. Colonel Carrington thought you'd like to greet him in person."

Not knowing if this was Fetterman's way of getting him out of the way so that he could give the crew of D23 a real "Come to Jesus" speech without him being there, Nathan thanked Fetterman, wiped his hands on his ACU pants and headed off to the helipad as quickly as he could, remembering to thank Plum and crew for the orientation and their time.

On his way across the compound, Nathan felt a sense of relief. He was glad that the other major from DA had finally arrived. Not only did it provide him with someone who was computer savvy and could analyze D23A's maintenance records, it would be good to have an ally in camp, another officer like himself he could talk to and bounce his thoughts and ideas off, especially now that D23A was about to be sent out again despite its record. Why it was being used instead of another M-10 borrowed from B Company, as had been previously discussed, and who had made that decision was something Nathan needed to find out.

The thought of going to the task force commander after meeting the inbound major and suggesting that D23A be left behind until the new officer had a chance to look it over was tempting. Only General Stevens's admonishment to him not to interfere with the operations of the unit unless it became absolutely necessary stayed Nathan's hand. At the moment, he didn't feel he was in a position to make that sort of call. There were still too many questions that needed to be answered and he simply did not have the necessary expertise to override decisions made by the UST contact team, the people who, he was sure, were really behind the decision to send D23A into the field again.

Whatever joy Nathan had felt over the news that the major being sent to review the maintenance records and examine D23A's computer programs was inbound evaporated the moment that officer hopped down off the UH-60 and headed over to where he was waiting. With a black civilian computer bag slung over one shoulder, a kit bag like the one he'd left back at FOB Al Kut and no field gear to speak of save a 9mm pistol, the newcomer looked exactly like what she was, an outsider.

That he wasn't doing a very good job of hiding his dismay was obvious as the five-foot-seven female major stopped a few feet from him and set her kit bag down before clasping her hands behind her back. "Can I assume by your expression, Major Dixon, that I am happier to see you than you seem to be to see me?"

Shaken from his uncharitable and most unprofessional ruminations, Nathan did his best to recover as he glanced down at his fellow major's nametape as he offered his hand. "You'll have to excuse me, Major Tucker. I was, ah, expecting . . ."

Taking his hand, she regarded him with a rather enigmatic expression. "There's no need to apologize, Major Dixon. You're not the first person I've come across in my travels that has been less than enthusiastic to see me."

While it wasn't quite as blatant as a slap in the face would have been, Major Tucker's comment was more than sufficient to remind Nathan that he was being an ass times two. Not only was his behavior most unprofessional, he was treating Major Tucker in a manner that would have enraged him had someone treated his wife that way when she'd been in the Army.

"I'm afraid I do need to apologize. And the name is Nathan, although I imagine there are a few names you'd prefer to call me that are probably far more colorful and quite appropriate, given my conduct."

In a heartbeat the tenseness between them passed as the corners of Major Tucker's lips turned upward into something akin to a smile. "In that case, Nathan, I'm afraid you're going to have to call me Debora. But let me warn you here and now, mister," she added trying to sound serious once more, "the first time you call me Debbie will be your last."

Playing along with his new confederate, Nathan nodded. "I see. In that case, Debora, grab your kit bag and follow me. I'll fill you in on the lay of the land along the way."

After dropping Tucker's gear at the conference room where Nathan took a few minutes to bring her up to date on what he'd accomplished so far, as well as his impressions of the personalities she'd be dealing with, he gave her a quick tour of the task force area. Since her focus would be on the records reflecting maintenance and repairs performed on D23A as well as D23A itself, he took her over to meet with the contractors.

The greeting they received from Peter White and his team was not what he had expected, leaving him to wonder what had changed since he'd last dealt with the retired Army colonel; it also caused Tucker to question Nathan's assessment of the UST team. Had he not been pressed for time, Nathan would have tarried a bit longer at the UST area to see if he could figure out what was up. Unfortunately, D Company's scheduled departure and his desire to accompany them that night did not permit it. Leaving Tucker to begin her work, Nathan hurried back to the conference room, grabbed the battle rattle he'd need and headed back down to the motor pool.

Unlike their comrades on the other vehicles in the column, the crew of D55 was busy during the entire road march from Camp Pacesetter to their assigned area of operation. With Nathan in the right seat, the one the executive officer used when he was onboard, and in the exact same position Captain Fetterman occupied on D66, the reconnaissance specialist to his left and the vehicle commander above and behind him used the time to fill him in on what he was seeing, and show him how to access and manipulate the command information network. Though he was suffering from a serious case of information overload and was barely able to keep up with what the track commander, Sergeant Mark Reyes, and Specialist Hector Cuevas, the recce specialist were telling him, Nathan was beginning to get a feel for the sort of information Fetterman had available to him on 13 September.

He was also beginning to wonder if all of this information might not be too much information, that the command and control network that 3rd of the 68th was testing provided the entire chain of command, from platoon leader to task force command with far too much freedom, freedom that allowed anyone in that chain to become too involved in what was happening on the front line. The temptation to interfere, to become so involved in tracking and focusing on the activities of individual vehicles might cause a company commander or even a task force commander to lose sight of the big picture. While timely and accurate information on what subordinate units are doing is absolutely critical to a commanding officer in battle, so is his ability to step back from the chaos of the close-in battle and take a moment or two to assess the overall situation of his own unit, as well as what was going on to the left of his unit, to its right, and even behind it. If a company commander allowed himself to become focused on one small piece of that mosaic, he'd lose his ability to issue effective and timely orders needed to orchestrate the activities of all the units under his command as well as coordinate them with adjacent commands and combat support elements. And while Nathan understood that this was not what happened on 13 September since only one UGV section was involved, the potential of this command and control configuration made the micromanagement of battles a reality.

Having allowed his mind to wander, it took Nathan a second to realize that he'd missed something Specialist Cuevas had showed him before moving onto something entirely different. Raising his left hand, Nathan waved Cuevas off. "Whoa there, cowboy! You've lost me, again."

Relying on the same affected easygoing manner that had put to rest any apprehensions D23's crew had about dealing with him, Nathan asked Cuevas to go over what he'd just told him. "And this time, Specialist," Nathan admonished in a jocular manner, "speak very slowly and use very small words.

Remember, you're dealing with an infantry officer here."

Both Cuevas and Sergeant Reyes chuckled before Cuevas reached over and pointed out the areas on the touch screen in front of Nathan he had been talking about. "Okay, sir. As I said, this is where you need to go when you want to select what's displayed on your tactical monitor. When the 'All' is highlighted, it will show you everything that's out there. If you want to eliminate something, just tap the appropriate box. For example, if you don't need to know where the combat service support elements are, hit the box labeled 'CSS' and all the symbols representing combat service support elements disappear like this." With a single tap of that highlighted item, Cuevas made Camp Pacesetter, where all of 3rd of the 68th's support elements were currently located, vanish from the monitor. "You can do the same to anything out there that a friendly vehicle or reconnaissance asset has eyes on and is reporting."

"Since we've been here," Reyes chimed in, "the UST folks added an additional discriminator. At first anything that was not friendly or definitely hostile was labeled as unknown. Since we operate where there are civilians, certain areas where there are known civilian populations are now tagged as such."

"We still cast a leery eye their way," Cuevas added, "since bad hajji likes to hide with not-quite-as-bad hajji. We're just a little more careful before we light them up when we see that it's a known civilian location."

Nathan paid no heed to the cold, almost cruel manner in which Cuevas explained how his unit viewed the locals. He'd heard it all before. His own men had expressed similar sentiments when he'd been a company commander. As with all soldiers involved in an insurgency where it was next to impossible to tell who was on your side and who was about to blow you up, Cuevas and the soldiers of 3rd of the 68th assumed all locals were hostile until proven otherwise. It was a smart thing to do, one that the insurgents counted on, for it fostered the sort of contempt and suspicion that all too often caused soldiers to overreact when dealing with innocent civilians, a response that alienated them from the foreigners in their midst and put teeth in the insurgents' propaganda. The war 3rd of the 68th was fighting was not as clean as the bright blue and red symbols on the monitor before Nathan sometimes made it seem. Like all wars of insurgency, it was messy, hard and took a long time. It was a war requiring virtues for which Americans were not particularly noted.

"If there's one thing we've become aware of through PW interrogation," Reyes pointed out as Nathan was scrolling through the options menu and seeing what each command did, "it's that hajji doesn't like going up against our UGVs."

"And why is that, Sergeant?" Nathan asked without taking his eyes off his monitor.

"Apparently there's no honor to be gained martyring yourself by blowing up a machine," Cuevas answered before his track commander could. "It seems you've got to kill at least one infidel in order to earn your seventy-one virgins."

From the driver's compartment, PFC Emit Snee, who'd been listening to all of this over the intercom, chuckled. "Hell, I'd kill a dozen infidels for just one virgin."

"Snee, you wouldn't know what to do with a virgin if she landed on your face," Cuevas called out.

"All right you guys, knock it off," Reyes commanded. "We don't want the major to get the impression we're total degenerates."

Cuevas winked at Nathan, who was looking at him out of the corner of his eye. "Yeah, we wouldn't want you to get the right impression."

Reyes ignored that remark, turning back to the subject they'd be discussing. "It seems the Shia Imams have debated this at great length and come to the conclusion that killing an infidel's machine does not fulfill a true believer's obligation to wage Jihad or earn him the right to skip the judgment and go straight to Paradise. So whenever they see a UGV headed their way, they run like jackrabbits."

"The downside of that," Cuevas added, "is that they ignore the UGVs when they can and target the hell out of the C2Vs."

Nathan grinned. "I hope you do realize, Specialist Cuevas, that's one piece of information I could have done without."

Cuevas, along with the rest of the crew, broke out laughing. "Always glad to be of service, sir."

Farther up the column, the crew of D23 had other, more immediate issues on their minds. Despite having passed all of its precombat diagnostics with flying colors, Staff Sergeant Plum had zero faith in D23A. In addition to instructing Cutty to leave the UGV's turret power off unless it became an absolute necessity, Plum had taken steps to ensure that should D23A go rogue on them again, it wouldn't be able to cause anything like the damage it had on 13 September. In this, they were greatly aided by a knowledge of their UGV that surpassed, in many ways, that of the UST contact team and the people who'd designed it.

While none of D23's crew could explain in great detail how everything inside D23A worked, a year of train-up at Fort Hood and three months in-country had given Plum, Cutty and Viloski an unrivaled feel for what it took to maintain and run an M-10 as well as what it was capable of. Plum knew, for example, exactly how much fuel D23A consumed during a mission such as the one they were running that night. Armed with that knowledge, he had Cutty drain the fuel tank before adding just enough back to allow D23A to make it out to their area of operation and conduct a few hours of surveillance of its assigned sector running on batteries alone. Though Plum knew they'd wind up towing D23A back and would catch hell for going out without topping off its tank, he figured he could deal with an ass chewing better than another massacre. To further ensure things didn't get out of hand should things go south, D23A had just five rounds of 25mm HE and 100 rounds of 7.62mm for its M240 coax. It was, Plum figured, just enough to scare off a curious hajji or buy him time to send D23B over to protect it in case there was a real threat to 23A. Again, he was taking a chance, but given 23A's track record, he figured he was more than justified. In this, he was supported one hundred percent by every man in his section.

From the corner of the task force TOC she shared with Jordan Sinclair from the UST contact team, Debora Tucker watched in fascination as the officers and enlisted men went about their duties. Reading about the unique command and control network 3rd of the 68th was testing was one thing. Actually seeing it in use for the first time, with all the brightly colored symbols representing real units maneuvering a stone's throw from the Iranian border was something else altogether. Tucker admitted as much to Sinclair, who agreed. "I know what you mean," the petite civilian whispered in a tone more befitting that of a church than the command post of a combat unit.

Despite an earlier warning by her boss, Peter White, Sinclair found herself unable to resist the urge to cozy up to the female major. It was more than the simple fact that they were the only two females in Camp Pacesetter. In Tucker, Sinclair found a kindred spirit, another person who shared her passion for computers and the challenge of discovering what made them tick. It was something that set her even farther apart from her male coworkers than their biological differences.

Tucker's motivation for getting to know Sinclair matched those of the civilian, as well as one more, something that mirrored the efforts Nathan was making by befriending the crew of D23. She'd be working closely with the UST contractor team over the next few days and figured she could use at least one ally in their camp, someone who would do a better job of filling her in on United Strategic Technologies internal politics than Nathan had. So rather than resorting to the, "Me Tarzan, you Jane," approach Nathan had employed in dealing with the civilians, Tucker sought to network with the UST folks by tapping someone who shared her values, views and interests.

All seemed to be going well, with Sinclair sharing some of her opinions on what needed to be done to make the command and control network more seamless, when Peter White entered the TOC. In the blink of an eye, the female engineer went from being relaxed and open to nervous and guarded as White gazed at her with eyes narrowed and an expression that told Tucker he was not at all pleased to see his employee consorting with the enemy. Using the index finger on his right hand, the retired colonel signaled Sinclair to come over to him.

Without hesitation she did so, making no effort to hide her nervousness. At first Tucker thought she was worried about being chewed out for speaking to her. That theory, however, took a serious hit when Sinclair reared back, folded her arms across her chest and defiantly shook her head after listening to White. Whatever it was they were discussing was definitely something that Sinclair was not happy with. White, it seemed, was even less pleased with his employee's stance on the issue, whatever it was, for he reached out and grabbed Sinclair by the arm before dragging her bodily out of the TOC, an action that raised many an eyebrow among the military personnel there and appalled Tucker. Even more telling was the expression on White's face when he returned, alone. It was one of guilt, but not over what he'd done to Sinclair. Something else, Tucker concluded, was going on as she watched White take a seat next to the task commander who was doing a masterful job of ignoring the tiff between the civilians.

Upon moving D23A and D23B into their assigned positions just short of the Ten-K Zone, Cutty asked Plum if he should shut 23A's engine down or leave it running until the last of its fuel was expended. Taking a moment to give the matter some thought, Plum considered his options. At present D23 was tucked away in a wadi five klicks away from D23A's position. If he let D23A crap out where it was, that would mean he'd have to escort D8, the recovery vehicle, forward and disconnect D23A's final drive there, almost within sight of the Iranian border before hooking D8's tow bar to D23A. It would be better, and easier, in his opinion to leave just enough fuel onboard their problem child and have it come back to them, rather than going forward in the dark, stumbling about looking for it. "Shut her down," Plum finally ordered.

Using the same procedures he'd used for well over a year to manually power down D23A's engine, Cutty complied. D23A did not. Instead, it lurched forward, trundling on at a stately five miles an hour, a predetermined speed used when an M-10 was set to function in the autonomous search-and-destroy mode.

It took Plum a few seconds to realize that something was wrong. "Cutty! What the hell are you doing?"

Without taking his eyes off his monitor or stopping his efforts to retransmit the halt command to D23A a second time, Cutty shouted back, "I'm trying to stop the damned thing."

"Why did you order it to move out?"

"I didn't. It did that on its own when I commanded the piece of shit to shut down."

"Well, stop it!"

"What in the hell do you think I'm doing?"

Confident that Cutty had his act together and was doing all he could, Plum was about to report up his chain of command when his platoon leader called him over the platoon net to ask Plum the same questions he'd just pelted Cutty with. As soon as Vanderhoff gave him a chance to do so, Plum relayed the news that D23A had gone rogue, again and at the moment, there wasn't anything they could do to stop it. Vanderhoff, in turn, passed the word on to Fetterman without hesitation, glad that he was but a link in the chain and not someone who was expected to actually do something to stop D23A and equally thankful that he didn't have to make a decision if Plum and crew couldn't stop their wayward UGV.

At the TOC, Carrington regarded White with a withering gaze. The urge to lay into the civilian for

talking him into sending D23A out again was tempered not only by the presence of his own staff, but
by the female major lurking in the corner, watching
and listening with great interest to everything. Instead, he turned to the duty officer and ordered him
to access D23A's override code and see if it could
be reined in from that location even before Fetterman was finished giving his initial report over the
task force command net.

Having expected as much, the young captain
seated behind the senior officers and civilians dutifully carried out his instructions, punched in a code
he'd all but memorized, and attempted to stop
D23A. He gave it three shots before he looked back
at Carrington and shook his head. "That's a no-go,
sir."

Barely able to suppress his smirk, Major Grummond informed Carrington that D23A was now in
the Ten-K Zone. After taking a moment to study the
main tactical monitor, Carrington ordered the duty
officer to indicate the most likely course D23A
would follow, including an estimated time it would
take the rogue UGV to breach the One-K Zone if it
continued to advance along its current heading. As
the officer on duty was doing that, Carrington
turned to White. "What do you recommend?"

Without hesitation, and to the shock of everyone
present except Tucker, who was only vaguely familiar
with what had occurred on 13 September here in the
TOC, White told the task force commander that there
was only one thing he could do. "Contact the Air
Force and request an air strike to take out D23A." In
an effort to make sure that he heard right, Carrington

asked White to repeat what he'd just said; the retired colonel did so.

Confused, Grummond looked at the data the
duty officer had posted on the tactical monitor at his
commanding officer's request. "What is the rush?"
he finally asked, turning his attention back to where
Carrington and White were staring at each other.
"So long as D23A continues at its current speed, we
have an hour before it gets anywhere near the One-
K Zone. That gives the crew of D23 plenty of time
to get out there and get D23A turned around. No
doubt they've done it before."

Carrington had no doubt about that either. In the
early days of testing and training back at Fort Hood,
it wasn't uncommon for an M-10 to suddenly wander off when operating in the autonomous mode,
headed in the wrong direction. To deal with those
situations, the crews of the C2Vs would simply
drive in front of the UGV, creating an obstacle that
the UGV's sensors would attempt to avoid by steering away from it. Done right, a trained crew could
keep an M-10 going around in circles for hours until
an UST technician managed to regain remote control of the rogue UGV or the UGV simply ran out of
fuel.

White was aware of this. That was why his suggestion that they destroy D23A—especially given
the fuss he'd put up on 13 September when both the
commander of D23 and Fetterman attempted to do
that very thing in a situation that was far more serious than the current one—struck Major Tucker as
being a little more than odd.

* * *

On board D23, the mood was far different than that at the TOC. Plum was chuckling to himself. "What do you guys think?" he called out to his crew over the intercom. "Should we tell the lieutenant that D23A is going to run out of fuel long before it hits the One-K Zone? Or should we let 'em sweat awhile?"

Cutty looked up at Plum over his shoulder and grinned. "Let the bastards stew. They deserve it, making us take that piece of crap out when everyone and their brother knows it's worthless."

They were still having a good laugh over this when their platoon leader passed the word down to them that the MQ-9 Reaper overhead was going to launch a Hellfire missile and take out D23A. Stunned, Plum and crew exchanged puzzled looks before he got on the radio and told his platoon leader there was no need for that. By the time he explained what he'd done and Vanderhoff understood, the pilot of the Reaper, located hundreds of kilometers away, had acquired D23A and was preparing to fire.

On board D55, Nathan listened to the frantic radio call by Fetterman on the task force command net, telling Carrington to check fire, explaining as best he could, as quickly as he could, that there was no need to destroy D23A. There was no way that either Nathan or the D Company commander could know that the decision to take out D23A in this manner had been made before it even rolled out the front gate that night.

With nothing better to do, Nathan moved up to D23A's location behind D8 to watch the recovery operations. As so often happens when things like this occur in the military, everyone who thought that they could justify doing so gathered at the site of the incident, resulting in a sizable crowd of spectators that far outnumbered worker bees. Nathan and the crew of D55 joined this gaggle of gawkers. The first thing he noticed was how little damage there was to D23A. When he commented on this, Captain Fetterman grunted.

"Apparently," he explained, "in addition to leaving barely enough fuel on board, all of which seems to have been gone when it was hit, the crew of D23 had removed most of the ammunition from the damned thing. I guess the pilot of the Reaper was told to stop it, which is why he aimed for the engine compartment. And since there was no fuel, there wasn't the sort of fireball that a full load of fuel would have created. And what little blast and fire the detonation of the Hellfire created apparently wasn't enough to set off the onboard ammo."

"So can D23A be salvaged?" Nathan asked.

Fetterman shrugged. "I don't know. I imagine some of the electronics and computers have been knocked about but, judging from what I can see, I don't see why not."

Nathan was about to move closer, to take a closer look at the damage, when Sergeant Jeff Kennedy, the reconnaissance specialist on D66, came up behind him. "Major, I just got a call from the TOC ordering you to get back there, ASAP."

"Did they say why they want me back?"

Kennedy shrugged. "They didn't say and I didn't ask, sir." With that, the sergeant headed back to his vehicle, leaving Nathan and Fetterman staring at each other, wondering what was behind that order.

TEN

To say that Chris Dixon was nervous was an understatement of the first magnitude. As she sat in the studio, seated behind a desk that did a marvelous job of hiding eight-plus months of gestation, she felt as if she were sitting in the eye of a hurricane. All around her there was a swirl of activity as people she didn't know went about doing all sorts of things. The strangest part of her first live TV appearance was the amount of fussing a girl from makeup had lavished upon her. Even now, as she waited to go on the air, a different young woman armed with an arsenal of brushes and a tackle box overflowing with makeup touched up Chris's face in an effort to ensure that everything was picture perfect.

Hidden behind Chris's apparent calm were a host of concerns she wasn't able to share with anyone, not even Jan, the woman who'd managed to talk her into doing this spot. While it did make sense that she be the one to break the story and thus, get credit for scooping *The New York Times* since she'd done the workup on it, the idea that she was breaking her promise to Nathan that she wouldn't go on the air until after she'd delivered, bothered her even more than her pending TV debut. If there was one thing Chris did take comfort in, it was that he wasn't there in the studio watching. Had he been, he'd no doubt be laughing his ass off.

Even before she'd received her commission, Chris had never been into the glamour scene. On her wedding day, much to the utter mortification of her mother, she'd insisted upon wearing her dress blues. Flanked by her maid of honor, who was also wearing her dress blues, and Nathan and his best man in theirs, Jan couldn't help but remark to her husband that it looked more like a changing of the guard than a wedding. Hair pulled back into a high ponytail or a tight French braid, and a moisturizer with enough SPF to keep her fair skin from matching her red hair, was about all she ever used. Those days, she realized, were gone.

With a clipboard in hand and a headset covering one ear, Beth Emerson, the producer, came over to Chris one last time to make sure she understood how the segment on Bob Brant's show would go down. "Bob will open it by describing the incident. You'll be able to hear everything being said by Bob through your IFB and see him in the monitor to the right of the camera. Your opening piece will be on the teleprompter, just like we rehearsed earlier. If there's a problem and you don't want the camera on you or you're not quite ready, simply motion with your right hand, like so." Already wound up tighter than a drum, Beth Emerson's rapid-fire review of things she'd already gone over before with Chris a half dozen times wasn't helping matters. "Do you have any questions?"

Chris did her best to keep a straight face. "Yes, just one."

"Yes?"

"Where do I throw up?"

Having handled countless rookies like Chris before, Beth placed a hand on Chris's. "Trust me, you'll do fine. I dare say, before you're finished tonight, you'll be hooked."

"Yeah," Chris replied, "and I'll probably be flopping about on the floor just like all the other freshly hooked fish Jan cons into sitting here like this."

From somewhere a person called out, "One minute." At that, everyone finished whatever it had been they were doing before taking up their positions or disappearing, leaving Chris alone on the set staring at a huge camera. In many ways briefing a senior ranking officer was far easier. Even the most demanding hard case was human, a person who conveyed certain visual cues that told her what sort of mood he was in, whether he was satisfied with what he was hearing, etc. The camera she'd be talking to was simply one big machine, a technological marvel that could do just about everything accept provide her with feedback, the sort that tells someone if they're hitting all their marks or are in the process of screwing the proverbial pooch.

Such thoughts were quickly shoved aside as Chris heard Brant, who was in the WNN New York studio introducing the story. Taking a deep breath, she prepared herself, remembering at the last minute not to overdo her smile. Jan had suggested that she try a Mona Lisa smile, something that was warm and inviting, not overdone. "You are, after all, supposed to be a military analyst," Jan reminded her, "not the weather girl."

"Joining us tonight from Washington is Christina Dixon," Brant announced crisply by way as a lead-in to her segment. For a split second, as the red light on the camera flicked on, Chris felt as if she was going to faint dead away. "Chris, a former officer in the Army, is new to the World News team and is here tonight to explain what UGVs are and help us understand some of the implications this incident could have on that program."

In the twinkling of an eye, any lingering apprehensions and nervousness evaporated as Chris went into her prepared pitch, delivering it like a pro. Using the same carefully measured delivery she had used countless times before, she explained what unmanned ground combat vehicles were, how they were currently being employed and how the Army envisioned using them in the future. By the time she finished running through her prepared spiel, she was comfortable enough that she was able to field Brant's questions without missing a beat. "Turning now to the incident involving the unit in Iraq that's currently testing the next generation of UGVs and an Iraqi Army unit, how do you see the Army handling the matter?"

"I expect the chain of command will treat this as they would any other friendly-fire incident," Chris explained. "There'll be an investigation to determine what, exactly, happened. Should that initial investigation determine that rules of engagement were not adhered to, standard operating procedures were ignored or someone in the chain of command disobeyed orders or conducted themselves in a manner that is contrary to the good order and discipline of the Armed Forces, an Article 32 investigation, the military equivalent of a grand jury, will be convened. The officer charged with conducting the Article 32 will determine who, if anyone, was at fault, what articles of the Uniformed Code of Military Justice were violated and make recommendations to the appropriate authority as to how the matter should be adjudicated."

"Chris, what happens if it turns out that no one was at fault? What if the problem was a mechanical failure or a simple computer glitch? Does the Army then haul the offending UGV before a firing squad and shoot it?"

Unable to help herself, Chris snickered. "Bob, that's like saying people don't kill people, guns kill people. Even if it turns out that everyone up and down the chain of command did exactly what they were supposed to do, somewhere someone either did something to the UGV that affected the performance of the UGV in question or made a decision to send out a machine that's not quite up to standards. In that case, the Article 32 officer must determine if the mistake, if it was a mistake, was an error of omission or an error of commission."

"So you're saying that the company that is producing the UGVs the Army is currently testing, United Strategic Technologies could be at fault here?"

Once more Chris allowed herself to snicker while

on camera. "Bob, you've got to remember, even though the price tag for each of these technological marvels is several million dollars and represent the latest advances in science and technology, they're still being manufactured by the lowest bidder. As my father used to say, you get what you pay for."

Unable to help himself, Bob Brant shook his head and laughed before asking a few more questions. When he was done, he thanked Chris, announcing to his audience that he hoped he'd be seeing a lot more of her in the future. With that, he wrapped up Chris's segment and moved on to his next story. In the Washington studio, when the red light on the camera finally flickered out and the producer gave the all-clear, everyone present applauded, causing Chris to blush. Coming over to her, Beth Emerson gave Chris a big thumbs up. "And here you said you were nervous," Beth admonished.

Chris grinned. "What can I say? Like my father-in-law used to say, never let the bastards see you sweat."

From somewhere on the set, someone yelled, "We're still on the air," causing Chris to panic until she saw everyone laughing. The cameraman stepped out from behind his camera and pointed a finger at her. "Got ya," an admission that caused a fresh round of laughter.

Seated on the sofa in her office, Jan couldn't help but smile as she watched Chris's segment on one of the large-screen TVs she used to monitor what was going on around the world. Angela Cardosa, her personal assistant, nodded. "You were right. She's a natural. And," Angela added, "Bob likes her."

"What's not to like?" Jan intoned. "She's smart, quick on her feet and," Jan added, glancing over at Angela and giving her a wink, "she's a hell of a lot easier on the eyes than some of those other military types we use."

"Now all we need to do is see if your opinion is reflected in the ratings and viewer comments," Angela warned.

Jan came to her feet and dismissively waved her hand. "Trust me, she's a success. No doubt about it."

"Is that the mother-in-law speaking or our hard-nosed, take-no-prisoners bureau chief?"

Taking a seat at her desk, Jan gave her assistant a rather prim, enigmatic smile. "Yes."

One vote that Chris was not going to be getting was Alex Hughes's. Told that there was the possibility that WNN was about to scoop his story, which was due out the next day above the fold on page one of *The Times*, he'd watched the Bob Brant show, something he had never done before. By the time the segment concerning the friendly-fire incident was over, Hughes wasn't sure who he hated more, the smug, obnoxious pig Brant or the redheaded twit.

While it was true that Brant's treatment of the story didn't even come close to the blistering assault his piece would be unleashing, the very idea that someone else had beaten him to the punch was galling. That it was a smug right-wing shill like Brant only added insult to injury. Jumping to his feet, he was tempted to lash out at something, anything but decided against doing so since it would do little to assuage his anger.

In the midst of this outburst, a phone rang. Pausing, Hughes looked at the phone but didn't reach out for it at first as an idea popped into his head. After deciding whom he'd need to call, he finally picked up the phone, told the person on the other end he'd call them back without having given them a chance to say a word and then hung up on them. Heading over to his desk, he opened his Day Runner and flipped through it until he found the name of an influential aide to a senator he knew very well. Not only did that senator owe him a big favor for all the favorable press coverage he'd given her during her last campaign, she was a member of the Senate Committee on Armed Services. While Hughes knew he might never have an opportunity to make Brant and the redheaded tramp he'd dug up from somewhere personally pay for their audacity, at least he'd be able to stick it to the people Brant and the rest of the World News hacks were always doing their best to defend.

ARLINGTON, VIRGINIA—SEPTEMBER 18

The speed with which Nathan completed his return trip was staggering. There was no waiting, no need to wander about in search of someone who could direct him to his next flight. At every stop along the way he was met by an officer or senior NCO who greeted him by name before escorting him directly

to his next point of debarkation. The downside to all
of this was that no one was able to tell him why he
was being recalled or why his travels were being
expedited in this manner. The standard response of
"Sorry, sir, I've no idea," didn't bode well.

A call to Colonel Kaplan didn't help matters either. It was short and not very informative. "You're
to report here as soon as you land at Andrews," Kaplan stated crisply. "There'll be someone there to
meet you."

Though Nathan was tempted to respond with a
cheeky, "No shit?" upon hearing that, he held his
tongue in check. Since he had, by now, concluded
that he was in seriously deep shit, Nathan figured it
would not be to his advantage to make things any
worse than they already were. He also decided
against calling Chris. Until he found out just what
was up, he'd figured it would be best if he kept her
in the dark. If his sudden recall was nothing more
than a desire by General Stevens to have a face-to-
face with him before booting him out the door and
all the way back to Iraq without a break, Chris
wouldn't be disappointed. If, however, he'd be in
town for a while, he could surprise his wife, something Nathan always enjoyed doing.

The one thing that seemed to bother Nathan the
most during his return trip was the state of his uniform. He'd gone to Iraq with just two pair of ACUs.
The training he'd conducted with the crew of D23
the day before and the need to get Major Tucker
settled in before moving out with D Company that
night had left him little opportunity to wash his
spare set of ACUs. The ones he had on now were

the same ones he'd worn the previous day while training on D23 and during his foray to the Iranian border with D Company. As a result, they reeked of diesel, gun oil, sweat and that strange, dry smell unique to desert dust. Around Camp Pacesetter and even at FOB Al Kut, no one paid any heed since just about everyone smelled the same. It was only when he began to mingle with people who were wearing freshly laundered uniforms that he noticed just how much he stood out. Even worse, everyone else did as well.

Upon arriving at Andrews Air Force Base Nathan was greeted by a sergeant he recognized as being on General Stevens's personal staff. Were it not for Kaplan's admonishment to report directly to General Stevens, he would have asked the sergeant to swing by his mother's place in Alexandria to change. That was when it finally dawned upon him that this would be a tactical error. The idea of standing out, as he surely would, no longer seemed to be a minus. Rather, his dirty boots, sweat-stained ACUs and the overpowering stench of diesel and gun oil would be a badge of honor in a perverse sort of way. He'd stand out from the hordes of staff toadies and high-speed lackeys that roamed the corridors of the Pentagon. The very funk that set him apart would announce to all who passed downwind of him that he was a real soldier, someone who'd been plucked fresh from The Shit and dropped in their midst to remind them what real soldiers looked and smelled like.

Whatever comfort Nathan derived from his rationalization over his appearance evaporated the second he entered the suite of offices belonging to the Chief of Staff. Rather than being greeted as a conquering hero fresh from the field of battle, everyone eyed him as if he were a leper visiting a day spa. In the outer office he shared with Kaplan, the colonel shooed him along into General Stevens's office with little more than a nod of his head.

Following his perfunctory knock, Nathan entered Stevens's office and presented himself to the general, who was seated behind his desk, slouched down in his chair and glaring at Nathan through narrowed eyes. After returning Nathan's salute, Stevens brought his hands together before him, resting his elbows on the arm of his chair as he took a moment to stare at the officer before him. "I selected you by name, Captain," Stevens announced in a low, menacing rumble, "because I assumed I could trust you."

The fact that Stevens hadn't given him permission to stand at ease, as well as his tone in addressing him as "Captain," told Nathan that he was about to be dumped on, big time. Still unsure of what he'd done to deserve this but beginning to suspect he already knew, he decided to go totally defensive and say nothing until he had a feel for the situation.

"When exactly," Stevens continued, "were you planning on telling me that your wife was an employee of the World News Network?"

With his worst-case scenario now in play, Nathan didn't hesitate. Though he'd be running a risk by answering the general's question the way he planned to, at this point Nathan figured he had very little to lose by doing so. "Chris was hired by my mother the day before you ordered me to Iraq, sir. I was going to inform you of that development when I came in the following day but, in the rush of events, the opportunity to do so never presented itself, sir."

The manner in which Stevens's eyes narrowed even farther told Nathan that his answer, one that created the impression he was shifting the blame for this oversight onto him had not gone down well. To his credit, Stevens didn't lash out. Instead, he took a moment to mull the matter over in his mind before ordering Nathan to stand at ease. "Just how much have you told your wife about the 13 September Incident and what you've been doing in Iraq?"

This was the opportunity Nathan had been waiting for, a chance to switch over to the attack, his preferred method of dealing with difficult situations. Making a show of drawing in a deep breath and affecting an expression that conveyed to Stevens that he felt he was being wronged, Nathan replied in a manner that was as close to being insubordinate as he dare go. "Sir, I've told my wife nothing, not even where I was going. If she somehow figured out where I was and what I was doing, it was only because she used to be a first-rate officer who knew how to accomplish her assigned duties, and not as a result of anything I told her."

Had Nathan been any other officer, Stevens would have been skeptical. But Nathan Dixon wasn't just any officer. He had three things going for him that made all the difference in the world to Stevens. First and foremost, he was Scott Dixon's son. It had been his relationship with that legendary soldier as well as Stevens's assumption that the man everyone called Little Dixon behind his back was cut from the same timber as his father had been that had caused him to take Nathan on as a special staff officer in the first place. The second thing that gave Stevens pause was Nathan's record. In his short military career he'd been in more than his fair share of difficult situations and had handled each in a manner that left no doubt in anyone's mind that Nathan Dixon was a pure warrior. He was the kind of officer who was all but incapable of the guile and duplicity that tended to infect far too many officers as they settled into a career pattern that took them further and further away from the smell of gunpowder, muddy boots and field commands. The final factor that Stevens found he could not ignore was Nathan's alma mater. And while he had little doubt that former VMI Keydets could be just as career oriented and willing to place personal gain above personal honor as anyone else, Stevens's dealings with other graduates from that esteemed Southern institution led him to believe that was not the case here.

Besides, he suddenly found himself thinking as he studied the defiant expression on Nathan's face and mulled over what he'd just heard, this was exactly the sort of officer he needed. After all, if he were willing to stand up to him and defend his ground, he'd have no compunction of doing so with any other man or woman further down the chain of command. A single wave of Stevens's hand served to brush aside the issue that had caused him to recall Nathan in the manner he had, as well as indicating that he was to take a seat.

"I doubt if you're up to date with what's been happening back here," Stevens stated as he sat up and moved onto the next order of business. "So I'll bring you up to speed." With that, Stevens filled Nathan in on the repercussions resulting from WNN's assessment of the 13 September Incident and Alex Hughes's minutely detailed account of it in the *New York Times*. "I spent an hour with the Sec Def this morning going over this incident. By then he'd already heard from several senators who serve on the Senate Committee on Armed Services, which just happens to be working on the appropriations bill for the next fiscal year. Not only do they expect us to find out who is responsible, they also made it known that they intend to look into the Army's UGV program once more before deciding on whether or not it should be funded at the levels we requested. And," Stevens muttered in disgust, "I expect the State Department, which has been doing its best to keep a lid on this, will be joining the chorus calling for the public excoriation of some poor sod, guilty or not, before the day is out in order to satisfy the Iraqi government's call for justice."

Nathan grunted. None of this surprised him. Even before he'd left for Iraq, he knew it would only be a matter of time before the shit hit the fan. "Do you have anyone in particular in mind, sir?"

Before answering, Stevens regarded Nathan. "That, Major Dixon, is for you to determine. Effective immediately, those hip pocket orders General Hannigan's SJA gave you appointing you as an Article 32 officer are in effect. The Sec Def will be making an announcement this afternoon that we will be conducting an investigation into the 13 September Incident."

That Stevens was, once more, referring to him as "Major" told Nathan that he was unofficially no longer at the very top of the general's shit list. That spot of good news, however, was more than tempered by Stevens's decision to charge him with the responsibility of conducting an Article 32 investigation into the 13 September Incident. In effect, Nathan had just been handed a hand grenade, minus the pin, and ordered to run an obstacle course, in the dark, with one hand tied behind his back. After taking but a minute to digest this latest challenge, Nathan decided to feel Stevens out in an effort to determine how he saw this going down. "Is 3rd of the 68th going to be stood down during the course of this investigation, sir?"

Stevens looked away as he considered how best to answer that question. "If this were a simple friendly-fire incident, we probably would. But there are other factors involved. First and foremost is the tactical situation on the ground. Even the Iraqi government realizes that standing down 3rd of the 68th is not possible. With the 11th Airborne already covering such a large stretch of the Iran–Iraq border and 3rd of the 68th responsible for a good chunk of that, it's not feasible to stand them down. So the Article 32 will be conducted while the unit continues to carry out its assigned duties."

"And if it does turn out that a court-martial is in order?"

"Then only those parties involved will be relieved of their duties and either replacements sent in or their second in command will be placed in charge."

"You realize, sir, that could very well strain an already tense command environment within 3rd of the 68th even further, perhaps to the breaking point."

Stevens grunted. "Unfortunately, that's not even the half of it. As I said, this incident has once more brought the debate over where the Army's UGV program is going to the fore. I expect there are many people, both in and out of uniform, who would like to see that program scaled back. That means that the UGV program, and specifically UST's M-10, will be on trial as well."

"Could I make a suggestion, sir?"

"Shoot."

"The situation within 3rd of the 68th is complicated. As you said, this is far from being a simple friendly-fire incident. We're going to need to do more than an Article 32."

"Go on, Major. I'm listening."

"I recommend we conduct two separate investigations. One, the Article 32, to determine if there was any misconduct on the part of any members of the 3rd of the 68th that resulted in the friendly-fire incident, and a second to determine if the UGVs the 3rd of the 68th are testing are suitable for the Army's needs and ready for prime time."

Unable to help himself, Stevens grinned. "I suppose you want to handle the latter and have someone else deal with the really messy investigation."

"While that is true, sir," Nathan admitted, "it's more than my personal preference. I do not feel I can be objective and impartial were I appointed as the Article 32 officer. I believe Major Tucker, who's only been there since yesterday, would be a better choice for that duty."

Stevens snickered. "Oh, she's going to love you for recommending her."

"She's a professional, sir. She'll understand."

"I wasn't talking about understanding. But I do see your point, and I've no choice but to agree with your assessment and your recommendation since you're familiar with the situation on the ground. Some people haven't been happy with the way some of the United Strategic Technologies representatives and contact teams have been conducting themselves during the development of the M-10, or with the M-10 itself. Those who know more about the UGV program than I do are telling me we should skip this generation and move onto the prototypes both General Dynamics and BEA are currently working on."

Rather than share his suspicions that there was something going on between the commanding officer of the 3rd of the 68th and Peter White, Nathan decided it would be best to keep that to himself, for now. Perhaps something would shake loose that would clue him in to what was going on between those two men now that there was an Article 32 in play. If he played it smart, Nathan figured he could use the threat of a court-martial to loosen tongues, particularly Carrington's.

Setting that thought aside for the moment, Nathan sought to clarify his status. "Then I assume, sir, that I am to return to Iraq and continue as before."

Before answering, Stevens paged Kaplan. With notebook in hand, that officer strolled in and stood by for orders. "Neil, as soon as Major Dixon fills you in on his activities and observations in Iraq to date, get him back downrange ASAP. But before you do that, have my aide get General Hannigan of the 11th Airborne on a secure line."

Glancing over at Nathan, then back at Stevens, Kaplan winked. "I'll make sure that Major Dixon is skids up and on his way first thing in the morning, sir."

Stevens nodded. "Sounds like a plan. Now, move out smartly."

Having finished briefing Kaplan on what he'd accomplished in Iraq as well as downloading his notes from his laptop to Kaplan's desktop computer, Nathan wandered over to his desk, where he plopped down in his chair and turned until he was facing the wall. From across the way, Kaplan watched in mild amusement until he couldn't take it any longer. "Look, Nathan, it's not her fault."

Bringing his chair partway around, Nathan regarded Kaplan out of the corner of his eye. It was obvious he knew everything about Chris, the Chief's real reason for hauling him back as he had and the delicate situation his current duties and her new career created. He was about to dismiss Kaplan's assessment as Pollyannaish, but took a moment to consider it. Casting his gaze back at the blank wall he'd been staring at, he realized that Kaplan was right. As improbable as it seemed, the circumstances that had led up to this strange convergence were all unrelated.

Well, Nathan corrected himself, *almost* all of them were unrelated. That Chris just happened to wind up at WNN was no accident, not when he factored in that they'd been living with his strong-willed and very independent mother for the past few months. Chris didn't just wake up one morning and decide to be a military analyst for WNN. And no doubt Jan didn't magically divine that Chris would be the most logical choice to cover a story such as the 13 September Incident. Just how much was pure happenstance and how much resulted from cold calculations would be impossible to sort at this point. Not that any of that mattered anymore. The only thing that mattered, in the end, was that it really hadn't been Chris's fault that things had become so complicated and balls-up. Everyone had simply been doing what they had thought was best at the moment. That they all collided head-on in the center of the same intersection was just one of those quirky little jokes Fate likes to play on people.

Finally coming to the conclusion that he was burning daylight, Nathan reached out, grabbed the phone and called Angela Cardosa. She'd be able to tell him where his mother and Chris were, allowing him to preserve the element of surprise. When he was finished with that call, he came to his feet. "Well, sir," he announced to Kaplan, "seeing as the general is finished chewing on my ass and you know everything I do, I think I'll make myself scarce."

Kaplan chuckled. "You do that, Major. I'll drop

your new travel orders off tonight after I'm finished here."

"Don't expect me to answer the door," Nathan warned.

"I'd be disappointed if you did," Kaplan added with a knowing wink.

Somehow the sight of her son strolling into her office in dirty ACUs, sporting an 11th Airborne patch on his left sleeve and reeking of sweat and gun oil, didn't surprise Jan in the least. She was used to her husband suddenly showing up from God knew where without warning. In fact, had the uniform been a blend of medium green, brown and black instead of the modern light green and gray, Jan would have found herself wondering if she was looking at a ghost. Even the silly grin Nathan was sporting bore an eerie similarity to his father's.

Coming to her feet, she came around her desk and met Nathan halfway. Without hesitation she hugged him, though she did make a show of turning up her nose when they pulled away. "The least you could have done was run through the lawn sprinklers outside before coming up to see me."

"What? And spoil all the fun?" Nathan beamed.

"You're just like your father."

"So I've been told. So, where do you have my wife chained up?"

A devilish grin lit up Jan's face. "She's down in the studio, getting ready to do a spot. What do you say we go cheer her on?"

Suspecting that his mother was just as anxious to

have some fun at Chris's expense as he was, the son readily agreed and followed the mother. In the elevator, Jan looked over at Nathan. "I suggest you take that airborne patch off unless, of course, you want Chris to know where you've been and what you've been up to."

As he was doing so, he glanced over at his mother, regarding her with a raised eyebrow. "Oh? And where would that be?"

"Nathan, you're not dealing with an complete idiot. I know where the 11th Airborne Division is and I know its order of battle. I also know the manner in which you were jerked out of the Pentagon and shipped out under the cover of darkness isn't how the Chief of Staff of the Army normally does things. Even without the patch I expect Chris will be able to connect all the dots, if she hasn't already done so."

"Chris was always too smart for her own good." Nathan chuckled.

"Oh, I don't know about that. After all, she married you, didn't she?"

Mother and son found Chris seated behind the desk they used to hide her pregnancy, receiving some last-minute touch-ups from the makeup girl. As she'd predicted, Nathan couldn't help but laugh. "My God, Mom. What have you done to my Chris?"

Proudly, Jan beamed. "She cleans up well, doesn't she?"

The two of them were in the middle of this exchange when Chris noticed them. Unable to help it, her eyes flew open and she began to turn beet red, causing the poor makeup girl who'd been working

on her to pull away and ask what was wrong. Before
Chris could respond, the producer announced they
were one minute from airtime. Stowing her brushes
and clearing away her tackle box, the young woman
beat a hasty retreat, leaving Chris struggling to regain her composure as she did her best to ignore
Nathan and her mother-in-law.

With an ease and confidence that belied her status as a newbie, Chris went about fielding the questions the host of a WNN daytime show hit her with
concerning the Army's UGV program, the story
she'd broken concerning the friendly-fire incident
involving 3rd of the 68th, the accuracy of *The New
York Times* piece concerning the 13 September
Incident and the just-concluded Secretary of Defense's announcement on that matter. Nathan was
both proud of the way his wife conducted herself
and appalled by the detailed knowledge she had
concerning the incident he was investigating. No
wonder, he found himself thinking, General Stevens had assumed that he'd been feeding her information, leaving him even more amazed that the
Chief not only accepted his explanation, but was
actually sending him back to finish the job. Had he
been in Stevens's seat, Nathan doubted if he would
have done either.

When her segment was finished, Chris wasted
little time staggering to her feet and making a bee-
line over to where Nathan was, barely giving the
sound tech time to remove her IFB earpiece and
transmitter. "Nathan Dixon," she admonished, doing her best to keep from making too big a scene,
"what are you doing here?"

Flashing her his best boyish grin, he reached out, took Chris by the arms, and pulled her into him, kissing her square on the lips as if they were the only two people in the room. Easing back a bit, he winked. "Does that answer your question?" Flustered and excited all at the same time, Chris simply blinked. "By the way," Nathan added, "I like what you did with your hair. Very nice."

Upon hearing this, Jan snickered. "You should have been there when they were cutting it. You would have thought we were torturing her."

At this Chris went all shy and defensive, looking up at her husband through her lashes. "You know how I feel about all that girlie stuff, Nate."

With the tip of his finger, he tilted Chris's head back until she was looking up into his eyes before kissing her once more. Unable to resist the urge to do so, Chris brought her hands up about Nathan's neck and drew herself up as close to her husband as her enormous belly permitted.

As he lay in the semidarkness of their bedroom with his head resting in the crook of his wife's arm, Nathan ran his hand over Chris's bare midsection, following the activities of their unborn child. "I don't think this little fella is too thrilled about us messing around like we did."

"How do you know it's a boy?" Chris asked, basking in the sheer pleasure of being with her husband like this.

"Don't tell me you broke down and let the doctor tell you what it is?"

"No, I didn't, though she's been dying to tell me something for months now."

"Is there something wrong?" Nathan asked, unable to hide the concern in his voice as he looked up at his wife's face.

Placing a hand on his head in order to gently guide it back to where it had been, Chris smiled to herself. "No, I'm sure of that. If there were a serious problem, I would have been told long before this."

Though still concerned, Nathan let the matter go. While they didn't always share all their little secrets, problems and concerns with each other, he was confident that if there were something seriously wrong with their child, she'd have told him.

"So, you're going back to Iraq tomorrow," Chris murmured.

Realizing it was rather pointless to deny where he'd been and where he was going, Nathan sighed. "I'm afraid so. Someone's got to keep the world safe for this little fella."

"When do you think you'll be back?"

Pulling away, Nathan shifted about and brought his head up to his own pillow, looking across to Chris, who'd turned to face him. "I don't know," he admitted in a low, mournful tone. "A week. Maybe more, maybe less."

"I hope you're here when this one decides to punch out," Chris murmured wistfully as she placed her hand on her stomach. A sudden thrust by a fetal limb into her bladder caused Chris to grimace. "God, I so hope most of this is water, 'cause if it's not, I'm afraid all of the king's horses and all the king's men won't be able to put poor old Chris back together again."

Suddenly concerned, Nathan placed a hand on his wife's cheek. "Don't say that. Don't even think that."

Realizing that she'd upset him, Chris craned her neck in order to plant a quick kiss on her husband's forehead before pulling away and smiling. "Don't worry about me, sweetums. I'll be all right. Just make sure you keep yourself healthy and out of harm's way. I don't relish the idea of being a single parent."

"Chris, you know me."

"Yeah, I do," she replied glumly. "That's why I'm worried."

ELEVEN

CAMP PACESETTER, IRAQ—SEPTEMBER 20

Word that there would be an Article 32 investigation into the 13 September Incident preceded Nathan's return, making his arrival an even less joyous occasion than it had been the first time, if that was possible. Only Debora Tucker was there to greet the Black Hawk carrying him back into the eye of a growing storm. "We have to talk," were the first words out of the female major's mouth as he approached her.

Not knowing whether her intent was to lash out at him for putting her in the unenviable position he had, or if there was something more important she needed to share with him, Nathan played it cool. "I expect we do," he replied as he followed her back to the task force conference room. There he divested himself of his kit and battle rattle, which he'd picked up from General Hannigan's aide on his way back through FOB Al Kut.

Pulling a chair out from the table, Tucker took a seat, speaking as she watched Nathan do likewise.

"I'm not even going to ask how you managed to weasel out of the Article 32."

"How do you know I did?"

"When the division SJA flew up here yesterday to brief me on my duties, drop off a copy of the *Manual for Courts-Martial* and answer any questions I had, he told me that orders came down from on high that revoked your hip pocket orders before issuing new orders appointing me as the Article 32 officer."

"The Chief of Staff decided it would be best if I focused on the nuts and bolts of the incident while you handled the Article 32."

"But I'm the subject-matter expert when it comes to computers," Tucker pointed out. "I should be the one handling that."

"We can work together," Nathan offered.

Folding her arms across her chest, the female major narrowed her eyes. "Do I have a choice?"

Nathan shrugged. "At this point, no."

"You know you're a sniveling little bastard."

In an effort to keep things from getting out of hand, Nathan grinned as he gave Tucker a wink. "I've been called worse. Now, down to business. Has anything of note happened while I was gone?"

With that the female officer filled him in on what had transpired during his absence. It seemed news that D23A had only been damaged and not totally destroyed created something of a panic among the UST personnel. Suspecting that something was amiss based upon what she'd witnessed in the TOC when the decision had been made to fire on D23A, Tucker had instructed the task force commander to keep the UST people away from it after it had been towed back. When Carrington told her that he had no intention of doing so, that the UST people had a right to examine and work on all UGVs and associated equipment, Tucker had found it necessary to inform Carrington that if he did not comply, she would have no choice but to notify his brigade and division commanders. Suspecting that he'd lose that fight, Carrington acquiesced to Tucker's demands, which sent Peter White over the edge.

"The man was livid," Tucker remarked. "I mean he became unglued, threatening Carrington, then me, then anyone who had the temerity to be in the same room with him."

"Sounds like he had something to hide."

Tucker nodded. "That's what I figured, so I started going over D23A with the help of some of the techno-geeks this unit seems to abound with."

"And?"

Tucker drew in a deep breath as she cocked an eyebrow. "While I can't quite pinpoint exactly what they did, or tell you who did it," she explained, "I *can* tell you that some of the computers and programming on D23A have been altered."

"Are you sure?"

"I've no doubt about it," Tucker replied without hesitation. "I compared what I was looking at on D23A with D23B."

"Could that have caused the 13 September Incident?"

"I can't tell you that for sure. According to AMC, since the M-10s here are still in the testing stage and the Army hasn't formally accepted the M-10, a

lot of the computer programs used to run the subroutines on the M-10 are proprietary. Without that
information, I'm only guessing."

"But you are confident that someone did mess
with D23A."

"Like I said, I've no doubt about it."

This gave Nathan pause as he mulled over what
Stevens had told him. Tucker couldn't help but notice. "Somehow I get the feeling none of this sur-
prises you."

"No, it doesn't. What about the Article 32? Have
you done anything on that yet?"

The female major looked away, averting her eyes.
"Well, yes, sort of."

"Sort of?"

"While the division SJA was here, I notified the
task force commander that I was conducting a preliminary inquiry in accordance with Rule 303 of
the UCMJ. To that end, I've gone over the notes you
left me and have reviewed all the audio and video
records as well as the written statements. I've also
requested that the SJA send a JAG officer up here
to help keep me from botching this before I start
talking to anyone."

"Smart move. This is one we don't want to bol-
locks-up. So," Nathan asked, unable to contain his
personal curiosity, "what have you come up with so
far?"

Turning to her notes, Major Tucker began to go
over what she'd been able to figure out thus far. The
operations order that set things in motion on 13 September, which was written by Major Grummond
and approved by Carrington, was sound but not

perfect, a conclusion Nathan had come to when he'd looked it over. The failure to establish a contact point on the ground manned by a representative of D Company and someone from the IA unit deployed forward of it was a glaring oversight by the task force operations officer but not, in Tucker's opinion, criminal. "The reliance of a single IA liaison officer at the task force TOC without dispatching an American officer to the IA battalion command post was insufficient to deal with a rapidly changing situation, as events proved. This deficiency needs to be addressed somewhere, but not using the UCMJ," Tucker summarized.

With nothing more than a nod, Nathan indicated that he both agreed and wanted her to continue. She next addressed the incident itself, starting with the actions of D23. In her opinion, the crew were the only ones who came out of the whole sordid mess looking good, coming up with an unconventional solution to the problem that not only put an end to the slaughter of IA troops but did so in a manner that caused minimal damage to valuable equipment that could, if things turned out the way they were going, be used as evidence in a court-martial. Their platoon leader, on the other hand, had come across to Tucker as being a total non-player. "If anything," Tucker stated dismissively, "Lieutenant Vanderhoff was an impediment, a useless clog that only served to confuse the crew and his company commander. While this incident makes him look as if he's something of a bungler, he really didn't do anything that could be deemed as inappropriate, negligent or criminal."

"By the same token he didn't do a damned thing to demonstrate that he is competent." Nathan grunted in disgust.

The fact that she skipped over Captain Fetterman's conduct on 13 September in order to address LTC Carrington's told Nathan that she had already come to the same sad conclusion he had when he'd first looked into the incident. Like Vanderhoff's behavior, the conduct of the people in the task force TOC that night, in her opinion, was anything but stellar, serving only to complicate matters and prolong the killing of IA troops. Here she differed with Nathan's thoughts on this aspect of the issue by a wide margin. To him, Carrington's failure to allow the commanding officer on the spot to deal with the situation bordered on being criminal. While he was well within his purview to override the orders of a subordinate commander, even to the extent of skipping over several links in the chain of command to ensure his orders were carried out, in this case Carrington had been wrong, dead wrong. His decision, one Nathan suspected Carrington had made for reasons that had nothing to do with the tactical situation was, in Nathan's mind, criminal, plain and simple. Even more egregious, in Nathan's eyes, was the fact that Carrington had allowed White, a civilian, to insert himself into the situation. The idea that a serving officer would allow a civilian to issue orders on a tactical radio net in the midst of a firefight was, to Nathan, mind-boggling.

The final person who Tucker saw as having played a role in the events of that night was, quite naturally, the company commander. Before she began, she looked up at Nathan, assuming an almost apologetic expression knowing full well what she was about to say wasn't going to go over well with him. She knew this because her own conclusions on the issue hadn't sat well with her either. "In all the confusion, all of the back and forth," Tucker surmised, "I can find only one clear violation of the UCMJ that would stand up in court."

Nathan saved Tucker from having to spell it out for him. Closing his eyes, he nodded. "I already know what you're about to say. Captain Fetterman's refusal to obey Carrington's order not to fire on D23A using D23B leaves him open to be tried under Article 92 of the UCMJ."

"Will that be enough to satisfy those who are looking for a scapegoat?" Tucker asked without thinking.

Nathan didn't honor that question with a response. While he glared at his fellow major, informing her that he was, to say the least, appalled that she would even consider such a thing, he also understood that if push came to shove and neither of them could come up with a better, more deserving candidate, Captain Fetterman would become the fall guy.

Once they had figured out how they would go about conducting their two investigations, both Nathan and Debora Tucker went to meet with LTC Carrington and his executive officer, First Lieutenant Austin. Since Carrington knew where Nathan had been, Dixon saw no problem in providing him with

a verbal summary of General Stevens's instructions. In doing so, Nathan was very careful what
information he shared and what he kept to himself.
The idea that he and Major Tucker were going to
have to come up with the name of an officer who
could be thrown to the wolves did not sit well with
Nathan, especially since the star candidate for that
honor was the one officer who, in Nathan's opinion,
had done exactly what he should have, including
disobeying an order that was inappropriate and,
more than likely, grounded on considerations that
had nothing to do with the tactical situation Fetterman and his people were dealing with.

As he had all along, Carrington did his best to
convince Nathan that he was fully cooperating with
him. Like Nathan and Tucker, he had evaluated
the situation in much the same way they had and
come to a conclusion that pretty much mirrored
the one reached by the two majors. While he
wasn't one hundred percent sure that he could depend upon Major Grummond in a court-martial if it
came to one, he had little doubt that everyone else
on his staff who had been in the TOC on the night
of 13 September would support whatever position
he took when it came time to justify his actions.
The fact of the matter was Carrington had managed
to convince himself that were it not for the behavior
of Peter White, his conduct during the crisis had
been flawless.

Nathan's meeting with Peter White later in the
day was far less congenial. Having been a full colonel before retiring and going to work for UST,
White knew exactly what was going on. He knew

Carrington would have no qualms whatsoever about throwing him, UST or the M-10 program under the bus if that man thought doing so would save his hide. But then, White was ready to do the same to Carrington if that's what it took to protect UST and the investment it had made in the M-10. In White's eyes, trashing a military career or two would be a small price to pay to keep a system that was so important to the Army from falling victim to political expediency. Were it not for his error in judgment on 13 September, as well as the failure of the MQ-9 Reaper to destroy D23A, he'd have nothing to worry about. Unfortunately, he'd allowed his temper to get the better of him in the first instance and was the victim of just plain bad luck when it came to the latter, leaving him little choice but to find a way of dissing Carrington and his people before they had a chance to do the same to him.

The one thing White could not depend upon unlike Carrington was the presumed loyalty of his subordinates. Of all the annoying little difficulties that White had when he'd made the transition from the military to corporate America, the worst was the dog-eat-dog mentality that governed corporate politics. If any of the people he had in his contact team felt threatened in any way, he had no doubt they'd sell him out in a heartbeat.

By the end of his first day back, Nathan found himself psychologically exhausted. Playing mind games with people who were much more practiced in that fine art took a lot out of him. As he sat out on the berm surrounding Camp Pacesetter that night, watching B Company's evening patrol roll out the front gate, he found himself envying the officers and men of that unit. Though their enemy were insurgents who hid among a population that was, at best, indifferent to the Americans, when they did reveal themselves the troopers in B Company could deal with them with shot and shell. The enemy Nathan was doing battle with was not only people who were supposed to be in the same Army he belonged to, it was a fight that was waged with regulations, paper and rhetoric couched in misleading statements, half-truths and outright lies. It was a way of war he was unfamiliar with and one that did not suit his personality. Whether he would be able to conduct an effective campaign, one that rewarded the just and punished the wicked, was a question he had no answer for. All he knew for sure was that at the moment, he was outgunned, outclassed and out of his league.

WASHINGTON, D.C.–SEPTEMBER 20

When she'd taken Jan's offer, Chris had been under the impression that it would be one that involved easy, flexible hours and wouldn't be stressful. Thus far her duties at WNN had been anything but. Much of the blame, of course, was due to the breaking of a story that threatened to impact the Army in much the same way the Haditha Incident had the Marine Corps. Not only did Alex Hughes's description of events surrounding the 13 September Incident cast serious aspersions upon American forces in Iraq and question the competence of their officers, the

wisdom of employing autonomous and semiautono-
mous ground combat vehicles was being openly debated in the press and would soon be the subject of
Congressional hearings. This, in itself, made the
story Chris had cut her teeth on something that demanded the best from everyone covering it.

Not all the pressure Chris was under was generated by the full-court press that WNN was putting
on its reporting of the Incident or Jan's determination to present a fair and balanced view of the incident, one that was sadly lacking in Hughes's account
of events. In part it was a self-inflicted wound, born
from Chris's habit of giving her assigned duties and
responsibilities her full attention. Unlike many of
the bright-eyed young journalists fresh out of college, she was not motivated by any great desire to
become a foot soldier for the Fourth Estate, righting
terrible wrongs and keeping the American public
informed of the world around them by shining the
bright lights of TV cameras on the story du jour.
The real reason Chris was throwing herself into the
story with such élan was far more basic, more personal than that. She simply needed to feel useful
again, to be a part of something bigger than herself,
although at the moment she felt as if there wasn't
anything bigger than her due to her pregnancy.

That the 13 September Incident involved an institution that he loved, one she'd dedicated her life to
only added to her desire to give the story her all.
With the unique power of television to shape and
influence the discussion of that incident at her dis-
posal, Chris threw herself into her job with the
same abandon and dedication that had made her an

outstanding staff officer and a rising star in her previous profession. And while journalism wasn't where her heart really was she realized, as all good soldiers do, that you seldom get to pick which battles you need to fight or where they're fought. All you can do is give it your all and do everything within your power to win and win big, which is exactly what Chris set out to do using her newfound platform.

To their credit, Bob Brant and Jan's bosses in New York recognized that in Chris they had someone who could do more than provide Brant and other WNN personalities with information and material that allowed them to put a different spin on the 13 September Incident, one that was more to Brant's liking. She provided him with a foil, one that he could use to parry some of the media critics of the military who were calling for blood. That she was also a very attractive young woman who came across as sincere and knowledgeable was a plus.

Even more impressive to someone like Brant was Chris's ability to shrug aside the caustic remarks that some TV experts and fellow journalists resorted to in an effort to rattle their critics, and come back with a measured, well-reasoned response that left her on-camera assailants looking like fools. It didn't matter to Brant, Jan or anyone else that Chris had learned how to do that the hard way, the way that most young officers in the Army do. All that mattered to the management of WNN was that she could look good while doing so.

There was a price to pay for this, one that Chris worried about but refused to give into. At the moment she was not a spry, young staff officer at the top of her game, physically or mentally. While she refused to treat her pregnancy as if it were a handicap, it was definitely a serious drag on her ability to put the sort of time and effort into the story that she wanted to, that she felt it demanded. Her determination and drive to provide the on air journalists of WNN with material that would allow them to set the record straight and present a more realistic and balanced accounting of the 13 September Incident was taking a toll on her, one that she knew she could not ignore forever. At some point, she knew she'd need to throttle back. Only the knowledge that her husband was in the forward area and, she suspected, involved in the incident kept her going when common sense and logic dictated otherwise.

So Christina Dixon shoved aside her personal concerns as she had done so many times in the past and pressed on.

CAMP PACESETTER, IRAQ—SEPTEMBER 22

Nathan's dealings with the UST contact team were turning out to be as contentious and difficult as he'd expected. Unlike the personnel in 3rd of the 68th who were forthcoming with reasonable answers and willing assistance because they either saw him as one of their own or understood what the consequences of not doing so would be, the civilian contractors treated him with barely concealed contempt. Were he not armed with a federal court order the divisional SJA had obtained, Nathan was convinced the UST team on Camp Pacesetter would have locked the doors to their hooch and pulled down the shades every time they saw him headed their way.

Fortunately, he found he didn't need to spend much time with them, at least not alone. As Debora Tucker had pointed out to him, some of the 3rd of the 68th personnel possessed a level of technical expertise that matched the UST team's. In the case of some, such as William Zhso, it actually surpassed them. This, of course, caused Nathan to wonder why the UST team was even there, a point that he made to Tucker. Being far more familiar with the ins and outs of the Army's procurement policies and regulations, she explained that since the Army had not yet made a decision on whether or not to buy into the M-10 program, UST provided all direct and general support maintenance to the 3rd of the 68th.

"It would be a monumental waste of time and resources to train military personnel who are needed elsewhere to take care of the higher-echelon maintenance needs of the M-10 if it turns out the Army doesn't type classify the UST version of the M-10. Only when a final decision is made will those duties be turned over to the Army. Of course, UST will receive a contract to conduct the initial training as well as provide all the specialized tools and test equipment needed to perform that maintenance."

"Of course," Nathan replied cynically.

It was because UST had a vested interest in seeing the M-10 succeed that Nathan found himself relying more and more on the soldiers of the 3rd of the 68th. They were only interested in one thing:

getting their hands on something that worked. Unfortunately, the enlisted personnel he was beginning to rely on in his quest to gain a better understanding of how the M-10 worked were not authorized to delve into the inners of the M-10s their lives depended upon. This left Nathan little choice but to use UST techs. While none were particularly thrilled about helping someone they saw as a threat, Jordan Sinclair was the most cooperative. Unlike some of her coworkers, she didn't run back to Peter White every time Nathan asked her to open up a maintenance access panel or remove a component so that Corporal Zhso could show Nathan what he was talking about.

This way of doing things was not without its problems. Unable to help herself, Sinclair would interrupt Zhso when she thought he was wrong. In addition to being proud of his own expertise and unwilling to concede a point to a civilian contractor when he suspected he was right, Zhso would go toe-to-toe with her, engaging in some very contentious debates over technical issues that were way over Nathan's head. Inevitably, he'd find himself having to put an end to their contentious and often heated arguments, claiming that he had enough of a grasp of the item under discussion even when he didn't have the foggiest idea what the two had been talking about.

Zhso and Sinclair were in the middle of one of their tête-à-têtes over a minor technical point, one that was causing Nathan's head to spin, when an NCO came up to the M-10 he was perched on. "Major, Colonel Carrington and Major Grummond would like to see you at the TOC." Taking full advantage of this opportunity to get away from the dueling techno-geeks, Nathan thanked them, told Zhso he'd get back with him when he had the time and fled.

Both the task force commander and his operations officer were waiting for Nathan just outside the entrance to the task force TOC when he arrived. The setting and their demeanor told Nathan that they were anxious to discuss something with him out of earshot with others. "We've just been handed a mission by brigade that's tailor made for a UGV company," Grummond stated in a guarded tone. "But before we went ahead with drafting any orders, both the colonel and I thought it might be a good idea to discuss the issue with you."

Confused, Nathan looked at Grummond, then over at Carrington. "There's really no need for you to clear this sort of thing with me, sir. Until such time as Major Tucker's initial inquiry is wrapped up and a decision has been made as to how to proceed, your unit is free to carry on as before."

"That may be so, Major," Carrington responded, "but in this case, I wanted to make sure that there won't be a problem further down the road."

Without needing it spelled out for him, Nathan realized that Carrington was in the process of covering his ass, in advance, should whatever it was he was thinking about doing turned out badly. Realizing that he would be the designated stuckie if it did, Nathan asked Carrington what, exactly, it was that he was talking about.

Grummond took over from his commanding officer. "The mission calls for us to send out an entire UGV company. According to intelligence, the Badr Organization will be making a major effort to slip heavy weapons and munitions across the border tonight. The IA is sending everything they can to cover as many of the likely infiltration routes as possible, but they can't cover them all."

"So they're calling on you to cover those that they can't," Nathan concluded.

"Unfortunately," Grummond continued, "we've been leaning on B Company so much since 13 September that better than a third of the UGVs are down for maintenance as well as a fair number of the C2Vs."

"In my opinion," Carrington stated taking up the discussion, "B Company is combat ineffective."

"What about the other line companies, Alpha and Charlie?" Nathan asked.

"Though they are rested and most of their equipment is ready to roll," Grummond explained, "you're talking about a unit that has only fourteen vehicles manning the forward picket line, vehicles that do not have the reconnaissance and surveillance capabilities that a single UGV does. A UGV company has eighteen combat vehicles."

"Seventeen," Nathan corrected him. "D23A is nonoperational."

Carrington shrugged. "We've already tasked B Company to replace it with one of theirs for tonight's mission."

Nathan successfully fought the urge to snicker. "Then you've already decided to send D Company." It was a statement that caused Grummond to glance over at Carrington out of the corner of his eye, and that officer to visibly wince. Having figured out their game, Nathan decided to leave them twisting in the wind a bit. "I should probably discuss this with Major Tucker. Though I'm sure she'll see no problem, given my special instructions, I need to ensure that something you do doesn't go against anything she might have been told."

Nathan was about to head off to the task force conference room when a thought crossed his mind. "Should you decide to send out D Company, I'm going with them."

Once more Carrington and Grummond exchanged glances before Carrington looked back over at Nathan. "I don't see any problem with that, Major."

TWELVE

A day that Chris had set side for a quiet, restful day
at home proved to be short-lived when Angela Cardosa called, informing Chris that she'd be appear-
ing on the Bob Brant show that night opposite Alex
Hughes, the journalist who'd written the story for
The New York Times. Had it been anyone else, Chris
would have dug in her heels and said no. The opportunity to have a go at him, however, was simply
too good to pass up.

"I'll be in," Chris agreed without having to give
the matter a second thought. "But you tell your boss
lady," she added, trying to sound as serious as she
could, "that if she doesn't give me the next two days
off, I'm going to rearrange her kitchen cabinets
again."

Knowing how Jan demanded that everything in
her personal space be just so, Angela couldn't help
but laugh. "I'll tell her. The car will be by to pick
you up at three."

CAMP PACESETTER, IRAQ—1900 HRS, LOCAL TIME, SEPTEMBER 22

From where they stood next to D55, both Debora Tucker and Nathan watched the armor crewmen of D Company go about making their final precombat checks and preparations.

"You know, there's really no need for you to go out tonight." Tucker never took her eyes off the crew of D23 as they finished checking out the track on the M-10 B Company was lending them.

"I know," Nathan quipped without hesitation.

"You're only doing this because you can, aren't you?" There was no ignoring the accusatory tone in the female major's voice.

"Yep!"

"It's not fair, you know," she continued. "You guys get to go out and have all the fun while I'm stuck here, in the rear with the gear."

"Didn't anyone ever tell you that's where all good combat service support officers belong, Debora?"

She glanced over at him. "Don't you mean that's where all female officers belong?"

Throwing up his hands as if to fend her off, Nathan backed away. "Oh no. You're not going to suck me into that argument, Major. I don't make the rules."

"But I'll bet you take advantage of them every chance you can, and break them when they don't suit you."

"I make it a policy only to break the little ones and only when I'm sure no one is looking," Nathan replied, trying his best to appear as if he was being serious.

Crossing her arms, Tucker cast a furtive glance behind her at D55. "I don't suppose I could talk you into breaking one of them tonight?"

Giving her a knowing look, he shook his head. "If things around here weren't as tense as they are at this moment, I probably would turn a blind eye to what you're alluding to. But . . ."

"Ah, yes," Tucker sighed. "Go ahead, hide behind the famous butt-monkey."

"I will. Now, if you'll excuse me, I've got some serious man's work to do."

His remark earned Nathan a withering gaze. "You're a bastard, you know. I hope you smash your fingers when you close the hatch."

With a broad grin and a wink, he acknowledged Tucker's comment before climbing up onto D55. "I love you, too."

"This track we got from Bravo is a piece of shit," Cutty whined over the intercom as D23 trundled along with the rest of the company toward its assigned sector. "It hesitates before responding to my commands."

From his seat, Alex Viloski snickered. "What did you expect B Company to do? Send us their best M-10?"

"The least they could have done was to send us one that wasn't on the verge of crapping out."

"Try using your head for something other than a place to store your CVC, moron," Staff Sergeant Plum called out from his perch above the UGV operators. "Bravo-One-Two Bravo has been having automotive problems for weeks. None of the assholes from UST seem to have a clue as to what's wrong with it."

Cutty snorted. "Where have I heard that before?"

"So rather than screw around with those people anymore," Plum continued, "Slattery and his crew have been pushing B12B, hoping they'll blow its engine and get a new one."

"And what better time for it to do that than when we're using it," Viloski added cynically. "That way we're the one's stuck doing all the dirty work preparing it to be towed as well as giving everyone in Bravo something else they can use when they're in the mood to pick on us."

Plum chuckled. "Now that's thinking like a true tanker."

Before Cutty could comment, a call from Lieutenant Vanderhoff over the platoon net alerted the crew of D23 that they were approaching checkpoint zero six, an imaginary spot on the road they were on where they'd leave it and head south, across the desert to their assigned sector.

"Well," Cutty admitted glumly, "at least the damned thing isn't going to go berserk when I hit the turret power."

"You hope," Plum muttered under his breath.

From her corner of the task force TOC, Debora Tucker could only imagine what Nathan and the crews like D23 were seeing, hearing, feeling. She knew everything there was to know about the M-10 and the electronic command and control suites mounted on the C2Vs that controlled them. She'd just never seen them functioning, at least not during the course of an actual combat operation.

That was something she would never have an opportunity to do. Despite all her knowledge and an exemplary record as an officer, she'd never be allowed to go where she wanted to go. Some rules were impervious to being bent, even by an officer like Nathan Dixon.

While his fellow major was back in the rear, sulking in her dark corner lamenting her pitiful fate, Nathan was struggling to stay awake as D55 made its way south across the open desert. Even though he found himself having to admit that there were certain advantages to going to war in an armored vehicle, being cooped up for hours on end in a hot, noisy sweatbox that lurched and swayed from side to side like a dingy on a storm-tossed sea was not one of them. How his father had endured this kind of punishment for so long and actually had the guts to claim that he loved it was beyond him. Perhaps, Nathan reasoned, you simply had to be an armor crewman long enough to have all common sense and logic rattled loose from their moorings in your brain housing group before you could reach that point.

The sound of Captain Fetterman's voice over the company net, directing his platoons to deploy to their assigned sectors caused Nathan to give his head a good shake in an effort to clear away his wandering thoughts and refocus them on where he was and what D Company was doing. Sergeant Reyes, seated in the track commander's seat of D55 behind him, ordered his driver to halt. They'd arrived in sector. Anxious to escape the heat and confinement of the company XO's seat, stretch and get some fresh air, Nathan made his way around Reyes's position and out the rear troop door as soon as the vehicle had settled into its final position for the night. Once on the ground, he took a moment to get his land legs back and allow his eyes to adjust to the darkness.

With the crescent moon still below the horizon, darkness engulfed D55 and everything around it. From where he stood, Nathan could barely make out the faint outline of D66 parked some fifty meters away. Though he could not see them, he knew that the 2nd Platoon was somewhere off to his right, with the platoon's four C2Vs deployed in a rough north–south line a hundred meters southeast of D66. The six UGVs belonging to that platoon were roughly five hundred meters farther east. First Platoon was deployed in a similar fashion, but to the northeast. The six M-11 recon UGVs from D Company's 3rd Platoon were once more deployed on the flanks of the company, with two sections at the extreme southern end of the company's forward line and one section at the northern end. In theory, these lonely sentinels were tied into company-sized elements of the Iraqi Army that were also deployed along the western boundary of the Ten-K Zone.

Before long, Nathan was joined on the ground by Sergeant Reyes who came up behind him. "Granola bar, sir?" Looking over to where Reyes was standing, holding his hand out to him, Nathan was about to refuse the snack when Reyes grinned. "It's got chocolate chips."

Unable to resist, Nathan took the treat, peeled back the foil wrapping and slowly began to munch away on the granola bar as he enjoyed the silence that had settled over D Company. He lived for moments like this. Somewhere out there, in the eerie stillness of the desert night, were fifty men and over thirty combat vehicles, some manned, some robotic. All of them were keyed up, watching and waiting for something that might never happen. All of them arrayed in a tiered line of battle, ready to spring into action at the drop of a hat. All, save a few sets of tired, blurry human eyes were pointed east.

WASHINGTON, D.C.–8:03 P.M., EASTERN TIME, SEPTEMBER 22

"You know Chris, it's getting harder and harder to cover up those dark circles under your eyes," Judy Miller mused as she worked furiously to finish up before airtime. "You really need to tell that mother-in-law of yours she needs to ease up on you."

"I'm getting all the rest I need, thank you very much." Chris sighed. "More, in fact, than I'm used to. Besides, if you guys can find a way of keeping my belly from showing up on camera, I'm sure you'll be able to figure out how to make me look good for the viewing audience."

Pulling back, the young makeup artist grinned. "Oh, I'm not worried about making you look good.

You already look good. It's my job to make you look great."

"At the moment, I'd settle for looking a little more . . ." Chris's comment was interrupted by a sharp pain that caused her to sit bolt upright in her seat.

Caught off-guard by this and worried that she'd done something wrong, Judy pulled away. "What's the matter?"

Chris didn't answer at first, taking a moment to decide if she needed to be worried. It wasn't the first such pain she'd felt like that. They'd started the night before. But since they weren't coming at regular or diminishing intervals, she knew they weren't contractions. At least she hoped they weren't. When it passed almost as quickly as it had come, she decided that it was nothing, just one of those things that comes with being pregnant.

"I'm fine," she finally muttered to a very concerned young woman. "It seems the Incredible Hulk here," she mused as she patted her belly, "is trying some new tricks."

The call that they had one minute to airtime caused the two women to set aside any personal concerns as Judy quickly stowed away her brushes and scurried off the set while Chris settled in, listening in on Bob Brant's introduction into the segment she'd be sharing with Alex Hughes. Hughes, who was the main attraction during this interview, would go first. Since she was there to counter some of the accusations Hughes had made in his initial piece and a follow-up story, Chris had an idea of what she was going to say, but not a prepared script.

Where the interview went, when she would be called upon to comment on something and what that something was would be determined by how Bob went about interrogating Hughes. There were certain things that Chris wanted to say and had made them known to Bob through her producer beforehand, but she couldn't be sure if he'd get to them. The one thing that she was sure of was that she needed to remain calm and keep her temper from getting the best of her. The last thing she wanted was for her emotions, which had been all over the place all day, from getting the better of her and distracting from her argument.

As expected, Hughes began by rehashing much of what he'd already said in two articles, adding nothing new or startling to what he'd already said. After letting him do so, Brant pitched in. "So, you've no doubt in your mind that this incident was preventable by the unit's chain of command."

"None whatsoever," Hughes responded without hesitation. "The blatant disregard for even the most commonsense precautions that would have prevented this incident from happening in the first place was compounded by an appalling display of incompetence at every level while it was occurring."

Making a show of shifting in his seat, even though he didn't need to do so in order to bring Chris into the conversation, Brant introduced her before asking for her views on the matter. In a masterful performance, Chris managed to not only keep her anger in check, but provided the audience with the image of a self-assured former Army officer who took pity on a poor, ignorant and ill-informed journalist. Tilting her head, she gave Bob, via the camera, a knowing smile. "While I believe that there is probably some truth in what Mr. Hughes alleges, it would have been impossible for him to be privy to everything that transpired at either company or task force level on the night of 13 September. By his own admission, he was in the rear of an armored vehicle during the entire operation, monitoring only the platoon's radio net and thus, unable to hear the radio transmissions made by Lieutenant Colonel Carrington and Captain Fetterman during much of the engagement."

Physically drawing himself up in his seat, Hughes's expression betrayed his feelings and thoughts. "I know what I saw and heard," he snorted. "The conduct of the officers involved in that incident is both reprehensible and inexcusable."

Once more Chris was able to affect an expression that belied her true feelings, one that she hoped would irritate Hughes. "Despite your expertise in military matters as well as your vast combat experience, I'm afraid I'm going to have to wait until the Army conducts a full and thorough investigation into the incident before I am able to state, with any degree of certainty, not only what happened, but if anyone was truly at fault."

"How can you even imagine that no one was at fault?" Hughes snapped.

"Unlike journalists," Chris patiently explained, "who have editors and proofreaders who pore over their work before it sees the light of day, a soldier in battle must make a decision like that," she stated while snapping her fingers. "A company commander, a platoon leader, a twenty-year-old soldier doesn't have the luxury of running each and every decision he makes by a team of experts to determine if what he is about to do is the right thing to do. They must respond to life and death situations that are staring them in the face, often times without even giving the matter a wit of thought. To hesitate in battle is the greatest sin a soldier can commit. And while every officer, NCO and enlisted man hopes that they make the right decision, sometimes they don't."

"In this case," Hughes shot back, "they didn't."

"That, sir," Chris replied in an even tone, "is for an Article 32 investigation to determine, not a journalist out to make a name for himself."

Sensing that things were about to get out of hand, Brant inserted himself back into the conversation. His timing could not have been better as Chris, once more, was wracked by another sharp pain that she could not help but react to. Without even knowing what was going on, Beth Emerson passed onto the producer of the Bob Brant show in New York to refrain from cutting back to Chris until further notice. When asked what the problem was, Beth simply said, "Technical problems," even as she was rushing out onto the set with an assistant.

Stunned, in pain, and not sure what to do, Chris gingerly pushed her chair out from the desk she'd been seated behind. Rather than scream out in horror when she saw the red-tainted liquid dripping down her legs, she screwed her eyes shut.

NORTHEAST OF CAMP PACESETTER—0308 HRS, LOCAL TIME, SEPTEMBER 23

Unable to face crawling back into the cramped confines of the C2V, Nathan had asked Sergeant Reyes if he didn't mind swapping places with him for a while. The NCO gladly took him up on his offer, reminding Nathan to keep an eye on their six. "We wouldn't want hajji surprising us in the middle of the night, now would we, sir?" Both men somehow found what Reyes said funny.

There was no one laughing when a flash, followed in quick succession by a whooshing noise and ending with the roar of an explosion shattered the calm, desert night. As so often happens at a moment like this, even to a veteran like Nathan, those who are involved in a sudden attack from an unexpected quarter blink in stunned disbelief. It's almost as if they're trying to convince themselves if what they've just witnessed is real. A quick glance from where he'd seen the flash and back to where D66 was engulfed in flames convinced Nathan of that as diesel fuel from the ruptured fuel tank of Fetterman's C2V fed the angry red flames lighting up the night sky.

Even before Sergeant Reyes had a chance to twist about in the XO's seat and ask what was going on, Nathan had dropped down into the track commander's seat and powered up the remotely operated weapons station. As he was bringing the M2 machine gun mounted in it to bear in the direction from which he'd seen the initial flash, Nathan was yelling down to Reyes without keying his intercom to get on the radio and report contact with dismounted insurgents.

Though using the remotely operated weapons station was strange to Nathan, it was not altogether unfamiliar. He'd first seen it at Fort Benning during the Advanced Course. He'd re-familiarized himself with it when he'd been learning how to operate the M-10. That he'd ever have cause to use it had never entered his mind. He simply knew that it was part of the Army's future and understood his need to know as much about it as possible. That the future was already here took Nathan by surprise, it didn't catch him unprepared.

"Sergeant Reyes, we've got an RPG team at nine o'clock."

From the driver's seat, PFC Emit Snee called out. "Should I crank her up?"

Having to concentrate on what he was doing, Nathan didn't answer. Grasping the joystick that controlled the weapons station, he aligned the sight on center mass of the target and lased to it. The insurgents made it all too easy for him. Having hit their intended target with their first round and caused so much devastation, they couldn't help but prop themselves up and enjoy the spectacle of watching D66 burn. In the same cool, dispassionate way that he conducted himself at times like this, Nathan let fly a killing burst. The results were both spectacular and deadly. One second, the computer screen before him depicted two well-defined human forms. The next, those same figures were being ripped apart by a hail of heavy, full metal jacketed rounds, each one half an inch in diameter. Throughout it all, Nathan felt neither joy nor sorrow. He'd never give the two men he'd just killed another thought. Neither of them would ever appear in his nightmares. To him, they were just two more people who'd chosen to become his enemy, a mistake they'd paid for.

Unlike the pair of freshly martyred insurgents, Nathan didn't dwell on what he had done. He didn't have the time. Instead, he turned his full attention to what needed to be done. Before doing so, he ordered Reyes to switch places with him. As they passed, Nathan told the NCO to keep his eyes open. "I only saw the two, but that doesn't mean there aren't more." Once in the XO seat, he plugged the cord of his CVC into the comms box there, made sure that the radio was set to the task force command net and called the TOC. Ignoring the assigned call signs for the night as published in the unit's CEOI, Nathan used Papa, the phonetic shorthand for "Pacesetter" when he went to raise the TOC on the radio. "Papa Three, this is Delta Five-five, over."

Rather than getting the operations officer, Carrington answered, something that didn't surprise Nathan. "Delta Five-five, this is Papa Six. Sit Rep, over."

"This is Delta Five-five, Delta Six-six has been destroyed by an RPG team. There are no survivors. The RPG team has been engaged and destroyed, over."

"This is Papa Six. Can you confirm Delta Six is dead, over?"

Keeping his temper in check, Nathan did his best to convince Carrington that Fetterman, Delta Six, was in fact dead. "This is Delta Five-five. Affirmative. Delta Six-six took a direct hit in the fuel cell. Secondary explosions and fire have engulfed the entire vehicle. No one bailed out. I say again, no one bailed out. How copy, over?"

There was a moment of silence. No doubt Carrington was either letting this sink in, trying to decide what to do now or was discussing this matter with someone. While he was waiting for a response, Nathan glanced at the monitor displaying D Company's tactical situation. That was when he noticed a number of moving target indicators along the eastern fringes of the Ten-K Zone. Even more ominous were a number of red symbols arrayed around the IA company to the north of D Company's sector. By the time Carrington finally did come back on the air, Nathan had a pretty good idea of what was coming his way.

"Delta Five-five, this is Papa Six. The Air Force is tracking a number of unknown MTIs east of your positions, over."

"This is Delta Five-five, I've got them on my screen, over."

"This is Papa Six. The IA unit to your north is under attack by an unknown number of insurgents. We have been requested to render assistance, over."

Nathan hesitated as he wondered who Carrington meant when he said "we." Knowing that this was no time to be shy, he keyed the radio. "This is Delta Five-five, over. If that mission is to be executed by this unit, I am prepared to assume command of Delta, over."

* * *

Nathan's transmission brought to the fore the thought that both Carrington and Grummond had already been weighing. While it was true that Nathan had gone out as an observer and nothing more, both officers could not deny that he was not only the most senior officer in a position to assume command of D Company, he was the only officer out there that had actually commanded a company in battle. The idea of turning the company over to the senior platoon leader, who happened to be Vanderhoff, was something neither Carrington nor Grummond found to be palatable. Holding off until one of them, or another officer of sufficient rank could be dispatched from Camp Pacesetter to the field was even less appealing. Far too many Iraqi soldiers would die while D Company sat in place, waiting for a new commander to mount up, roll out the front gate, traverse the twenty-five kilometers to where D Company was located, assume command, brief his new and unfamiliar platoon leaders on his plan and then put that plan into effect. The idea of running D Company personally from the TOC was even less inviting to Carrington and Grummond. While that was technically possible, it went against the instinct of every officer present. With more dead Iraqi soldiers to his credit than he was comfortable with, Carrington made the only call that made sense to him.

Besides, Carrington was able to add one more good reason for turning D Company over to Major Dixon, one that he shared with no one. Dixon was an outsider. If things did not go well, 3rd of the 68th and all of its officers, including him, would be off the hook. While even he couldn't deny that this was one hell of a time to be thinking along those lines, Carrington labored under the greatest of all frailties that crippled even the most brilliant commanders: he was only human.

After ordering the duty officer to put him on D Company command net, Carrington keyed the hand mike. "All elements this net, this is Papa Six. Effective immediately, Major Dixon is in command of Delta, acknowledge, over."

Rather than answer the responses from D Company's platoon leaders, Carrington handed the mike back to the duty officer and took a seat as he prepared to watch how the next hour or two played out on the large monitor. He had done all he had intended to do. It was now up to Nathan Dixon, a man he had once viewed as his executioner, but who now could very well turn out to be his savior.

THIRTEEN

Jan had been at home relaxing on her sofa, watching the Bob Brant show. Unable to help herself,
she'd beamed with pride as Chris had systematically
and publically destroyed Alex Hughes. The ease
with which she'd done it and the poise she main-
tained throughout the interview left no doubt in
Jan's mind that she'd made a great call, one that she
expected her boss in New York would, no doubt, be
seconding, just as he had when Chris had first broken the story. Even before the segment was over,
Jan had found herself wondering what she could do
by way of celebrating tonight's journalistic triumph
when Beth Emerson brought Chris home after
they'd finished in the studio.

She'd just about decided to rush out to the local
Giant supermarket and buy Chris a quart of Häagen-
Dazs chocolate chocolate chip when Jan saw Bob
Brant frown before announcing that they'd lost their
link with the D.C. studios as a result of technical
difficulties. In a heartbeat, Jan's self-congratulatory

mood was replaced with acute irritation. As she reached for the phone, she found herself hoping for Beth's sake that the problem was on New York's end and not theirs. It came as no great surprise that the phone began ringing before she could hit the speed-dial. It was, of course, the WNN studio. What Beth told Jan when she answered it, however, wasn't anywhere close to what she'd anticipated, news that turned her mood on its head once more.

Her drive to the Washington Hospital Center was, perhaps, the most nerve-racking experience in Jan's life. All sorts of thoughts ran through her mind, none of them very good in light of what she'd been told over the phone. Things did not improve in the least when she reached the hospital. A very worried Beth greeted her with the news that Chris was already in surgery. "They wouldn't tell me much," Beth lamented. "Something about the placenta pulling away from the cervix."

The sight of Beth's bloody clothes and what she was telling her thoroughly rattled Jan. "The baby?"

"I don't know, Jan. They didn't mention anything about the baby other than they'll be doing a C-section."

Though she knew what she should have done next, Jan hesitated. Rather than passing on a fragmentary report like the one she'd gotten when Scott's chopper had gone down in the Philippines, Jan decided to wait to find out how Chris and the baby were doing before notifying the Red Cross or going directly through General Stevens in an effort to contact her son. Despite all evidence to the contrary, the news could be good. At least she hoped it would be good, Jan found herself praying. At the moment, hope was the only thing she had.

NORTHEAST OF CAMP PACESETTER—0335 HRS, LOCAL TIME, SEPTEMBER 23

Hope had no place in the scheme of maneuver that Nathan had come up with for D Company. After making a quick assessment of the situation, Nathan issued his orders using both the company's secure FM radio net and computer graphics he was able to digitally transmit. Those plans were based, in part, on the assumption that the movement the Reaper had been monitoring east of D Company's position was part of a ruse, an assessment Major Grummond agreed with. Yet neither man was prepared to strip D Company's assigned sector of all combat elements. In order to guard against the possibility that the activity was a real threat, Nathan had no choice but to leave part of D Company in place. To this end, he ordered the 3rd Platoon to spread itself out to cover the entire sector, using the Class I UAVs each M-11 carried to patrol any gaps between the M-11s. That would allow him to pull both the 1st and 2nd Platoons back and take them north to the relief of the IA company using his most powerful combat elements. Splitting his force in that manner was risky, but one that couldn't be avoided.

That wasn't the only risk that Nathan would have to take that night. By far the greatest challenge he faced was in finding a simple and effective way of operating in close proximity to an IA company that was in contact with the enemy when he had no direct link with that unit. Sergeant Omer Mohajeri, the IA liaison who'd been assigned to D Company had been with Captain Fetterman. Like Fetterman, he was now gone. Task force wouldn't be able to help him overcome this handicap either. Such was the animosity between the IA units in the area and 3rd of the 68th in the wake of the 13 September Incident that the staff of the IA battalion operating along the Iranian border that night hadn't even bothered to brief their liaison officer in the 3rd of the 68th's TOC on exactly where all their units would be. No one had to tell Nathan that this operation had potential disaster written all over it.

In an effort to get a better handle on what was going on to the north using the resources he had at hand, Nathan requested that the Air Force Reaper be sent out ahead of his company to pinpoint the IA company's positions. While he had a vague idea of where they were, he insisted that someone at the task force TOC plot each and every known and suspected IA position before doing the same for the insurgents. While it would be important to take out as many insurgents as possible, Nathan understood without having to be told that it was absolutely critical that no one from the 3rd of the 68th kill a single IA soldier.

Doing so would be a neat trick. To pull it off Nathan ordered 1st Platoon, which had been closest to the threatened IA company, to swing north and deploy in an east–west line with its right flank anchored on the western boundary of the Ten-K Zone. The lack of a discernable terrain feature that marked that buffer zone was of no consequence to the UGV equipped company. All the 1st Platoon UGV operator who was serving as the anchor on the platoon's right flank had to do was keep the symbol that represented his UGV just to the right of the line that showed up on his monitor marking the Ten-K Zone. The gun sights and navigational sensors of his UGV would see nothing. But its onboard GPS transmitter would keep the task force's digital network fully updated on its exact location, the same network that created the symbol that the operator and everyone else in the chain of command saw on their monitors.

Once 1st Platoon's skirmish line reached a point two kilometers southeast of the IA company's position, it would stop. As part of the orders he'd issued to 1st Platoon, Nathan had established rules of engagement that allowed them to fire on any targets that were acquired by that platoon to the right of the eastern-most IA position with any weapon. Any target that appeared west of that line, on the other hand, had to be positively identified as enemy before being engaged, and could only be taken under fire using the UGV's M240 7.62 coax machine gun. Should the platoon's 25mm Bushmasters be needed to deal with an insurgent target that cropped up in the area that lay between 1st Platoon and the IA company, it could be employed only if there was no way that a 25mm HE round could sail over the insurgent position and into the IA Company's perimeter.

His 1st Platoon did more than provide Nathan with a base of fire around which he could maneuver

2nd Platoon. Should it become necessary for the encircled IA company to break out before the balance of D Company completed its maneuver, the Iraqi soldiers could escape by fleeing south, toward the 1st Platoon's skirmish line. No one wanted to try this, not at night and especially not without any prior coordination. But it did provide the IA company with an out if the situation deteriorated any further.

As demanding as the rules of engagement Nathan had imposed upon 1st Platoon were, the restrictions 2nd Platoon would be laboring under were even more stringent. Once 1st Platoon was set, Nathan intended to personally lead 2nd Platoon around the outer perimeter of the IA company's positions, pushing aside the insurgents in the same way a plow clears away snow. To accomplish this in a manner that was easily controlled and reduce the chances that 2nd Platoon would accidently fire into the IA positions, Nathan intended to hug the IA outer perimeter with D55 as close as he dared go. The 2nd Platoon would be deployed to his left and in echelon, with D23 to the left and a little behind D55. D24 would, in turn, be to the left and a little behind D23. D22 was next, to the left and behind 24. D21, not having any UGVs but mounting an M19 grenade launcher, would serve as the far left flanker of this staggered line. With all M-10s deployed fifty meters or less in front of their C2Vs and all guns oriented straight ahead or to the left, Nathan was as sure as he could be that he'd taken every precaution possible in order to ensure that there would be no friendly-fire incidents.

Having issued his orders, Nathan now had no choice but to wait and see if the officers under his command could translate a scheme of maneuver that made perfect sense to him into action. Having been in combat before, he knew there'd be problems. He just hoped that he'd be able to anticipate those problems and come up with a solution before they turned his plan into a disaster.

As they listened to Nathan's orders and mentally tracked what he intended to do, Carrington and Grummond looked at each other. "It makes sense," Grummond finally concluded.

Carrington grunted. "I wonder if that's what the Earl of Lucan said when Captain Nolan handed him his orders to charge the guns at Balaklava."

"Sir, those aren't Russians D Company are charging into the middle of."

Once more, Carrington grunted. "I hope the hell not. Otherwise we're all in deep shit."

Unable to resist the urge to do so, Debora Tucker left the corner of the TOC she'd been watching from and moved to the front, taking the seat that Peter White usually occupied. No one commented on his absence. No one seemed to care, not even Carrington. At the moment all attention was focused on the enemy out there, out where Major Tucker so longed to be.

The crew of D23 understood their role: to a man they found it comforting to know that D55 would be

to their right and Sergeant First Class Bohnslav and
D24 on their right. In many ways, having his M-10s
serve as the right-hand anchor for the platoon made
things easier on Plum. Instinctively he knew the
major on D55 wouldn't do something unexpected or
boneheaded. He might be new to mechanized warfare, but this definitely wasn't his first rodeo. Plum
also suspected that if anyone could make the weird
maneuver they were about to execute work, it was
that officer.

Cutty also found the position his UGV was assigned very much to his liking. It would, after all,
be the lead M-10. All the other 2nd Platoon operators and their UGVs would have to conform to his
maneuvers and keep up with him. Other than keeping his UGV twenty to thirty meters to the left of
D55 and its main gun aimed straight ahead, the
only thing he needed to worry about was the conditions of B12B's engine. Thus far it was holding up,
but she was still behaving sluggishly, especially
when it came to making sharp turns. This caused
Cutty to think that B12B had more wrong with it
than a failing engine. The turning problem could
only be due to a faulty transmission that, according
to the information being transmitted from sensors
on B12B, was now running hot.

He was about to tell Plum about this new concern
when Vanderhoff passed word down on the platoon
net that they were coming up even with 1st Platoon.
"All Delta Two elements, this is Delta Two-one. Execute echelon left now. Conform the maneuvers of
your vehicles to those to the right. Maintain a twelve

o'clock to nine o'clock orientation of all weapons. Acknowledge, over."

In sequence the three section leaders responded, both verbally and by slowing down in order to allow the vehicles to their right to surge ahead.

On board D55, Nathan found the experience of going into battle cooped up in a tracked vehicle to be extremely unnerving. As an infantry officer he'd learned to gauge the ebb and flow of battle by paying attention to what he heard and saw with his own ears and eyes. Relying on digital displays and secondhand information wasn't to his liking. While he understood what he was seeing and was satisfied everything he'd directed his subordinates to do was being executed in accordance to his orders, his lack of experience in waging war in this manner was proving to be all but impossible to deal with. In time he knew he would be able to master both the skills needed to do so and the nerve required to fight a battle as if it were nothing more than a video game. This, however, was not a good time for that. He needed to lead this company of strangers in the only way he knew how.

Twisting about in his seat, he looked up at Sergeant Reyes. "Switch places."

Confused, Reyes looked down at Nathan. "What?"

"I want you down here," Nathan yelled over the rumbling of the C2V's engine while pointing down at his seat with his index finger.

Before he could say another word, Reyes watched

as the major unplugged the cord of his CVC and began to climb out of his seat. Seeing that he had no other choice but to comply, he slipped out of the track commander's seat and waited till Nathan squeezed past him before easing into the XO's position.

After reconnecting his CVC cord to the radio/intercom cord located at the track commander's position, Nathan popped the hatch above him and stood up on the seat, leaving him exposed from the waist up. While the C2V's remote weapons station still obstructed his view to his direct front, forcing him to lean left or right in order to see around it, Nathan was convinced that this would be a much better place from which to control D Company. Even without night-vision goggles, the waxing moon provided just enough light for him to see D23's lead UGV off to the left of his track and the remaining UGVs beyond it and trailing off behind. Where 2nd Platoon's C2Vs were didn't really matter, a fact that Nathan was only now beginning to appreciate. Had he been smart, he would have left them behind 1st Platoon's skirmish line. There had been no need to order them forward as he had. His was the only manned vehicle that needed to be up on the firing line. Even that, he found himself thinking, was something that could be debated. This new way of war, he finally admitted to himself, was going to take a lot of getting used to.

Nathan was in the midst of trying to figure out how he could correct this oversight without causing undue confusion when the 25mm cannon on the UGV next to him lit up the night. Quickly glancing to his right, he watched where the tracers were go-

ing, more concerned that they stayed clear of any
IA positions than whether they were hitting their
mark.

Without letting up on the trigger, Cutty whooped
and howled. "Look at the bastards run!"

Plum watched the monitor at his position as the
lone figure to their front Cutty had acquired and
fired on was joined by others the second B12B's
first three-round burst of cannon fire impacted. Apparently they were no more willing to die at the
hands of an inhuman machine tonight than they had
on previous occasions.

In the middle of this engagement, Plum heard
Vanderhoff's voice in the earphones of his CVC.
"All Delta Two elements, watch your sectors of fire.
Do not, I say again, do not engage anything beyond
twelve to nine, over."

"Yeah, yeah, we hear you," Cutty muttered without taking his eyes off his monitor or easing up off
the trigger that controlled B12B's main gun.

"Just shut up and watch your sector," Plum
snapped. He watched Viloski open fire on a group
of insurgents who'd fled Cutty's fire and straight
into his designated kill zone.

With the cry of *"Allah akbar,"* Viloski opened up
with D23B's 7.62mm, cutting a wide swath into the
gaggle of fleeing men.

Trying to steady himself with one hand as D55
pitched and swayed while holding his NVGs up to

his eyes with the other was proving to be impossible, causing Nathan to curse the bean counter who
had made the decision not to put a mount for NVGs
on the CVC he was wearing. Abandoning the effort
to use his NVGs, he shoved them back into the
pouch attached to his body armor and turned sideways in the hatch, looking off to the left and to the
rear of D55's direction of travel. The sound of Reyes
directing D55's driver using the monitor in the XO's
position to follow a path Nathan had designated just
beyond the IA perimeter mingled with contact reports coming in over the radio from both 1st and
2nd Platoons. In the semidarkness, Nathan caught
glimpses of figures moving away from the IA perimeter. Few seemed to be getting far as the staggered line of UGVs opened fire in sequence. Second
Platoon, it seemed, was moving faster than word
was able to spread to the insurgents that still lay
ahead.

Much to Nathan's surprise, his plan seemed to
be working. After taking a moment to check, one
more time, that all tracer streams were staying
within the designated kill zone that he'd assigned
second Platoon, Nathan switched his radio to the
task force command net and began to verbally report his observations to the task force commander.

With the senior man on board oriented to the left
of D55's direction of travel and busy talking on the
radio, Sergeant Reyes watched the monitor before
him as he did his best to keep the symbol that represented D55 on the imaginary line that marked its
planned route. Specialist Cuevas keeping an eye on
the information coming in from all sources, it

should not have come as a surprise that it was the driver, PFC Snee, who was the only man on D55 who spotted the danger to their immediate front. His scream of "RPG! Twelve o'clock!" only served to give everyone plugged into D55's intercom time enough to distract them from what they'd been doing, but not enough time to do anything about it.

The slamming of the shaped-charge rocket-propelled grenade against the flat surface of D55's upper hull blinded Nathan and showered him with shards of hot shrapnel from the antitank rocket's warhead and bits of D55. Instinctively, Nathan dropped down inside as Snee, rattled by the hit, brought D55 to a full dead stop. Reyes was the first to react, twisting about in his seat and looking up at Nathan. Unaware that he was injured, Reyes yelled, "Shoot!"

Stunned, bleeding and blinded by the blast, Nathan lowered his hands from his face. "I can't see."

Without giving the matter a second thought, Reyes rose up from his seat, yelling as he went. "Get out of the way!"

Unable to do so gracefully, Nathan literally pitched himself off to the left, making just enough room for Reyes to climb into the track commander's seat. Fighting back the urge to rush things, he took the time to align the remote weapons station sight onto the pair of insurgents who were, at the same time, doing their best to reload their RPG. Hitting the laser rangefinder button, Reyes forced himself to wait until he had a good ballistic solution before opening up with a killing burst.

At his feet, Nathan was struggling to pick himself

up off the floor. Leaving his seat, Cuevas helped the
stunned officer settle into the jump seat located behind and to the rear of the track commander's position. In the faint glow of computer monitors and
overhead crew compartment lights, Cuevas took to
examining Nathan's wounds. But before D55's recon
specialist was able to do much, Nathan blindly swat-
ted his arm away. "Is the track dead? Can we move?"

Understanding what the officer was getting at
and the urgency of his concern, Cuevas turned to
Snee. "Emit! What's the story?"

Intently focused on the mayhem his UGV operators
were creating, it took Sergeant Plum a minute,
maybe two before he realized that D55 had stopped
and B12B was surging ahead of the vehicle that it
was supposed to be staying abreast of. Using the
thermal sight of his remote weapons station, he oriented it until he caught sight of the stricken C2V to
his right. It was clear to him that the vehicle had
been hit and was stopped. "Cutty, Ski, stop advancing your UGVs." Then remembering that his own
vehicle was in motion, he ordered his driver to halt
as well before keying the platoon radio net. "Delta
Two-one, this is Two-three. Delta Five-five has
stopped. I say again, Delta Five-five has been hit
and has stopped."

The other UGV section leaders didn't need to
wait for Lieutenant Vanderhoff to come up on the
net and order them to cease their advance. Now
alerted to the situation on their right and fully cog-
nizant of their orders, they followed Plum's lead.

* * *

"We've got a problem," Grummond muttered as he leaned forward and focused his attention on the staggered line of blue symbols on the TOC's tactical display. One by one those representing 2nd Platoon were stopping. He was in the process of picking up the radio mike to call Major Dixon when the duty officer pointed out that the vehicle status display off to the left of the tactical display indicated that D55 was suffering from multiple system failures.

"He's been hit," Carrington grumbled. "I knew it was a bad idea for him to lead off with his own vehicle like that."

Ignoring his task force commander's comment about an opinion that no one in the TOC ever remembered him making, Grummond took the hand mike and tried to raise D55.

By the time Grummond's call came in over the task force command net, a modicum of calm had returned to the stricken vehicle. Cuevas had tried to remove Nathan's CVC but was stopped. "I need to hear what's going on," Nathan uttered in a manner that told Cuevas that the major he was tending to was in shock. Understanding what the officer was saying, the recon specialist did his best to cover the most grievous wounds and Nathan's eyes with a large field dressing.

Even as this was being done, Nathan managed to resume his duties. "Sergeant Reyes, get this thing

moving, now! Continue around the Iraqi perimeter."
From the track commander's position, Reyes looked
down to where Cuevas was working on the major
before ordering Snee to move out. Once he felt the
C2V lurch forward, Nathan brushed Cuevas's hand
aside and ordered him to connect his CVC cord to
the closest radio control box. The moment he was
plugged back in, he heard the babble of voices that
were crowding both the company and the task force
command net. "Put me on company," Nathan demanded.

"You're on company, sir."

Keying his radio, Nathan proceeded to order 2nd
Platoon to continue their advance. Once Vanderhoff
acknowledged this, Nathan directed Cuevas to switch
the radio over to the task force command net. Once
again, as soon as he was told it had been done, Nathan informed Major Grummond that they'd taken
an RPG round but were still in the fight.

"Delta Five-five, this is Pacesetter Three. Do
you have casualties on board."

"This is Delta Five-five, nothing serious, out."

In silence, Reyes looked down at Cuevas, who
stared up at his track commander. Both imagined
the worst. Neither man, however, was unwilling to
override the major's assessment. Ever so slowly,
they continued to circumnavigate the IA perimeter
with 2nd Platoon in tow. It wasn't long after D55
had been hit that 1st Platoon was able to join in on
the slaughter of insurgents as 2nd Platoon came
around and began to converge on 1st Platoon's positions like a hammer falling upon an anvil. Throughout it all Nathan remained calm, doing his best to

maintain control of D Company as Reyes and Cuevas did all they could to keep him and D55 in the fight. Under different circumstances Nathan might have relinquished command to the next man in the chain of command. That would have been the recommended Fort Benning school solution. At the moment, however, he knew it wouldn't be the smart thing to do.

Besides, he found himself rationalizing as he listened to the reports from his platoon leaders come in, the fastest way to the aid station was through the insurgents. Relying on the tactical graphics that he could only see with his mind's eye, Nathan continued to direct D Company.

FOURTEEN

Debora Tucker found Nathan sitting on a stretcher next to the medevac vehicle parked within sight of the shattered remains of D66. "How come you're still out here?"

Tilting his head back as far as he could so that he could see out from under the bandage that was partially covering his one good eye, Nathan grunted. "I'm waiting for a lift. Rather than taking me overland to Pacesetter inside this rattletrap and then by chopper to Al Kut, someone decided it would be better to fly me all the way."

"It must be nice to get special treatment."

Nathan chuckled. "You'll not hear me complaining. What are you doing out here?"

Tucker looked over at the smoldering remains of D66 before answering. "When I called back to my boss and told him what had happened to D66, he became rather agitated."

"I hate to sound cold and unfeeling given that five men died in it, but what's the big deal? We were attacked and it was hit with an antitank round. Antitank rockets are designed to kill tanks and a C2V is no tank. Or so I've been told," he added sarcastically.

"True," Tucker admitted quietly. "But the C2V shouldn't have gone up like that, not after taking a single RPG round."

"A lucky shot."

Tucker looked down at Nathan. Despite the possibility that he could very well lose one eye, she still envied him. Last night she'd come as close to combat as she ever had in her long career. It was the closest she would ever get and she knew it. Dixon, on the other hand would, in all likelihood, be patched up and sent back again, and again, and again.

Then, remembering a message she'd been given to relay to him by the task force operations officer, she reached into a pocket and pulled out the satellite phone she'd found in his kit back at camp. "By the way, I was told to have you call your mother as soon as you could." She was about to offer the phone to him when she realized how dumb doing so would be. "Do you want me to dial the number for you?"

"Yes, please. Her cell phone number is on speed-dial. Just hit the 3."

When she heard ringing, Tucker passed the satellite phone over to Nathan. Ever so gingerly, he lifted the bandage covering his ear so he could place the phone against it.

"Hello? Nathan?" The sound of his mother's voice sent a chill through him. She'd never have called unless there was a problem with Chris.

"Mom, is Chris all right?"

"Yes, she's doing fine. And congratulations. You're a father, times two."

Confused by his mother's comment, still not hearing clearly and suffering from a combination of shock from being wounded and post-combat jitters, Nathan wasn't sure he'd heard right. "Two? I don't understand."

"Yes, it turns out that all that extra bulk wasn't water or one oversized baby, but twins."

Stunned, it took Nathan nearly a full minute to process this news and a prompting by his mother before he was able to speak. "What are they? Boys?"

"One of each."

Unable to believe it, Nathan pulled the phone away from his mouth. "I'm a father!" he announced, not realizing that Tucker had already wandered off to D66 in order to take a closer look at it.

A medic, who happened to be passing by slowed as he looked down at Nathan. "Congratulations, sir."

"And Chris? Is she okay?" Nathan continued as he turned his attention back to the call. "Can I talk to her?"

"Chris is fine but she's asleep. It was, ah, hard on her." The guarded manner with which she answered his question was totally lost on Nathan. "Wendy Marie and Scott Alexander are also doing well," she added quickly, using the names that he and Chris had agreed upon before he'd left home. That both had been needed was the only thing they hadn't counted on. "How are you?"

The thought of telling his mother the truth never

crossed his mind. Instead, Nathan did his best to sound as cheerful and upbeat as he could. "Oh, you know me."

"Yes, I know you all too well, Nathan Dixon," Jan replied in that tone all mothers use when they're doing their best to let their children know that they're not fooling them.

The faint beating of a chopper's blades slicing their way through the early morning air and the sound of the medics preparing to pop smoke and guide the dustoff in told Nathan that he needed to end the call. "Mom, I've got to go. I'll call you as soon as I can, okay?"

"Nate, when will you be home?"

"Soon, I expect," he replied. "Give Chris my love and kiss Wendy and Scott for me. Love ya Mom." With that, he ended the call. Sitting upright, he beamed. "I'm a father." The statement caused a passing soldier to look over at the wounded major as if he were nuts. Then, after giving the matter some thought, the soldier shook his head. Of course he was nuts, the soldier concluded as he continued to go about his duties. He's a major.

After clicking off her cell phone and slipping it absentmindedly back into the pocket of her jeans, Jan let out a sigh of relief. Thank God he didn't push her for details, she thought. There'd be time enough after he'd returned home to fill him in on the whole sad story. Besides, it wasn't her place, nor was it a good time to tell him that little Wendy and Scott would be the only children he'd ever have with

Chris. There'd come a day, no doubt, when the two of them would lament over that hard truth.

This, however, wasn't it, Jan concluded as she drew herself up. This was a day to celebrate, she told herself as she prepared to head back to Chris's room. Today she would celebrate life and the fact that she was a grandmother. And while it was true that there wasn't a drop of her blood that ran through Wendy's or Scott's veins, Jan had reached a point in her life where she was more than satisfied to enjoy whatever joy and happiness happened to come her way. If anyone knew just how precious life could be and how important it was to enjoy it with those you loved when you had a chance, it was someone who was, or in Jan's case, had been, married to the Army, an organization that had but one purpose: to kill people and break things. That it often ate its own while doing so, as it had to Jan's husband, was just one of those things you learned to live with.

ARLINGTON, VIRGINIA—OCTOBER 19

Looking up from the report before him, General Stevens regarded the major across the table from him. "This is the report you intend to go with?" he asked as he placed his hand over Nathan's written account of D Company's operations on the morning of 23 September against Badr insurgents.

Having had an opportunity to coordinate what he had planned to say in his report with Carrington, Grummond and Major Tucker and found them all willing to agree to his written recommendations,

Nathan nodded as he stared at the report he'd penned while recovering from surgery. "Yes sir, every last word of it."

Having gotten wind of another version of the events that had taken place that night from other sources, Stevens knew Nathan was lying to him. Still, as he looked over at Nathan, who now sported a black eye patch that made him look more like a character out of a novel about the French Foreign Legion than a Pentagon staff officer, Stevens understood why Nathan and his coconspirators had placed their own careers on the line in order to protect the reputation of a fellow officer. What they were trying to pull was wrong, of course. But by the same token, the spirit that had caused them to band together and protect one of their own was just the sort of thing Stevens so admired about the men and women who wore the same uniform that he did. The loyalty and spirit they were showing was a rare thing in an Army that was on the verge of entering a new age, an age when warriors sat hunched over computer screens manipulating whole battalions of robotic combatants hundreds, maybe even thousands of miles away. The greatest challenge he faced as the Chief of Staff of the Army was how to lead that Army into that age while preserving the warrior spirit that had seen it through grim wars and lean times. If it required him to turn a blind eye to an occasional little white lie, so be it.

Easing back in his seat, Stevens laced his fingers together and brought them to rest on his stomach. "I spoke to General Hannigan of the 11th Airborne this morning and discussed this and Major Tucker's investigation into the 13 September Incident. He agrees that, in light of Captain Fetterman's efforts on the night of the twenty-third it would not reflect well on the Army if we continued with Tucker's Article 32."

Nathan made a show of thinking over what the Chief of Staff said before sagely nodding in agreement. "I imagine that's true, sir, especially in light of the fact that Captain Fetterman had been the focus of Major Tucker's investigation."

"We also agreed that it wouldn't be right to let the performance of the officer who commanded D Company on the twenty-third go without recognizing it in some way. General Hannigan thought the Distinguished Service Cross would be appropriate. I convinced him a Silver Star would do. What do you think, Major Dixon?"

Knowing that he'd already pushed his luck way beyond the red line, Nathan nodded. "I don't see a problem with that at all, sir. I'm sure Captain Fetterman's parents will find comfort in knowing that their son died heroically in the performance of his duties."

Stevens didn't respond at first, taking a moment to peer into Nathan's one good eye as he deliberated on whether he wanted to delve into Nathan's role in that action. Eventually he came to the conclusion that there was no good way of doing so, especially in light of what Nathan had said in his report. Instead, he sat upright.

"Good!" Stevens announced crisply in the way

generals do when they're about to wrap up something. "Since you were the senior officer present and know everything there is about the action, I want you to write up the commendation."

Ignoring the manner in which his superior phrased his remarks, Nathan nodded in full agreement, glad that Stevens was willing to accept his fictional account of Captain Fetterman's actions on that night. "No problem, sir."

"Your other report," Stevens stated as he changed topics, "isn't going to go down well in certain circles."

Unable to help himself, Nathan smirked. "Somehow I didn't think it would, sir."

"You realize that you're going to make a fair number of enemies, don't you?"

Reasserting his previous deadpan expression, Nathan rattled off a response that he found to be distasteful but unavoidable. "I have no doubt that there is a future for robotics in the Army, sir, especially for UGVs like the M-10. Employed properly and under the control of officers who understand their capabilities as well as their limitations, they will prove ideal in certain situations.

"Unfortunately," he continued having managed to deliver that statement without choking on his own words, "I do not think the UST's version of the M-10 is right for the Army. Major Tucker was kind enough to send me a copy of her findings, which I included in my report. In addition to some technical problems with the UST version of the M-10 UGV, she was able to document numerous irregularities in what the UST personnel did to keep the M-10s and M-11s the 3rd of the 68th were using operational. We both agree that UST does not have the best interests of the Army in mind."

Lifting the corner of several pages of the report they were discussing, Stevens exhaled. "You do realize that some of what you say in here exceeds the scope of your charter. Because of what you said about White and the conduct of the other UST personnel at Pacesetter, I've no choice but to refer this matter over to the justice department."

Pleased at hearing this, Nathan found it all but impossible to keep from smirking. "If I am guilty of exceeding my orders, then I did so only because I believe that the situation called for it, sir."

"I hope you do appreciate that exceeding your charter by inserting yourself into situations that you don't belong can be dangerous, Major."

Nathan returned Stevens's stare, knowing he was talking about more than the report. "Our profession is an inherently dangerous one, sir. Sometimes we've no choice but to take chances, consequences be damned."

Stevens nodded. "Yes, yes, we do." With that, he came to his feet, prompting Nathan to do likewise. "While that may be true, Major Dixon," he stated with a sly grin, "I've found that ignoring our domestic duties can be even more hazardous than anything we face here or on the field of battle. Now, I expect you to walk out that door and keep going until you reach home, is that clear?"

Coming to attention, Nathan rendered a crisp hand salute before carrying out the second best orders he'd been given since being assigned to the Pentagon.

ALEXANDRIA, VIRGINIA—OCTOBER 19

Opening her eyes, Chris was pleasantly surprised to find Nathan kneeling down next to the sofa she'd been napping on. Stretching, she yawned before smiling at her husband. "What time is it?"

"A little after three."

"You're home early."

"Colonel Kaplan got tired of watching me practice winking with my one good eye and sent me home."

Though he'd meant it as a joke, Chris frowned as she gently placed the tips of her fingers on the side of Nathan's scarred face, the side without an eye. Realizing that he'd managed to upset her, he quickly changed the subject. "I take it Mutt and Jeff are also enjoying an afternoon siesta."

Pulling her hand away from his face, she gave him a playful slap on his arm. "You know I hate it when you call them that."

"You also hate it when I call them Frick and Frack."

"Their names are Wendy and Scott."

"So you keep saying. Still, I like Mutt and Jeff much better."

Pushing herself upright, Chris patted the sofa cushion next to her. As he was getting settled, Chris folded her arms and looked away. "Nathan," she started slowly, "we've not had much of a chance to talk since you've been back."

Having expected a moment like this would come, Nathan reached over, took his wife's face in his hand and slowly turned it toward his. "We're not going to go there, Chris."

Chris, however, could not let it go, not without saying what she'd been wanting to say since he'd returned from Iraq. "No, Nathan, you have to hear me out, please. I was wrong to go to work when I did. I should have known better, I should have realized that I'd be incapable of half-stepping once I was in the thick of things. Maybe if I'd followed the doctor's advice, I'd still have a uterus and I'd be able to give Wendy and Scott a brother or a sister."

"And maybe," Nathan countered, "if I'd done what I should have in Iraq, I'd still have both eyes. But we both did what we thought was right. You had no way of knowing that something like the 13 September Incident was going to be dropped in your lap. You couldn't, just as we both know you couldn't do a half-ass job of covering it when it did. Besides," he added in a more conciliatory voice, "didn't the doctor tell you that there's no way of knowing for sure why things turned out the way they did?"

"I know she said that but . . ."

Placing a finger on her lips, Nathan tried to end this pointless discussion. "Let's just be happy for what we have, okay? You've got a great job that you love, I have one good eye, and we both have two healthy babies. What more could you ask for?"

Realizing that he was right, Chris lowered her chin a smidgen before looking up at him through her lashes. "How about a kiss?"

Hooking her chin in the crook of his finger, Nathan tilted it back. "You do realize what a kiss can lead to, don't you?"

Chris grinned as she came to her feet, took Nathan

by his hands, and pulled him up. "Oh, believe me, mister, I am sooo counting on that."

With a wink, Chris led Nathan away, two flawed humans enjoying what they had as they did their best to find their way, together, in an imperfect world.

AUTHOR'S NOTES

JANUARY 2009

This is a work of fiction, a story. All the vehicles, weapons systems, and equipment mentioned in it, however, are already in the Army's inventory and are currently undergoing testing or are based upon advanced prototypes. The love/hate relationship that exists between those who serve their country by wearing a uniform and the people who make a living by reporting what they do is also very real.

The M-10 and M-11 unmanned ground combat vehicles, or UGVs mentioned in this story, are based upon BEA's Black Knight unmanned robotic light tank, a twelve-ton vehicle that bears a striking resemblance to the M-1 tank but is in fact based upon the Bradley. It was tested throughout 2007 at Aberdeen Test Center in Maryland. The UGVs in this story are a blend of what currently exists and what I think can be added without stretching current technological boundaries.

The MQ-9 Reaper unmanned aerial vehicle is currently in use by the U.S. Air Force, the Royal

Air Force, as well as U.S. Customs and Border Protection. The Class I unmanned aerial vehicle mentioned as being part of the M-11 in this story is being developed by Boeing and, in all probability, will be in use by the time this book is published.

The M1209 Command and Control vehicle, or C2V, is part of a family of armored vehicles based upon a common chassis called the Future Combat Systems. General Dynamics is currently developing this family of manned combat vehicles. The layout of the interior of the C2Vs depicted in this story was based upon the Army's Crew-integration and Automation Test bed. The manner in which the UGV companies are organized is purely my own creation.

A more detailed description of weapons and equipment mentioned in this story as well as a definition of terms, acronyms, and military slang can be found in the glossary.

My depiction of the media is based upon historic and current practices. There has always been a close relationship between those who wear the rapiers and those who wield a goose quill. It can be argued that the efforts of George Washington and his army would have been for naught had it not been for the writings of Thomas Paine. The call to war against Spain in 1898 would not have been nearly as shrilled without the stories William Randolph Hearst published. George S. Patton III would have just been another footnote in dusty old history books had the media not decided to make him their darling.

The flipside is also true, as is evidenced by the

manner with which the facts surrounding the Haditha incident became less important than the manner in which it was dealt with, by both the military and the media. That incident has become the Iraq War's My Lai Massacre, an incident that I, as a young officer, had my nose rubbed in more times than I cared for. Both served as the foundation for this story.

Journalists are not the only people who use words to influence popular opinion, either, for or against the military. Stephen Crane's *Red Badge of Courage* is an American classic. While not necessarily prowar, it does counter the brutality of war with glimpses of nobility and courage. Dalton Trumbo's 1938 novel, *Johnny Got His Gun,* on the other hand, was outright antiwar, a work that was well received at the time by a nation anxious to stay out of the growing European war. In 1940 it won the prestigious American Booksellers Award, the same year Hitler crushed France and brought Britain to her knees while Russia overpowered Finland, and the Japanese Empire continued its efforts to absorb China. And the beat goes on. The Navy loves Tom Clancy while the Marine Corps wishes it never heard of Evan Wright, author of *Generation Kill.*

Today much of our news and information about war is derived from other sources, in particular 24/7 news channels. As with their predecessors, they are not immune from tilting their coverage one way or the other. On one channel, you have the management promoting Oliver North and his *War Stories* series while elsewhere a story like Operation Tailwind gets top billing.

If we were to be honest, most people would have to agree that it is almost impossible for the American public to determine where the truth lies. Decisions about what is true and what is not are made not by facts, but what we, as individuals, are predisposed to believe. Oftentimes this is based upon our personal, political, religious, and cultural beliefs. Whether this is right or wrong, good or bad, is beyond the scope of this modest story.

Finally, the unit designations used are all based upon historical units that are no longer in existence.

11TH AIRBORNE DIVISION (ANGELS): The division was activated in February 1943. It was the only airborne division to serve in the Pacific in World War II. After the war it performed occupation duty in Japan until 1949. In 1958 it was deactivated but enjoyed a brief reprieve in 1963 when it was reactivated as the 11th Air Assault Division (Test) and assigned the mission of developing airmobile/air assault tactics and doctrine. On 25 June 1965, it was reflagged as the 1st Cavalry Division (Airmobile).

It is said that the founders of the motorcycle gang, the Hell's Angels, were former members of the 11th Airborne Division, nicknamed the Angels, who returned from World War II but found reintegrating into society difficult. To recapture some of the excitement of living on the edge of danger, they purchased war surplus motorcycles and spent their weekends riding about, drinking hard, and raising hell. Whether this is true or not is all but impossible to determine.

3RD BRIGADE, 4TH ARMOR DIVISION: The division was activated on 15 April 1941. Although it did not have an official nickname, the Germans are said to have called the 4th AD Roosevelt's Butchers. On 26 December 1944, a battalion commanded by LTC Creighton Abrams and assigned to Combat Command C, which would have been the division's 3rd Brigade, broke through to the 101st Airborne Division at Bastogne during the Battle of the Bulge. The division remained in Germany after the war, forming part of the Constabulary force for a period of time. It was reflagged in 1971 as the 1st Armored Division.

3RD OF THE 68TH ARMOR (PACESETTERS): The 68th Armor began life as the part of the Tank Corps, American Expeditionary Force in World War I when it was equipped with the 6.5 ton French built FT-17 Renault tanks that had a two-man crew, no radios, a 37mm gun or a 7.92mm machine gun and moved at a stately rate of 4.2 miles per hour. In World War II it was an amphibious tractor unit that saw combat in the Pacific, earning members of the Pacesetter Battalion the right to wear the Presidential Naval Unit Citation. During the Cold War the battalion was stationed at Sullivan Barracks outside of Mannheim, Germany with its sister battalion, 5th of the 68th Armor as part of the 3rd Brigade, 8th Infantry Division. In the summer of 1986, 3rd of the 68th Armor was reflagged as 5th of the 77th Armor.

I served in the 3rd of the 68th from January 1975 through December 1979. During that time I was a tank platoon leader and a tank company executive officer in C Company, an S-3 Air on battalion staff and the commanding officer of A Company.

When I was with 3rd of the 68th Armor there were five battalions that carried on the lineage of the 68th Armor. Today there is only one, 1st of the 68th Armor, part of the 4th Infantry Division. The Silver Lions have been bouncing back and forth between their home station of Fort Carson, Colorado, and Iraq since 2003.

All information concerning weapons systems, vehicles, equipment, and programs has been drawn from open sources, which are available to anyone who can open a book or click a computer mouse. All characters mentioned in this book are fictional as is the World News Network. Any similarities between any characters or organizations mentioned in this book are unintended and purely accidental.

GLOSSARY

Article 15: Also known as nonjudicial punishment. It is punishment that can be imposed by a commanding officer for minor disciplinary offenses.

Article 31: The military version of the Miranda warning. Arresting officers or officers conducting an investigation utilize the Article 31 warning and waiver as a means to prevent self-incrimination and advise the individual of their right to have legal counsel present during questioning.

Article 32 Hearing/Investigation: An investigative proceeding under the United States Uniform Code of Military Justice, similar to that of a preliminary hearing or a grand jury proceeding in civilian law. Its name is derived from UCMJ section VII ("Trial Procedure") Article 32 (10 U.S.C. § 832), which mandates the hearing.

Badr Organization: The Iranian-trained wing of the Supreme Council for the Islamic Revolution in Iraq (SCIRI), the largest Shiite party in Iraq. It operates mainly in Shiite-controlled southern

Iraq where a number of regional governments are dominated by SCIRI representatives.

Battle Rattle: Combat gear; consisting of body armor manufactured by Point Blank Solutions, Inc. of Pompano Beach, Florida, a helmet and a variety of pouches, primarily manufactured by BAE Systems, that are designed to hold ammunition, personal first-aid kits, radios, and other equipment a soldier requires in battle and while in the field. An armed soldier tricked out in full battle rattle can find himself hauling close to one hundred pounds of equipment.

Boondoggle: A trip that has no useful military function, usually taken in a location that allows the personnel on it to enjoy themselves at government expense. The Congressional equivalent is a fact-finding trip.

Bumper Number: Alpha/numeric tag used to identify vehicles within a unit. Normally the letter identifies the company the vehicle is part of and the number identifies the platoon and the vehicle's sequence within that platoon. For example, D-23 means that the vehicle is the third vehicle in D Company's 2nd Platoon. Commanding officers, company and above normally use the number Six as their designation with a single six used on their Humvee and "66" to identify their tracked or fighting vehicle if they have one. When using the radio, people often use these designations to identify themselves. It's easier than looking up your official call sign in the CEOI.

C2V: An XM1209 Command and Control Vehicle is part of a family of armored vehicles based upon a common chassis called the Future Combat Systems, or FCS. General Dynamics is currently developing this family of manned combat vehicles that include the following:

XM1201 Reconnaissance and Surveillance Vehicle (RSV)
XM1202 Mounted Combat System (MCS)
XM1203 Non-Line-of-Sight Cannon (NLOS-C)
XM1204 Non-Line-of-Sight Mortar (NLOS-M)
XM1205 Recovery and Maintenance Vehicle (FRMV)
XM1206 Infantry Carrier Vehicle (ICV)
XM1207 and XM1208 Medical Vehicles (MV)
XM1209 Command and Control Vehicle (C2V)

CEOI: Communications-electronic operating instructions; a listing of all radio frequencies, call signs, and other communications-related instructions and procedures to be used by a unit in the field.

Class I Unmanned Aerial Vehicle: Unmanned Aerial Vehicle (UAV) designed to provide the dismounted soldier with Reconnaissance, Surveillance, and Target Acquisition. Estimated to weigh less than thirty-five pounds. It is designed to use autonomous flight and navigation, but it will interact with the network and soldier. It is being developed by Boeing.

CVC: Combat Vehicle Crewman's helmet. It features an outershell, innerliner, and communications, offering head protection inside armored vehicles as well as access to the vehicle's intercom and radios.

DA: Department of the Army.

Desert Fox: A female soldier that is considered more attractive because she is currently deployed in Iraq or Afghanistan.

Downrange: Any destination a group of soldiers are headed to, normally used when referring to moving out into combat or a combat zone.

Dustoff: A term coined in the Vietnam War used to describe the aerial evacuation of wounded.

FOB: Forward Operating Base. These are major installations that provide all the support needs of units operating in active combat theaters. Think Fort Apache without the wives and families.

Frock(ing): One of several ways the military has of promoting personnel, at least temporarily, for special requirements.

GAA: Grease, Artillery, and Automotive, the military's equivalent of axle grease and udder balm.

Hajji: Literally, "Hajji" means a Muslim that has gone on the Hajj, but American soldiers use it when referring to Middle Eastern civilians or Arabs in general. Also used to refer to local markets that sell cheap goods of questionable authenticity.

IA: Iraqi Army.

IFB: Interruptible fold back systems are designed for use in broadcast and motion picture production to provide high-quality monaural audio for crew communications, program audio monitoring, and talent cueing. It's the little thing you see in a journalist's ear that the producer uses to tell him what to say or that his fly is open.

IFF: Identify, friend or foe. IFF is an electronic system used to determine if an aircraft or a vehicle is friendly. Most IFF systems are a two-channel system, with one frequency used for the interrogating signals and another for the reply. An IFF that transmits a friendly code is said to be squawking.

JAG: Judge Advocate General; military lawyers who provide legal services to the Army at all levels of command.

Javelin: The FGM-148 Javelin man portable, fire-and-forget, self-guidance anti-tank guided missile with a range of 2,500 meters. It was jointly developed and is manufactured by Raytheon and Lockheed Martin.

Jump Seat: A spare seat for passengers or individuals not operating the vehicle. It is usually folded up and out of the way when not in use.

Klick(s): Military slang for kilometer(s) which is 0.621 miles.

LADAR: Laser detection and ranging sensors provide a 3D terrain estimation for medium- and close-range obstacle detection, allowing for the safe navigation of an unmanned vehicle. It is being developed by General Dynamics Robotic Systems.

LD: Line of Departure.

M240: A 7.62mm machine gun designed and originally manufactured by Fabrique Nationale of Belgium, who produced it for the Belgium Army under the designation MAG-58. It was adopted by the U.S. Army in 1977 and is manufactured in the U.S. by the American division of FN Herstal, in Columbia, South Carolina. It is a belt-fed, gas-operated weapon with a rate of fire that can be set as low as 650 rounds per minute or up to 950 rpm. Its maximum effective range is 900 meters. The M-240 replaced the Vietnam-era M-60 machine gun and the tank mounted M-219, which was the world's only single shot machine gun and was best used as a doorstop for the unit armory's door.

M242: A 25mm automatic cannon currently mounted on the M-2 and M-3 Bradley as well as the USMC LAV-25. It is an electrically powered, chain-driven automatic cannon with a rate of fire up to 200 rounds a minute capable of firing armor piercing or high explosive rounds out to an effective range of 2,500 meters.

Manual for Courts-Martial: A detailed listing of military law as well as duties and responsibilities.

MOS: Military Skill Identifier, an alpha/numeric tag that identifies an enlisted soldier's military specialty. For example, an infantryman's MOS is 11B.

MQ-9 Reaper: This is a medium-to-high altitude, long endurance remotely piloted aircraft that is currently in service with the U.S. Air Force, the RAF, and U.S. Customs and Border Protection. It has a cruise speed of around 230 miles per hour, a range of 3,682 miles, a ceiling of 50,000 feet, and can be armed with a combination of AGM-114 Hellfire missiles, GBU-12 Paveway II, and GBU-38 Joint Direct Attack Munitions. It is operated by a remote crew of two, a pilot and sensor operator. It is manufactured by General Atomics Aeronautical Systems.

MTI: Moving Target Indicator. Many reconnaissance and surveillance radars can detect motion but cannot identify whether the vehicle or personnel that are being tracked are friend or foe. Until such time as a more definitive description can be applied, they are referred to as MTIs.

NVGs: Night vision goggles, also known as NVDs or night vision devices. Generally, those used by individuals or crew-served weapons rely on amplifying ambient light. The image they create in the user's field of vision is green and black. Currently the Army is working toward NVGs that detect heat, as most of the vehicle and aircraft mounted weapons sights do.

Pogue: A derogatory term for a soldier who spends all of his time back at camp or any noncombat arms soldier. In the Infantry, this term applies to anyone who isn't infantry.

RPG: Rocket-propelled grenade, a short-range, shoulder-fired, antitank weapon.

Remote Weapon Station: A remotely controlled weapons station (RWS) that can be mounted to vehicles and stationary platforms. It is used on a variety of vehicle platforms and supports the MK19 Grenade Machine Gun, .50 Caliber M2 Machine Gun, M240B Machine Gun, and M249 Squad Automatic Weapon.

The Shit: The combat zone, battle. Originally used to refer to Vietnam.

Sec Def: Secretary of Defense.

Sit Rep: Military shorthand for situation report. It's a commander's way of asking, "What in the hell is going on?"

SJA: Staff Judge Advocate, the military counsel on staff. The military equivalent to a state or Federal attorney general.

Tango-uniform: Tits up. Broken, nonfunctional, dead.

Task Force: A battalion-sized unit that includes a mix of combat elements, normally a combination of four tank and infantry companies along with a headquarters company. In the case of Task Force 3rd of the 68th as depicted in this story, A Company is a tank company with M1A1 tanks, B Company is a UGV company, C Company is a mechanized infantry company equipped with M2 Bradley fighting vehicles and D Company is another UGV company. All staff, support and combat support elements organic to 3rd of the 68th are assigned to Headquarters and Headquarters Company.

TDY: Temporary Duty, the military version of a business trip.

TOC: Tactical operations center, the location where the battle staff of a battalion/task force plans, monitors and directs the battle. It's a place where there are a lot of maps, a lot of radios, a whole lot of paper and lots and lots of officers who all too often feel the need to talk at the same time.

UAV: Unmanned aerial vehicle. These are now categorized by the Army in four classes, with a Class I UAV being a man portable unmanned aerial vehicle (provided you consider something that weighs thirty-five pounds man portable), designed to allow combat troops to peek over the next hill, while a Class IV UAV weighs well over a hundred pounds, has a loiter time of eighteen to twenty-four hours and an operating range of seventy-five kilometers or more.

UCMJ: Uniformed Code of Military Justice. It is the military law book that describes responsibilities, legal procedures and lists violations that a soldier, sailor, airman, or Marine can be tried for.

UGV: Unmanned Ground Vehicle, which includes both combat and unarmed robotic vehicles. The Army is currently testing this concept. Its first armed version was known as the SWORD, a 350-pound tracked robot mounting an M249 machine gun built by QinetiQ. Another test bed is the Black Knight, a twelve-ton unmanned combat vehicle that bears a striking resemblance to the M-1 Abrams tank. It mounts a 30mm cannon. The M-10s and M-11 UCVs mentioned in the story are based upon the Black Knight, developed by BAE Systems, Inc.

XO: Executive officer, a unit's second in command who, at task force and company level, is usually saddled with handling all the minute administrative details the commanding officer doesn't want to deal with.

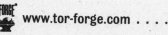